GOLDEN ARM

GOLDEN ARM

CARL DEUKER

Clarion Books

An Imprint of HarperCollinsPublishers

Clarion Books is an imprint of HarperCollins Publishers.

Golden Arm
Copyright © 2020 by Carl Deuker

Library of Congress Cataloging-in-Publication Data
Description: Boston ; New York : Houghton Mifflin Harcourt, [2020] |
Summary: Lazarus Weathers, a high school senior from the
wrong side of the tracks, seeks to protect his half-brother while
pitching his way out of poverty, one strike at a time.
Identifiers: LCCN 2019006525 |
Subjects: | CYAC: Baseball—Fiction. | Poverty—Fiction. |
Stuttering—Fiction. | Single-parent families—Fiction. | Family
life—Seattle—Fiction. | Seattle (Wash.)—Fiction.
Classification: LCC PZ7.D493 Gol 2020 | DDC [Fic]—dc23
LC record available at https://lccn.loc.gov/2019006525

ISBN 978-0-35-801242-9 hardcover
ISBN 978-0-35-866794-0 paperback

The text was set in Dante MT Std.
Typography by Kaitlin Yang
22 23 24 25 26   PC/LSCC   10 9 8 7 6 5 4 3 2 1

First paperback edition, 2022

For **AARON, MARIAN, AND IMOGEN**

The author would like to thank Ann Rider, the editor of this book, for her advice and encouragement.

PART ONE

ONE

I LIVE IN A SINGLE-WIDE in Jet City, a trailer park in Seattle. I got my baseball glove for two bucks at Goodwill and found my Mariners cap in a garbage can by the RapidRide E bus stop on Aurora Avenue. I don't have baseball cleats or an authentic jersey. I've never been to a major-league baseball game, and we don't have cable TV. I follow the Mariners on my radio.

My mom has worked as a custodian at Northwest Hospital for so long that she has her name—Timmi—stitched on her uniform. She named me Lazarus because I almost died while I was being born, and there's a guy in the Bible named Lazarus who came back from the dead. I'm not good at school, and I'm not good at talking, probably because I was born two months early. When I get nervous, I tilt my head sideways and my eyes roll back, and that's how I stay until something frees up and the words move again. I went to speech class all through grade school, and that helped some. Still, if I'm with Antonio, my younger brother, I let him do the talking for both of us.

When I'm on my game, none of that matters, because my

pitching speaks for me. The hitters all look more like baseball players than I do, but their fancy gear does them no good. My arm is free and loose like a whip, and everything slows. Everything except the ball coming out of my hand. The batter might slap a soft ground ball or manage a pop fly, but squaring up one of my fastballs and driving it far and deep?

Not happening.

When I'm in the zone, I *know* I'm good enough to get drafted by a major-league team, and maybe even good enough to make it all the way to the major leagues. But to take even one step down that road, I need a scout to see me when I'm on my game. Until that happens, nothing happens.

My school, North Central High, is a tough school. The kids are poor like my brother and me. Some are immigrant kids who don't speak English at home. Some are in gangs, or are gang wannabes. Teachers and coaches desert North Central first chance they get.

Mr. Kellogg coaches our baseball team, and he does it alone. No assistant coaches, no parent volunteers. Just Mr. Kellogg. He was a third baseman in high school, so he knows hitting and fielding, but not pitching.

That's nothing new for me. I've never had a real pitching coach. I've had games when my stuff is unhittable, but when I'm not in the zone, I guide my pitches instead of letting them fly. I don't know if my stride is too long or I'm releasing the ball too soon, and there's never been anybody to ask. My fastball comes right down Main Street, and it isn't all that fast. Then I get hit, and hit hard, which is why my overall stats are mediocre.

Major-league teams don't draft mediocre pitchers.

TWO

MY LAST NAME IS WEATHERS; my brother Antonio's last name is Driver. Since we have different fathers, it's no surprise that we don't look alike. I'm six-two, long-armed, skinny, have light brown hair and a little peach fuzz on my face. Antonio is four inches shorter but fifteen pounds heavier, has dark hair and eyes, is thick through the chest, and could grow a beard in a week.

It's not just looks—our personalities are different, too. My stutter makes people uncomfortable, and that makes me uncomfortable. Antonio's the guy who lights up a room when he walks in. Partly it's because he's fast and funny with words. But it's more than that. It's as if he got an extra dose of life, so people want to be near him, talk to him, hear him talk.

It's baseball that has held us together. I pitch; he plays shortstop. Half brothers, but full teammates.

We've both always known that our mom isn't like most moms. Her last name is Medina, which makes it seem as though she's not related to either of us. She smokes a pack a day, except for when she's quitting. She has tattoos of barbed wire on her arms and neck, and her hair always has purple or green streaks.

Antonio once asked her to wear a long-sleeved, high-necked shirt to back-to-school night to cover up her tattoos. "You got the mom you got," she said. "Get used to it."

When we were in middle school, some high school kids started hassling Antonio and me as we walked home. "You know why you've got different last names, don't you?" a wiry-haired kid called out.

I looked over, not getting it, but Antonio understood. It doesn't matter whether it's on the street or in the classroom — he always understands before I do.

"Shut up," he shouted.

"You do know, don't you?" the kid said, pointing at him and grinning. "But Laz there doesn't, because he's stupid. Isn't that right, L-L-L-L-Laz?"

Moments like that are the worst for me. When I really want to say something, I can't. Antonio jumped in. "I said, shut up."

The kid kept his eyes trained on me. "It's because your mom's a slut. You do know what that means, don't you? Or do I need to explain it to you?"

I'm older by eighteen months, so it should have been me who went first, but it was Antonio. He flew at them, fists windmilling. I followed. We took some punches and got some cuts and bruises, but we gave out punishment, too. I must have caught one of those guys solid, because my right hand hurt for two days.

When Mom saw our bloodied faces, she was mad. "What do you mean you had to fight?" she barked at Antonio.

"They said stuff about you."

"What did they say about me?"

"Stuff," Antonio repeated.

Their eyes locked, and Mom went quiet. Then she took a breath and exhaled. "All right. If you had to, you had to. Just don't be out there looking for trouble. You hear me?"

THREE

MOM SAYS THAT because of the tough time I had getting born, I needed an extra year to get ready for school. I want to believe her, but the truth is I've *never* felt ready for school. I understand enough of what I read, but I don't get math. At North Central Middle and North Central High, I studied hard and barely pulled Cs. Antonio, one year behind me, got As even though he hardly ever studied.

Both of our dads were long gone, so taking care of us was one hundred percent on our mom, which is why she hated summer vacation. "You two are not getting yourselves in trouble while I'm at work," she said every June. "You're joining every league and camp I can get you into, and you're going to play baseball on the community center team, too."

She got no argument from me. The first time my fingertips felt those raised stitches and that smooth cowhide, I was hooked. The only thing better than holding a baseball is throwing one.

For years she got no argument from Antonio, either. But toward the end of middle school, he started complaining. The camps were dumb; the community center team was lame. "Laz pitches, so it's okay for him. I just stand out there kicking dirt. And it's not even a real team."

And there was Garrett Diehl.

Garrett is almost two years older than me, which makes him three years older than Antonio. His parents were killed in a car crash, so he and his sister, Selena, live with their grandfather. I don't know what happened to the grandmother.

Girls must think Garrett is good-looking, because they hang around him. He's tall, with long dirty-blond hair that he keeps in a man bun. He's got blue eyes, a bony face, and a loud laugh. He says he got his GED after he quit North Central High, but I don't believe it. For the last few years he's practically lived at the back fence of Jet City Trailer Park, smoking cigarettes or weed. A year ago he started getting expensive things: an iPhone, a leather jacket, a Seahawks parka, and finally a used black Subaru WRX.

My mom drives an old Corolla. For Christmas a couple of years back she bought Antonio and me pay-as-you-go flip phones. They're burners—throwaway phones—only we don't throw them away. We get our clothes at Value Village.

I'm not saying that I wouldn't like new clothes and a better phone and a fast car, but it's not like I'm wearing clothes that don't fit, and it's not like I don't have a phone, so I'm okay with it. Not Antonio, though. Somewhere in there it started eating at him that he couldn't have new Nikes or expensive jeans or an iPhone.

I remember the day Garrett sucked Antonio into his circle. It was last January, the middle of my junior year, Antonio's sophomore. We were walking back from school on a cold, windy Tuesday when we saw what looked like a fire burning by the fence.

Mobile homes can go up in flames fast, so we hustled down the path, rounded the corner, and then slowed. No emergency, just Garrett burning old pieces of wood in one of the empty barrels back there. With him were a couple of guys and a girl with long black hair who was wearing tight jeans and a jean jacket. She was new at North Central; I'd noticed her, but I didn't know her name.

"Hey," Garrett called when he saw us. "Come back here, both of you. Tell me about the old school."

He sounded high.

I struggled to answer. "I have stuff t-to d-d-do," I finally managed.

Garrett grinned. I don't know if he was laughing at my stutter or at me for being a wuss. Probably both.

"How about you, Antonio? You afraid to hang out with the bad kids?"

"I'm not afraid of nothing," Antonio said.

Garrett motioned with his head. "Come on, then. You can give Jasmine a heads-up about North Central."

Antonio glanced at me. Our eyes caught, and then he headed toward Garrett. The girl smiled at him, and the guys stood up a little taller.

As I watched him go, my pulse quickened. This wasn't a good place. I wanted to say something that would pull him back, but the right words never come easily for me, and none at all came that day.

FOUR

THE WEEK BEFORE baseball season started, I was working on a writing assignment with Suja, a girl I've known since fourth grade. She was supposed to edit my essay and I was supposed to edit hers, as if I could possibly help her. "Your brother is headed for trouble," she whispered as she marked up my paper.

My back stiffened. "What do you m-mean?"

She moved closer. "You know Selena, Garrett's sister?"

Selena was a couple of years older and a lot friendlier than Garrett. We had a joke together: Whenever our paths crossed, she'd asked me how math was going. "Not so good," I'd say. She'd smile. "I never could find X, either."

"She got a job with Seattle Helpers, working for old people, doing their laundry, heating up soup, and keeping them company."

"So?"

"So old people take lots of pills. Vicodin, Percocet, OxyContin —the drugs you hear about all the time. If Selena thinks the old people won't notice, or if they die, she takes their pills and gives them to Garrett. He puts out the word and then stands at the back fence waiting for the druggies to come to him. Our trailer is close to the fence. At least ten guys buy from him every day. And when he sells, your brother is standing right by him."

That afternoon, as Antonio and I walked home, I sucked up my courage and confronted him. "Don't g-go to the back fence," I said when we reached the spot where we split up.

"What's wrong with the back fence?"

I took a deep breath; I needed my words to be clear. "The stuff G-Garrett has. He buys it with d-drug money."

Antonio looked up at the sky. "Who told you that?"

"It's t-true, isn't it?"

Antonio opened his hands. "Yeah, I guess. But it's no big deal. Sometimes he gets a few pills from his sister. When he does, he sells them to old Jet City guys who can't get them from their doctors anymore. That's it. He's not El Chaco, or whatever that guy's name is."

"It's still a crime. He c-could g-get arrested. You c-could g-get arrested."

Antonio tilted his head. "This is coming from Suja, isn't it?"

I didn't answer.

He smiled. "You know what a drama queen she is. Remember the day she started bawling because she was sure the North Koreans were going to drop an atom bomb on Jet City? The girl is not happy unless she's unhappy." He paused. "I hang out there, tell stories and listen to stories. That's all."

I was silent for a moment. "If I told Mom, she wouldn't think it was n-nothing," I finally said.

His smile disappeared. "Seriously, Laz? You're going to tattle on me? I'm sixteen, not six." He paused. "How about you take care of you and I'll take care of me. Deal?"

I didn't answer.

"Deal?" he repeated, his smile back.

"I guess," I mumbled.

He waited a beat. then he grabbed me around the neck and we wrestled a little. When he let go, he headed to the back fence as I walked to our trailer.

FIVE

ANTONIO WAS RIGHT—I did need to take care of me, especially on the baseball diamond. I'd grown, and I'd gotten stronger, making my fastball faster. And for the first time, North Central had the makings of a decent team. My junior season had a chance to be my breakout season.

We started with a run of five straight wins. The defense was strong, especially up the middle. Dawit Senai, our center fielder, ran down every fly ball anywhere near him; catcher Tory Nelson was solid behind the plate. Antonio was a vacuum cleaner at shortstop, and he sparked the offense, rocketing a slew of doubles into the gaps and driving in runs by the handful.

On the mound, I wasn't in the zone all the time, but I was there most of the time. And even when I was off, I was never way off like I had been other years. "This is going to be a special year for us," Mr. Kellogg said after win number six. "A really special year."

Then the North Central curse hit. Our right fielder, Trey Lister, flunked two midterms and was ineligible. James Xiong landed an afterschool job working at Century Link and quit the team. Cam Hinton moved to Renton without telling anyone, not even his girlfriend. By May, we were down to eleven players, and we'd lost six of seven games.

Even though the season had fallen apart, I still had one game circled on my schedule: Laurelhurst High, the defending city champions. They'd lost in the state playoffs to Tacoma's Jesuit High, but only because Jesuit had a pitcher named Fergus Hart that the *Seattle Times* said might be the next Clayton Kershaw.

Laurelhurst had a future major-leaguer of its own, a center fielder named Ian Thurman. Thurman had been all-league as a freshman and all-state as a sophomore, and he had a good chance to be Washington State Player of the Year as a junior if Laurelhurst could beat Fergus Hart and take the state title.

Websites that covered high school sports posted articles and stats on Thurman. After lunch, I went to the computer lab and pored over them. I knew his height, his weight, how many pounds he could bench-press, how fast he ran the fifty-yard dash. His coach, an old guy named Pop Vereen who'd been at Laurelhurst for a million years, said that Thurman was the best high school player he'd ever coached. Top baseball colleges were recruiting him, and a major-league team was sure to draft him, probably in the first round.

Ian Thurman was such a big star that even when the lowly North Central High Eagles played Laurelhurst a *Seattle Times* writer would be there, and so would major-league scouts. They'd come to see Thurman, but if I could dominate, then one scout from one team might write my name down in his notebook, and that team might someday give me a chance to prove myself in their minor-league system. That's all I wanted: a chance.

I couldn't do it alone, though. I needed the guys behind me to play the way they had early in the season. I thought about calling a team meeting, pictured myself standing tall on a bench, rallying the guys to give it their best shot: *We play hard and smart, and we can beat these guys!*

Then I reran the film, the second time seeing how it would actually play out. *We p-p-play hard and s-s-smart, and we c-c-can b-beat these g-g-guys.*

SIX

MONEY IS TIGHT around our house, so Antonio and I both have jobs. He works at Home Depot watering plants; I work at the Aurora Driving Range, which is directly behind the trailer park. Mr. Matsui, the range pro, hired me when I was fifteen, and I've worked there ever since. I drive a John Deere Gator with a metal cage around me so I don't get conked in the head by golf balls. The Gator has roller arms that gather up the golf balls and spit them into attached metal baskets. When the baskets are full, I dump the balls into a chute that leads to a ball dispenser, starting the cycle again.

I have a driver's license, but I almost never get a chance to drive my mom's Corolla, so tooling around in the utility vehicle is almost fun. There's nothing fun about refilling the ball dispensers, though. A single golf ball doesn't weigh much, but lifting basket after basket over your head makes your muscles burn. Still, I push myself to heave those baskets high. More arm strength means more miles per hour on the fastball.

When I finished work on the Friday night before the Laurelhurst game, Antonio wasn't at the back fence with

Garrett, which was great. Instead, he was waiting for me by the entrance to Jet City. "The guys are going to a movie at Oak Tree. Eight thirty. You in?"

I always play catch the night before a game because I want my arm to be a little tired when I take the mound. If I'm too rested, I overthrow and I'm wild. For years, Antonio had been my partner. Since he'd started hanging with Garrett, Mr. Leskov, the grizzled old guy who runs the community center, had taken his place.

"Come on, Laz," Antonio said after I'd turned him down. "The movie is supposed to be hot. Lots of nice-looking girls. Nicer looking than Leskov."

"C-C-C-C—"

Antonio waited. He always did.

"C-Couldn't we go tomorrow night? After the game?"

He shook his head. "The guys are going tonight."

At eight, while Antonio and the rest of them were walking to Oak Tree Cinema, I was playing catch with Mr. Leskov on the grass under the parking lot lights. The baseball went back and forth. Finally Leskov caught one of my throws and held the ball. "We stop now," he called out. "You have good pitches in your game tomorrow. You strike three those boys."

SEVEN

IT DOESN'T TAKE a genius to figure out what happened. Somebody—or a couple of somebodies—sneaked jugs of wine into the movie theater, and the wine got passed around.

The movie was one of those *Girls Go Crazy* films. Every time one of the girls took off her top, the guys stomped their feet, whistled, and hollered. They made such a racket that the manager turned on the lights and told them to hold it down.

They didn't.

People watching other movies in the cineplex complained. The manager turned on the lights again and told them to leave.

They didn't.

The manager called the cops. As the cops rousted the guys out, they found the wine. Nobody owned up, so the cops gave every kid a Minor in Possession citation and drove them home.

I was in my room listening to the Mariners game when the police knocked on the door of our trailer. Antonio wasn't drunk and he hadn't copped an attitude, and the officer told my mom that.

"What happens next?" she asked when she saw the citation.

"Juvenile court, then a class on drug and alcohol abuse. Your boy stays out of trouble, and they'll wipe this off his record. He doesn't, they won't."

Saturday morning, when I came out from my room, Antonio was eating cereal at the kitchen table, his face glum. As I moved to join him, Mom's cell, which was sitting on the kitchen table, started ringing. Coach Kellogg's name popped onto the screen. Antonio and I looked at each other, unsure what to do. Before we had to decide, Mom's bedroom door burst open. She grabbed the phone and took it to the sofa. We stopped eating and listened.

Kellogg did most of the talking. All Mom said was, "Yes . . . Yes . . . That doesn't seem fair . . . If there's no choice, there's no choice . . . I'll tell him."

After she cut the connection, she glared at Antonio, then turned to me. "Laz, that was your coach. He knows about last night. Your brother and the rest of them are off the team. League rules. Your coach says he won't have enough players to field a team, so he'll have to forfeit all the remaining games. Your season is over." Her eyes returned to Antonio. She started to say something, but stopped.

After I finished my cereal, I walked the gravel roads of Jet City, kicking at rocks, my head pounding, my guts empty. Sure, I still had my senior year, but I'd be a no-name senior pitching on a terrible team, and when my senior year ended, I'd be just another guy who pitched a little in high school.

• • •

I followed every game of the state playoffs, even though it was like picking at a scab. Laurelhurst made it to the quarterfinals before getting shut out—again—by Jesuit High's Fergus Hart. The *Seattle Times* article said it was the seventeenth time Pop Vereen, their coach, had taken a Laurelhurst team into the state playoffs and the seventeenth time they'd been knocked out, making him the winningest losing coach in high school baseball history. Jesuit went on to capture the state championship for the third straight year, and Fergus Hart, not Ian Thurman, was Washington Player of the Year.

EIGHT

SELECT BASEBALL TEAMS cost money, so that was never happening for me or anybody from North Central. But every summer, Mr. Leskov rounded up enough guys to field a sandlot team, wrangled a local sporting goods store into donating T-shirts and a few bats and balls, and then called coaches of real teams to arrange games.

Considering the way the school season had fizzled, I didn't think Mr. Leskov would be able to put together a summer team. "I'm not sure any g-guys will want to p-play," I told him.

He waved his hands above his head. "Don't worry, Laz. We'll get a team together. You and me."

North Central Community Center has a basketball court, a swimming pool, tennis courts, a weight room, a video room, a TV room, foosball, Ping-Pong tables, and fields for soccer and baseball. It's the best thing in North Central, and it's where kids who want to stay out of trouble hang out.

Mr. Leskov quickly signed up Dawit and a handful of other guys who'd played on the North Central team. We needed more players, though, so Mr. Leskov and I walked around, badgering guys who barely spoke English into signing up to play a game they barely understood. Actually, it was Mr. Leskov who did the badgering. He knew about my stutter, so he had me stand next to him holding the sign-up sheet. "What else are you going to do?" he demanded of random kids. Then he pointed a finger at himself and tapped it hard against his chest. "You see me, old white man with funny Russian accent? But I was once young buck like you. Trouble call for me like it calls for you. You play baseball, then no drugs, no drinking, no getting girlfriend with baby. Here, put your name down. Baseball is America."

Eventually, six more guys did.

"And your brother, right?" Mr. Leskov said as he wrote Antonio's name at the bottom.

"Yeah, my b-brother," I answered, even though I hadn't asked him yet.

"Okay," Mr. Leskov said. "Now—let's arrange the games."

We went into his cramped office at the community center. For two hours I searched the Internet for the names of teams who played in leagues like American Legion or Babe Ruth or Northwest Premier Baseball. When I found a telephone number, Mr. Leskov would call. Other coaches tried to say no, but he was like a dog with a bone. "We'll play at your field!" he shouted into the phone. "One innings, four innings, ten innings. You choose. Just name the date and time and we'll be there."

When he had sixteen games scheduled, he turned to me, half-moons of sweat around his armpits. "Enough?"

I bumped knuckles with him. "Yeah. Enough."

He slapped the table as he got to his feet. "We win them all! You strike three everyone, and we win them all!"

That night at dinner I told Antonio I'd signed him up for the team. He groaned, but Mom stepped in. "Why wouldn't you play?"

"I've got my job at Home Depot."

"Two hours in the morning watering plants? What are you going to do with the rest of your day?"

"I don't know. Just hang out."

"At the back fence with Garrett Diehl? He's way older than you." She paused. "What goes on there anyway?"

Antonio flashed me a look. "Nothing goes on there."

"Yeah? Well, in my experience a bunch of teenage boys doing nothing usually ends up as *something*." She paused. "You get a full-time job and you can drop baseball. Until then, you play."

NINE

THIRTEEN GUYS SOUNDS LIKE plenty for a baseball team, but signing your name to a piece of paper isn't the same as showing up. Most of the guys on the team lived in Jet City, and in Jet City you never really know what's coming next.

Once in a while it's good stuff. Somebody appears who has been gone for months or years. A mom, a dad, a sister, a brother. Maybe from jail, maybe from across town, maybe from across the world. When that happens, music blasts from the lucky trailer and people celebrate.

Sometimes it's bad stuff. A man goes after his wife, or two brothers get into it, or somebody steals something. Police cars show up, gravel flying, sirens wailing. The cops handcuff the guy and haul him to jail. Every once in a while it's a *she* who gets cuffed.

Even when there are no police, there's still alcohol and drugs and girls selling themselves on Aurora Avenue. And there's the uncertainty. You have a neighbor one day, and the next, they're gone. So thirteen players isn't really thirteen.

I just hoped it would be nine.

• • •

On the day of our first summer game, Mr. Leskov—driving the community center van—pulled up in front of our trailer and honked. I grabbed my glove and hurried out the door, Antonio trailing behind.

Once we were inside the van, Pushkin, Leskov's black lab, jumped on Antonio and licked his face. "Look what I got," Mr. Leskov said, shoving a black plastic bag at me that was filled with bright orange T-shirts. "Uniforms. There's even one for Pushkin."

Leskov had the addresses of the guys on a sheet of yellow paper. I read them to him, and he cruised around, trying to corral guys who had signed up. When we got ten, Leskov punched an address into his GPS and we were off. As he drove, Antonio passed out orange T-shirts to the guys while I patched together a lineup.

I could see from Leskov's GPS that our opponent practiced on a field near Husky Stadium. As we pulled into the parking lot, I couldn't believe all the gear they had—a pitching machine, batting nets, a speed gun. And that was the stuff that was out. A bunch of bulging mesh bags emblazoned with the words **SEATTLE MARAUDERS** sat along the sideline.

We milled around in the parking lot while Mr. Leskov talked to their coach. Leskov pointed at us and then pointed to his clipboard.

"Their coach forgot all about the game," Antonio snickered. "A buck says we don't play."

Right then, Leskov waved us forward. As we headed toward the infield, I could see some of the guys on the other team smile at our orange T-shirts, ratty jeans, and old sneakers.

I kept my eyes forward and my back straight. I picked one guy to stare at. He had a cocky way of standing and a smug grin on his face. As we neared the baseball diamond, I kept staring —only now I could feel my pulse in my ears.

The kid smirking at me was Ian Thurman.

TEN

"FOUR INNINGS," MR. LESKOV SAID when we circled around him. "Five minutes to loosen muscles, and then we play."

I've never needed more than a dozen throws to get warm. With the adrenaline rush from seeing Ian Thurman, I was ready after six.

We were the visitors, so we batted first. Dawit, who'd come to Seattle from Ethiopia, led off. He had long arms, long legs, and a mischievous gleam in his eyes. Soccer was his passion; baseball was strictly for fun. That made him fearless at the plate. When your bat is loose and quick and you're an athlete, good things can happen.

The Marauders pitcher went into his wind-up and delivered. Dawit swung and missed, taking such a huge cut that he did a complete three-sixty and fell down, landing on home plate. When he got back to his feet, he raised the bat above his head like some kind of warrior, and everybody laughed, including the Marauders guys.

Dawit got set in the batter's box; the pitcher delivered. Again Dawit swung, but this time he caught the ball square, rocketing a line drive over the first baseman's head that landed just fair. Dawit stood at home plate for a beat, watching in delight before he took off.

He should have stopped at second, but we hadn't thought about base coaches, so he just kept running. The third baseman had the tag down in time, but Dawit's hard slide caused the ball to pop out of his glove. "Safe!" the umpire yelled, and Dawit stood on the base clapping his hands together as we all cheered like madmen.

Tory Nelson, our catcher, was batting second. He was a stocky guy with good hands and a good eye. Their pitcher, rattled by Dawit's surprise triple, threw his first two pitches a foot outside. The next two were closer, but they weren't strikes. Tory trotted down to first as I stepped up to the plate.

Their third baseman was playing back. I wanted to make sure we scored at least one run, so when I got a low fastball on the outside corner, I pushed a bunt past the mound toward second. The second baseman charged, fielded the ball, and threw me out, but Dawit came flying down the line. He didn't need to slide, but he did, kicking up another cloud of dust and then shouting for joy as he leaped to his feet.

The poor kids in the stupid orange shirts were ahead, 1–0.

The Marauders coach—a tall man with wavy gray-black hair who looked as if he belonged on a yacht—marched out to the mound, said something to the pitcher, and then retreated to the sidelines.

Their pitcher—I learned later his name was Kevin Griffith

—rubbed up the baseball and looked toward center field. I knew what he was thinking—that he hadn't given up anything. A lucky triple on a wild swing, a walk, and a bunt.

Antonio stepped to the plate and took a couple of smooth practice swings. The pitcher stretched, looked back at Tory Nelson leading from second base, and delivered—a fastball right down the middle.

Hit it if you can.

And Antonio could.

He unleashed his short, powerful swing, catching the ball in the sweet spot and driving it into the left center field gap. Nelson scored easily. Antonio wanted the glory of an inside-the-park home run, but the relays from the outfielder to the shortstop and from the shortstop to the catcher were perfect. The catcher put the tag on Antonio, and the umpire's thumb went up.

After our next hitter, Rafael Rodriguez, struck out to end the inning, the Marauders players charged in, faces set, eager to pound out a bunch of hits, score a slew of runs, and put us in our places.

Their leadoff hitter took slow, measured practice swings, but I could feel his impatience. I started him off with a changeup, and his swing was early. He tried to check, but instead tapped a slow roller toward first. Ivan Burgos, our first baseman, fielded it and stepped on the bag. One pitch; one out.

As the hitter walked back to his dugout, he shook his head, as if his out had been a fluke. His teammates on the bench nodded. But when I struck out the next batter on three pitches, I saw worry on their faces.

Ian Thurman, batting third, strode into the batter's box. All the Marauders players and coaches were up, expectant. I took a deep breath, exhaled. The matchup I'd wanted had finally come my way.

I rubbed up the baseball as Antonio started the regular chatter: "No hitter. No hitter." From center field Dawit, picking up on the idea, screamed, "Loser! Loser! Ugly, ugly loser!"

Dawit had had his crazy moments on the school team, so the guys on my team laughed, but the Marauders didn't think it was funny. Thurman stepped out of the batter's box, disbelief in his eyes. The umpire—one of the Laurelhurst coaches —came out from behind home plate and glared out to center field. Antonio motioned for Dawit to stop. Dawit shrugged and went quiet.

The weirdness of it all calmed me. I went into my wind-up and threw. Thurman swung from the heels, fouling the pitch straight back.

I thought about throwing a changeup for the second pitch, but I didn't want to get Thurman out by fooling him. So my second pitch was another fastball; this one he popped down the first base line, out of play.

He stepped out to adjust his batting gloves. When he stepped back in, I made sure he was set, and then delivered. This fastball had late movement, jamming him. For a second I didn't see the ball, but there it was—a soft liner toward first. Burgos made the easy catch for the third out.

Thurman slammed his helmet down. It bounced straight back up, hitting him in the face. Antonio, jogging in from short-stop, saw it and laughed. "Sweet! Do that again!"

Thurman, fuming, took a step toward Antonio, trying to intimidate him. It was a mistake because, though my brother never looks for a fight, he never backs down either. Antonio dropped his glove, his hands balling into fists, his whole body screaming *Let's go!* Before anything stupid happened, their first base coach jumped between them and led Thurman back to the Marauders sideline. As he walked off the field, Thurman pretended he wanted a piece of Antonio, but you could see in his eyes it was all show.

ELEVEN

IN THE TOP OF THE SECOND, the Marauders pitcher set us down one-two-three and then walked off the mound, with an *I'm done fooling around* look on this face.

He was trying to unnerve me, and so was their cleanup hitter, a kid named Jay. He smacked his bat against the outside part of the plate, pulled it back into hitting position, and glared.

I'd overpowered Ian Thurman. I had a two-run lead. Did he really think I'd toss up a fat fastball for him to drive into the gap because he pulled his cap down and furrowed his eyebrows?

I started him off by blowing a fastball right past him. He stepped out, took a couple of vicious practice swings, and stepped back in. He was geared up for another fastball, so I threw him a change. He was way out in front, lifting an easy fly to Kevin Snead in short left.

The next hitter wouldn't expect a first pitch changeup, so I threw one. That's how baseball is—lots of thinking about what the other guy is thinking. He didn't swing, giving me a quick strike. Two fastballs later he was dragging his bat back to the bench. I struck out the next guy, too, though he did hit a long foul fly down the first base line.

Nothing happened in the third for either team, and we went down in order in the top of the fourth. When I took the mound for the bottom of the fourth, the Marauders coach stepped onto the field. "This is it. Last at bat."

It wasn't a full game, and it wasn't a real game, but if I could get three more outs, we would have beaten the Seattle Marauders and I would have held them hitless.

I wanted the W so badly that my nerves took over. I overthrew my first pitch; it sailed inside and plunked their leadoff hitter in the back. He grimaced as he made his way to first.

The Marauders bench came alive, half of the guys screaming at me for hitting the batter and the other half screaming encouragement to their teammate as he settled in at the plate.

The wild pitch made me aim the ball instead of throwing it. My next delivery came in fat, and the Marauders hitter smacked it into right center for a double, their first hit. That put runners at second and third with nobody out and Ian Thurman stepping up to the plate.

I knew the correct baseball strategy, even if nobody else on my team did: walk Thurman to set up a force at every base.

But there was no way I was walking Ian Thurman.

Thurman took a few slow, easy practice swings.

He knew what was going to happen. Everybody on his team knew what was going to happen. Kids from North Central don't beat kids from Laurelhurst. Not in baseball, not in anything.

Thurman would drive one of my pitches over the fence. Then he'd trot around the bases as his teammates high-fived one another. We'd have lost—just like we were supposed to.

I held the ball gently, as if it were a small bird and I was feeling for its tiny, beating heart. There'd be no changeups, no sliders, no pitches in the dirt. I was coming right down the middle, trusting the ball to move late.

He swung over the top of the first pitch, a fastball that darted down and in. He stepped out, took two breaths, and stepped in. I came with pure heat again. Again he swung, a long, powerful swing. Too long. The ball was by him before his bat reached the hitting zone.

Strike two.

Ian followed his same routine, stepping out, taking his two breaths, stepping in. A strange peace came over me. Everything loose and light. Everything fluid. The zone. The ball exploded out of my hand. His bat ripped across the plate. His teammates yelled in anticipation. But all he caught was air.

Strike three.

I don't remember pitching to the final two hitters. All I know is that my arm felt as light as air, and the ball came out of my hand like a missile. When the final hitter struck out, the guys behind me raced toward the mound, jumping around as though we'd won the World Series. Pushkin, wearing his orange shirt, barked insanely as he ran in circles.

As we walked toward Leskov's van, the Marauders head coach came over to me. "What's your name, son?"

"Laz Weathers."

"That's a helluva fastball you got, Laz. What high school do you play for?"

"N-N-North Central."

His mind worked for a moment. "Oh, the team that forfeited. No wonder I didn't recognize you." He nodded. "Well, you've got a golden arm there. Take good care of it."

TWELVE

WE PLAYED FOUR GAMES in the next two weeks, and they all followed the same pattern. Mr. Leskov drove us to some nice field. We piled out of the van, and our opponents snickered at our raggedy pants and our bright orange T-shirts. Then I took the mound, fired a few fastballs past them, and the smirks disappeared.

I wasn't perfect on the mound. Some ground balls got through; some fly balls fell in. And if a ball was hit hard to some-body other than Antonio, the chance for an error was pretty good. But we scratched out at least three runs in every game, and I never gave up more than two, so we won them all.

On the rides back, we drank the orange soda—Mr. Leskov's joke—that he always had for us. Antonio and some of the other guys took turns telling stories, keeping everybody loose. It was all so much fun that I could almost convince myself that playing for Leskov was better than playing with a select team.

Almost.

When I wasn't working or pitching, I'd go to the community center and play foosball or pool or just hang out. Every so often

I'd log onto one of the computers to check how Ian Thurman and the rest of the Seattle Marauders were doing.

While I'd spent the Fourth of July driving the Gator back and forth at the driving range, Thurman had been banging out doubles and home runs at a tournament in Boise. He'd played in another tournament in Missoula in the middle of July, and the Marauders would later play at Cannon Beach, Oregon, before finishing the summer with three games in Vancouver, British Columbia.

Thurman was the biggest star on a team of stars. A picture of him crossing home plate after a grand slam was at the top of the Seattle Marauders homepage. He was batting over .400 and was the leading RBI guy on the team.

So what if I'd struck him out? So what if I'd shut down the whole team? No scout had seen it. No reporter had written about it. It might as well have happened in an ice cave in Antarctica.

THIRTEEN

I HUNG OUT WITH ANTONIO during our baseball games, but that was it. He had his morning job at Home Depot; I worked afternoons at the driving range. As soon as Antonio was out of Leskov's van, he headed to the back fence.

As I swept up golf balls in the John Deere, I'd see him with Garrett and the others. They'd be leaning against the fence or sitting on old plastic chairs just outside an abandoned toolshed. It looked like nothing—Antonio hanging out, telling stories, making other kids laugh. And that's what it was most of the time. Nothing. But every once in a while a guy would wander back. Then everything would stop as he bought pills from Garrett. The guy would leave, and the stories would start again.

As the weeks rolled by, though, *every once in a while* became *every hour* and then *every half-hour*. Some of the guys were from Jet City. Others walked in off Aurora Avenue or rode in on bicycles. They'd work their way down Jet City's gravel lanes to where Garrett and Antonio were hanging. There'd be talk and then an exchange. After a handclasp, the guy would pedal or walk away. About every tenth person was a female.

The first time a car drove in was on July 20. I know the exact date because we'd beaten Stanwood the day before. I was replaying the game in my head when a black Kia came in the side entrance of Jet City, drove slowly to the back fence, and pulled to a stop.

The driver's window rolled down, and the exchange with Garrett was made. The window closed; the Kia backed up and then glided out of Jet City. The next day, two cars pulled in. The Tuesday after that, I counted four cars—and that was just while I was driving the John Deere.

When Antonio left for his job at Home Depot the next morning, I walked out of the trailer with him. He'd gotten me to agree not to say anything to Mom, but that didn't mean I couldn't speak my mind to him.

"What's up?" he asked as we headed toward Aurora Avenue.

"G-Garrett."

He rolled his eyes. "Suja again?"

"No. Not Suja. I c-can s-see what's going on with m-my own eyes. You s-say it's n-nothing, but G-Garrett is selling more and m-more."

He blew out air. "Laz, Garrett is so smalltime that he doesn't exist. He's like a fly surrounded by jets at SeaTac. Nobody cares about a kid selling a few pills at Jet City."

"I d-don't g-get it. Why hang with h-him?"

His face clouded. "Look, you're happy playing Ping-Pong at the community center with Leskov watching. But I'm not you. The walls just push in on me there. I feel like I'm going to suffocate. But when I'm at the fence with Garrett and Jasmine and the rest of them—I can breathe. I don't sell; I don't buy; I don't use. I just hang out and tell stories with my friends. Have some laughs. So stop worrying about me."

FOURTEEN

MOM HAD BEEN GETTING HOME late lots of nights that summer. I figured she was working overtime, but a few days later I found out the real reason. Coming back from the driving range, I spotted a GMC pickup parked behind her Corolla. Cleated logger boots were outside our front door, and the music pouring out of the trailer was Megadeth, not Pearl Jam or Nirvana or any of the old rock Mom listens to.

I opened the door and stepped inside. Stretched out on the sofa, his feet up on the cushions, was a burly guy with dark hair and a thick black beard. He was wearing a muscle shirt that showed off tatted biceps.

"Laz," Mom said, standing up to meet me, her voice strangely high-pitched. She motioned with her head toward the guy. "This is Curtis Driver, Antonio's dad. You remember him, don't you?"

I did, sort of.

He'd lived with us in an apartment in the Central District when I was in preschool, the year before Mom bought our trailer in Jet City.

Curtis stood and stretched a hand toward me. His hand-shake was so strong it hurt. "Good to see you again, Laz."

"G-G-Good to s-s-see you," I said.

"Last time I saw you," he said, grinning, "you were having trouble keeping the sheets dry at night. You better with that now?"

Blood rushed to my face.

"Don't tease him," Mom said. She looked at me. "Do you know where Antonio is?"

I shook my head. "I'm g-going to change."

I stepped into my room, closed the door, and dropped onto my bed. I belched, and it tasted like puke.

I didn't want to go back out and face Curtis, so I just stayed there. Finally, I heard the front door open—Antonio.

The walls in the trailer are about as thin as a cracker. Mom did most of the talking. Sometimes Curtis would say something, usually followed by a big laugh. When Antonio spoke, his voice was so quiet I couldn't make out his words.

I started to feel like a spy so I switched on my radio, plugged in headphones, and tuned to KJR. I'd been listening to fans rip the Mariners for about ten minutes when Mom tapped on my door. "Laz, Curtis is taking us to Northgate Mall for dinner."

We went in Mom's Corolla, but Curtis drove. Mom asked questions about how the day had gone, and I answered. Antonio stared out the window, grim.

As we parked and walked to the food court, Curtis said, "I've been thinning hemlocks all day, and I'm starved. I think I'll get myself a twelve-inch hero sandwich. How about you, Antonio? You feel like a hero?"

"Not really," Antonio mumbled.

Irritation flashed in Curtis's eyes.

"I'll get a hero," I said.

Ignoring me, Curtis opened his wallet, took out two ten-dollar bills, and held them out to Antonio. "Get whatever you'd like."

Antonio stared at the bills. "I won't need that much."

"Then bring me back the change."

Mom was full of cheer while we ate, going on about how good her fish and chips were. Once everyone had finished, Curtis looked to Mom. She nodded, and then Curtis stood. "I'm going to take a walk," he said. "Down to the end of the mall and back. Heroes need to keep moving."

FIFTEEN

"SO HOW DOES YOUR FATHER seem to you?" Mom asked Antonio.

"He's okay," Antonio answered, picking at his fingernails.

"Just okay?"

Antonio kept picking at his nails.

"Antonio?"

Antonio frowned. "I don't know him. I can't say anything about a guy I don't know."

"How about you, Laz? What do you think of Curtis?"

I looked at the table. "I d-don't know him either."

She folded her hands together as if she were praying and looked from Antonio to me. "Well, I hope that eventually he is more than okay for you boys, because Curtis and I have decided that we're going to reconnect."

Silence.

"What's that m-mean?" I finally asked.

"Duh," Antonio mocked.

"Antonio," Mom snapped. She turned to me. "It means he's going to move in, Laz."

Antonio dropped his head. Five seconds went by. Ten.

Fifteen. "Does he expect me to call him *Dad?*" Antonio said, breaking the silence.

"Do you want to?"

The answer was immediate. "No."

"Then call him *Curtis.* Laz, you can call him that, too."

I nodded.

"And you'll be respectful. Both of you."

I nodded.

"Antonio?"

"Whatever you say."

"But where will he sleep?" I asked.

As soon as the words were out, I felt like a fool. Antonio laid his forehead on the table. Mom paused, and then answered. "He's going to sleep with me, like a grown man does with a grown woman."

I looked toward the mall and saw Curtis approaching. When he reached our table, he opened the bag he was holding. "I got us pretzels."

"Thanks," I said, taking one.

Mom also took one, but Antonio shook his head. "Not hungry."

Curtis drove the Corolla back to Jet City, got into his pickup, and returned to his own place, wherever that was.

Back inside the trailer, I lay on my bed, listening to my mom through the wall, moving around. Soon Curtis Driver would be in her room, in her bed. They'd have sex sometimes, and I'd hear them. Just thinking about that made my whole body ache.

SIXTEEN

TWO DAYS LATER he moved in. I was coming home from the driving range when I saw him unload a box from the back of his pickup and carry it up the three stairs that led to the trailer.

When he stepped back out, our eyes met. "Let's talk," he said.

He went to his truck and leaned against it. I stood in the roadway and waited. Nothing. Finally he scrunched up his face and spoke. "I know you don't want me moving in, Laz. And I get it."

I shook my head. "I n-n-never—"

"Just listen," he said, stopping me.

I nodded.

"You're going to be a senior. Once you graduate, you'll be wanting to move out, right? That's just natural. Start your own life and all that. So how long is that? Nine? Ten months? That's all we're talking about. We can make this work that long, right?"

I swallowed. "Y-Yeah."

Curtis stuck out his fist and we bumped knuckles. Then he nodded toward his truck. "How about giving me a hand with my stuff?"

Nothing was heavy, not even his big-screen TV, but my legs were wobbly, as if I'd been hit by a sucker punch. Sure I was planning on moving out of the trailer someday, but I always figured that I'd decide when I was ready. Now Curtis Driver was calling the shots. Ten months, and then he wanted me gone. I could feel time rushing at me like a train.

That night, Mom ordered Domino's for Antonio and me, and then she and Curtis drove off somewhere. When the pizza came, we ate in the front room, the Mariners game on the TV.

"What do you think?" Antonio asked, his head down.

"About what?"

"Come on, Laz."

I thought about Curtis shoving me out the door in ten months, but that's not what I said. "It's okay."

He snorted. "It sucks."

I shrugged. "He's your f-father. You should g-give him a ch-chance."

Antonio's eyes narrowed. "I'm dead to him for twelve years and I'm supposed to act like it's Christmas because he's back for a couple of weeks?"

"Maybe he'll st-stick around this t-time."

Antonio stared at me for a moment. Then he pushed his chair back and headed for the front door.

"You g-going out?"

"Yeah."

"You want some c-company?"

"I'm good," he said, and the door closed behind him.

I finished the pizza and dumped the box in the trash. Curtis's TV was ten times nicer than Mom's, but instead of following the game, I kept picturing those TV shows where families reunite after years apart. Everybody hugs and cries and they're all happy.

That wasn't going to happen with Antonio and Curtis.

Around eleven I went to bed. I couldn't sleep, so I channel-surfed FM stations until I found a murder mystery full of creaking doors and howling winds. It was fake-y, but it was okay.

Around eleven thirty, Mom and Curtis returned. I could hear them moving in Mom's bedroom, and I panicked. Then an idea came to me. I rooted around in a drawer until I found my earbuds. I plugged them into my radio and turned up the volume. I followed the story for a while, but then I must have fallen asleep, because I don't remember the ending. The next morning, jazz was playing when I awoke.

A wave of relief broke over me. All I had to do was sleep with the radio on and the earbuds in, and I'd never hear anything from my mom's bedroom.

When I came out that morning, Antonio had already left for his job at Home Depot. Mom was in the kitchen drinking coffee, and I could hear Curtis walking in her bedroom. He was a big man, way over two hundred pounds, and with every step the floorboards groaned.

"You want scrambled eggs?" Mom asked.

I heard the shower go on; Curtis would be a while. I could eat and get out without seeing him.

"Okay," I said.

As Mom scrambled the eggs I put two slices of bread into the toaster.

"This can work," she said when she put a plate in front of me a few minutes later, "if we all make an effort."

She wasn't eating—I guess she was waiting for Curtis—but she sat with me. "What are you thinking?" she asked when I was about done.

"N-Nothing."

"Something's on your mind. Laz. Tell me."

I used a crust of the toast to push the last of the egg onto my fork. I kept my head down. "What was my d-dad like?"

I hadn't planned on asking. I'm not even sure I knew I was thinking about him until the words came out.

Mom sat back. "Your dad was just a boy, Laz. Just a boy."

I kept my eyes on my plate. "Do you ever t-try to g-get in touch with him?"

"No."

"Do you think he m-might—"

"Laz, your dad is gone, and he's not coming back. I'm sorry."

SEVENTEEN

WE HAD A GAME a couple days later. Antonio had missed two of the last three games, and when it was time to head over to the community center, he was missing again. Whenever he didn't play, the team was flat, the effort not there. If he kept skipping games, other guys would skip, too.

I texted him. **Game. North Acres. 1 hour. U there?**

I stared at the phone, waiting for a reply. It came ten minutes later: **try 2 b**

As I warmed up, I kept looking for him.

Then, as the game was starting, Garrett's Subaru pulled into the parking lot. The passenger door opened, and Antonio stepped out. He made it to the bench as Dawit, leading off, strode to the plate. The guys on the bench all called out to Antonio, glad he'd shown up, but I was angry.

"Where were you?" I asked.

He picked up on my irritation. "I'm here, Laz. Okay?"

We were playing Bitter Lake, a team not even close to the Seattle Marauders in talent. If I'd been on my game, I would have dominated, but I couldn't get settled. And I was unlucky, which made everything worse. They hit some balls hard, but even their weak hits seemed to find holes. We lost 10–0.

During our last at bat, I'd seen Antonio on his phone. And while the rest of us were shaking hands with the Bitter Lake guys, he was driving off with Garrett.

When we got back to the community center, I helped Mr. Leskov unload the equipment, got Pushkin out of his orange shirt, and then walked to Jet City. Inside the trailer, Curtis was sprawled on the sofa, his feet up, watching *SportsCenter* on his big TV. I headed into the kitchen, where I made myself a peanut butter sandwich, and was just sitting down to eat when Curtis appeared in the doorway. "Where's Antonio?"

"I d-don't know."

"He wasn't at the game?"

"He was there. "

"So why didn't he come back with you?"

I shrugged.

"You two don't hang out?"

"Not t-too m-much."

I took a bite of my sandwich, hoping Curtis would go back to the sofa, but he stayed. "So, are you kind of the nerdy older brother? Is that what I'm seeing?"

He was smiling, as if he were making a joke, but I felt a sting.

"I g-guess."

"His friends. They're okay, though. Right?"

Just then the front door opened and Mom stuck her head in. "Hey, can somebody give me a hand with the groceries?"

"You got it," Curtis said. Within minutes, grocery bags were on the kitchen table and I was in my room.

EIGHTEEN

I HAD ANOTHER ROTTEN START against the Kirkland Owls, maybe because Antonio had skipped out again. In the van, Dawit said he'd seen him and Garrett heading downtown on Aurora Avenue. "Did he quit the team?" Dawit asked. "Because if he quits, I think I'll quit, too."

"He didn't quit."

My mind wasn't on baseball when I took the mound. I walked the first two guys and then threw a wild pitch to the third hitter, allowing the runners to move up to second and third.

Then came something I wasn't expecting. Mr. Leskov, for the first time all season, called time and strode out to the mound. "What's wrong with you?" he demanded. "Your head in sky."

"I'll do better."

"We get new pitcher? Maybe Dawit. Maybe Nelson."

"N-No. I can p-pitch."

He glared at me. "You pitch then. You strike three these guys or someone else try." With that, he stomped back to the bench.

I turned and looked out at my teammates, comical in their bright orange T-shirts. They didn't know Joe DiMaggio from Joe Montana. Still, they were doing their best, just like Leskov —who knew nothing about baseball. With or without Antonio, I needed to do my best.

I didn't worry about painting the corners. I poured pitch after pitch across the plate, trusting my stuff. And it worked. I struck out Kirkland's three-hitter and their cleanup guy. I thought I'd strike out the side, but the number-five batter looped a soft line drive toward short right. Ivan Burgos raced back and then dived. The ball stuck out of the top of his glove like a scoop of vanilla ice cream, but he hung on for the third out. The guys came in from the field excited, pounding Ivan on the back and giving me knuckle bumps.

We scored twice in the second to take the lead. In their half of the inning, I got the first two outs quickly. With two strikes on the next hitter, I threw a curve that sat in the middle of the plate like a pumpkin.

The Owl batter swung from the heels and caught the ball in the sweet spot, sending a towering drive to center. I was sure it was over Dawit's head, but that guy can fly. At the last moment he reached up and snagged the ball before tumbling head over heels to the ground.

Dawit grinned as he ran in. When he reached second base, he stopped and did a little dance on the bag. The infielders, who'd all waited for him, gave him high-fives. We ended up winning 8–0—the first game we'd won without Antonio.

In the van going back to North Central, with Pushkin's paws digging into my thighs, I texted Antonio, giving him the score and a couple of highlights. No response. I held the phone as the miles clicked away. Where was he? What was he doing?

Finally it vibrated.

C grats.

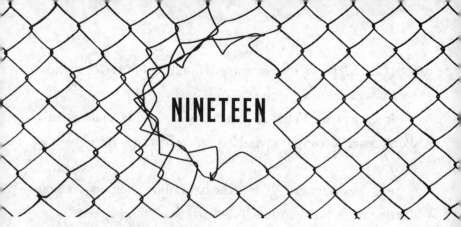

NINETEEN

BACK AT THE COMMUNITY CENTER, I helped Mr. Leskov put away the bats, balls, and gloves, then headed to my job. When someone called my name, I turned and saw Coach Kellogg walking toward me. None of the teachers or coaches at North Central High lived near the school. Why was he here?

"Laz, good to see you. How'd your game go?"

"P-pretty good."

"Did you win?"

"Yeah. Eight to zip."

"Shutout. That's more than pretty good." He motioned to a couple of chairs by the window that looked out at the jungle gym. "Got a minute?"

We sat, and he tugged at his scruffy beard. "My wife just had a baby, a little girl. I've taken a teaching job at Lake Stevens High, which is close to my home, so I can help out more. I wanted to tell you in person and to thank you for all you've done for the baseball program at North Central."

I paused, trying to figure out what to say. "I'll m-m-miss

you, Coach," I said, the right words finally coming. "The whole t-team will."

It wasn't true. Kellogg's practices were boring, and he really didn't coach. Most guys wouldn't care when they heard he was leaving.

His eyes went sad. "That's the hard thing about moving on. Cutting those bonds. You tell the guys that I'll miss them."

"Sure."

An awkward silence followed before he spoke again.

"Did you hear you've got a new principal at North Central?"

I shook my head. "No."

"Mrs. Park. And she's not a big fan of team sports. She had me give her the number of kids who participated in the baseball program, and asked about the cop thing at Oak Tree Cinema. Then she started going on about how intramurals get more kids involved."

I didn't understand why he was telling me all this, and my confusion must have shown. "Long story short. Mrs. Park wants to eliminate the baseball program and use our field for Ultimate Frisbee, kite flying, rocketry. With me gone, she'll get her way."

My blood ran cold. "You mean North Central won't have a b-baseball t-team next year?"

"That's exactly what I mean." Then Mr. Kellogg leaned toward me and spoke in a whisper. "But Laz, North Central dropping baseball could be a good thing for you."

I felt dizzy. "How? If there's no t-team, I'm done."

He slid his chair closer. "There's a rule about this. If your high school doesn't offer a sport, you can go to any Seattle high school and play for them. Broadview High is closest, but they're no good. Laurelhurst High is only a mile farther away. I called their coach and told him about baseball being canceled at North Central. At first he was bored, but that changed when I mentioned your name. A parent who coaches a select summer team had told him about you. The point is—Laurelhurst wants you."

I swallowed. "M-Me? They want me?"

Kellogg's smile grew wider. "Yeah. And they don't mess around. They've got an off-season program that starts soon. I checked on the buses. One goes down Thirty-fifth right after school lets out, so getting there will be easy. I don't know how you'll get home afterward, but you're a North Central kid, right? North Central kids figure out a way." He paused. "Interested?"

I was so excited my voice squeaked. "Yeah. I'm interested. A-And thank—"

He cut me off. "Nothing to thank me for. North Central wasn't doing right by you, not with the talent you have. I'll call their coach tomorrow and tell him you want in." He looked at the clock above the main desk. "I need to go. My wife and I are going to her parents' for dinner."

He stood, shook my hand, and headed out. "Coach—" I called out before he reached the door. "Way to go. With the baby I mean."

He laughed. "Thanks, Laz. I appreciate it."

I stood stock-still for a long moment, until I remembered

the driving range. As I hurried to work, the excitement slipped away and fear took its place. The Laurelhurst kids would have designer clothes and smartphones and money in their wallets. Some would have their own cars. Even my duffle bag would suck compared to the ones they had. I wouldn't know anyone, so my words would get stuck. I could see my head tilting sideways as I repeated some sound three, four, six times while the Laurelhurst players exchanged half-hidden smiles.

Going alone would be miserable, but I'd be okay if Antonio tried out, too. He had the talent to make the Laurelhurst team; all he had to do was put in the effort. Yeah, he was skipping out on Leskov's games. But Laurelhurst was different. It was a real team—he wouldn't be ashamed to play for them. He'd be in my corner, and I'd be in his, and together we'd show them.

TWENTY

ONCE CURTIS MOVED IN, he was after Antonio to do things with him, but Antonio always put him off. *Can't—going to Green Lake. Can't—meeting friends at the arcade . . .*

Finally, one morning in late August, Curtis laid a Mariners schedule in front of Antonio as he was scarfing down a bowl of Cheerios. "You point to a day you *can* go to a Mariners game and I'll buy tickets. And once I buy them, you're going. No backing out."

Antonio looked to Mom, and she looked right back at him. "Laz is coming with us. Right?" he said.

Curtis didn't even glance at me. "Sure, Laz can come. Now pick a game."

Antonio looked at the calendar. "Tonight's fine."

The Mariners were playing the Angels. Curtis tried to get Antonio talking as we drove to T-Mobile Park, but all he got were grunts and a few *yeah*s and *nah*s and *maybe*s.

Curtis had used StubHub to get the seats, and he hadn't cheaped out: third level, right behind home plate, four rows up. Antonio tried to make it so I'd be sitting in the middle, but Curtis didn't let that happen.

In the early innings Curtis would say normal stuff to Antonio. *Trout has one sweet swing . . . The air is dead in this park . . . You got to wonder if the Mariners will ever make it to the World Series.*

Antonio gave him nothing back.

"Give the m-man a break," I whispered to Antonio in the bottom of the fourth.

He got up. "I've got to take a leak," he said as he pushed by me.

Half an inning went by, then an inning. Curtis kept looking at the aisle. Finally he stood and scanned the entire area. "He didn't get himself lost, did he?"

I shook my head. "N-no way. We're directly behind home p-plate."

Right then he spotted Antonio working his way toward us. "Here, Son," he called out, waving his hand. It was the first time I'd ever heard him call Antonio *Son*, and Antonio flinched.

The Mariners rallied to win on a two-out ninth-inning hit by some guy just up from Triple-A. Around us, fans went crazy, but the three of us were zombies. We returned to the car in silence.

As Curtis drove back to Jet City, I could feel his fury building. I was waiting for him to lash out at Antonio, but instead he went after me. "Laz, has your mom ever told you about your dad? How he ended up in prison?"

My throat went dry. I hadn't known my father was in prison.

He chuckled. "She hasn't, has she? It's some story. Your old man stole something like thirty-eight dollars from a 7-Eleven over in Spokane. When he came out with his loot, he discovered that his partner had panicked and driven off. So your genius dad decided to—"

"Stop it," Antonio interrupted.

"What?" Curtis said.

"Leave Laz alone. He hasn't done anything to you."

There was a long silence, and then Curtis spoke in a steely voice. "All right. You don't want me to talk to Laz, then you talk to me."

"Okay," Antonio said. "I will."

And he did. For the rest of the ride home, they talked about the game, about Jet City, about movies and food and Husky football. "Was that so bad?" Curtis asked when he pulled up in front of the trailer.

"No," Antonio said as he opened the door and stepped out. "It wasn't."

TWENTY-ONE

OUR LAST SUMMER GAME was on August 31 against the Green Lake Gophers. Leskov spread the word that after the game he'd pay for us to go out on paddleboats in Green Lake and then have a pizza lunch, so everyone showed up.

Since the Mariners game, Curtis and Antonio had been getting along. When Curtis heard where our final game was being played, he told Antonio he'd be there, which meant Antonio had to be there too. "We're cutting down a couple of old cedars in Woodland Park," Curtis said, "so I can stop by during my lunch. You'd better do something good. You hear me?"

At noon, when the game started, gray clouds were heading our way from Puget Sound. Trees were swaying in the breeze, dropping the first leaves of fall; some of the walkers circling the lake were wearing long-sleeved shirts.

I'd found my rhythm against the Kirkland Owls, and I'd stayed in the zone after that. Against the Gophers, I threw easy—so easy—yet the ball shot across the plate. They had no chance.

Curtis arrived as I took the mound to pitch the bottom of the third. As he walked from his pickup truck toward the diamond, he waved. For an instant I thought he was waving to me, but his eyes were on Antonio. That threw me off for a few pitches, but then I rediscovered my rhythm. Three up; three down. Two pop-ups and a groundout.

In the top of the fourth, Dawit razzed me on the bench. "This is boring, Laz. Let them hit. We want some action."

"Make some action f-for yourself," I joked, looking down the bench. "Get some h-hits; score some r-runs."

And they did, banging out three singles and a double. Two runs had already scored when Antonio stepped to the plate with two on and two out. He worked the count to 2-0 and then smoked a line drive into right center that plated both runners and brought Curtis to his feet. "Yes! Yes!" His voice boomed from behind me as Antonio slid safely into third.

"Last at bat," their coach called out as I headed to the mound for the bottom of the fifth. I took the ball in my hand, turned around, and checked the fielders. Then, from nowhere, a wave of sadness broke over me.

Summer was done. Summer baseball was done. There wouldn't be a North Central baseball team in the spring. This was my last time pitching with my guys from my neighborhood behind me.

"Let's go!" a parent shouted from the sideline, and I snapped out of it.

It took eleven pitches for me to strike out the side.

Shutout.

No-hitter.

Perfect game.

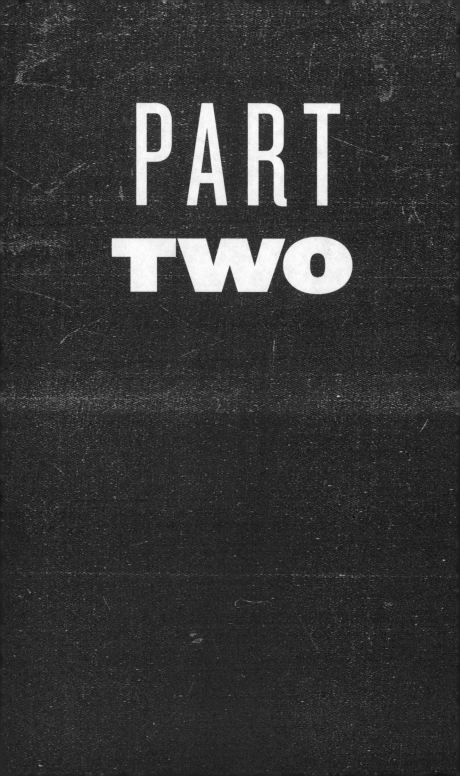

PART
TWO

ONE

WHEN I WAS LITTLE, the first day of school had been exciting. When had that stopped?

Antonio and I left early, trudging off in a light drizzle. "It's going to be weird at school," Antonio said as we neared North Central. "All those years, with everybody knowing I didn't have a dad, and now I've got one." He paused. "For as long as he stays."

"He'll s-stay."

"How do you know?"

"I just feel it."

Once we reached the campus, kids started calling out to him. "Hey, Antonio what's up?" . . . "Antonio, who you got for gym?" . . . "Antonio, when's your lunch period?"

It was as if I were invisible. The same thing happened every year and—in a smaller way—every day. I gave him a quick nod, and he nodded back. Then I headed to my first period class.

I'd barely passed Algebra I, so Algebra II—a state requirement for graduation—had me terrified. My teacher, Mr. Eagan, was new to the school and also looked like a brand-new teacher.

Eagan's voice was shaky and his smile way too big as he

introduced himself. It was the first period of the first day, but ten minutes into the class, kids got rowdy, leaning back and talking to kids rows behind him. Thirty minutes in, they had cell phones out and were texting or playing games. A girl made a phone call and then covered one ear so she could hear. Mr. Eagan—his smile gone—said, "Please, no phone calls during class," but she kept talking.

During lunch, I joined a long line outside my counselor's office. It took nearly the entire period before I was able to see Ms. Wilhelm, and she was not in a good mood. When I told her I wanted a different algebra teacher, she leaned forward, her eyes wide. "Seriously, Laz? One day? Not happening."

I started to argue, but she flapped her hands in front of her face. "Goodbye, Laz. Door is right behind you."

I had my hand on the doorknob when she suddenly snapped her fingers. "Wait one second. You're the baseball player, right?"

I nodded.

"Sit back down."

As I settled into the chair, she fumbled with papers on her desk. "You heard there's not going to be a team this year?"

"I h-heard."

"A man from Laurelhurst High called this morning," she said as she shuffled through a stack of papers on her desk. "Here it is. Bill Thurman. He's someone involved with their baseball team. He wants to talk to you about playing for them." She slid the slip of paper to me. "You must be pretty good. Normally Laurelhurst doesn't want anything to do with us."

TWO

FOR THE REST OF THE DAY, I kept feeling in my pocket for that piece of paper, afraid I'd lost it. When sixth period ended, I headed to the library and found a study carrel in the back. I'm always in dread that I'll stutter on the phone, and Mr. Thurman had to be Ian Thurman's father, which made it worse. I took deep breaths for a few moments before I punched in the numbers.

"Bill Thurman," a gravelly voice said after one ring.

"Hello," I said, making myself speak slowly, "this is Laz Weathers returning—"

"Laz, glad to hear from you. You might remember me. You had quite a game against my son's team this summer. The Seattle Marauders. We talked a little after."

"I re-remember," I said.

For the next few minutes he asked how I was doing, how my arm was feeling. In the dark of the carrel, my stutter mostly stayed hidden.

"Well, here's why I called. Since your school won't have a team this year, we here at Laurelhurst would like you to pitch for us. How's that sound?"

"It sounds g-great."

"Good. Listen, our off-season training program begins in a couple of weeks. It's totally voluntary and has nothing to do with Coach Vereen or the school team, though most of the Laurelhurst players will be there. You're welcome to participate, get a feel for what Laurelhurst baseball is about. Interested?"

"Y-Yes."

"Officially, it's the YMCA that runs the program, and they have forms that need to be filled out and signed. Talk to your parents and then call me with a good time for me to stop by. Okay?"

"Okay."

"Any questions you have for me?"

I swallowed. "My b-brother plays baseball, too. He's a g-good hitter and a g-good fielder. He's the one who g-got a d-double against your pitcher. He c-can come, right?"

There was a pause. "Sure he can. Like I said, the workouts are open to everyone. No guarantee that he'll make the Laurelhurst team, though. No guarantee for you, either, for that matter, but you're both welcome to try out."

I thanked him and cut the connection. Then I carefully folded up the piece of paper with his phone number on it and tucked it into my wallet.

I'd never told Antonio about the chance to play for Laurelhurst. I was afraid he'd say no, and I wasn't sure I'd have the guts to go alone. But in the darkness of the study carrel I knew that it didn't matter what Antonio did. It didn't matter that I stuttered, that my shoes were old, my glove ratty, my jeans ripped.

Laurelhurst was my last chance.

THREE

WHEN I REACHED JET CITY that afternoon, a crowd of people was milling around the main entrance, staring at a large sign. As I moved closer, I saw the words **PROPOSED LAND ACTION** in foot-high letters, but I couldn't read the smaller words below.

Jasmine, the girl who was new to Jet City, was in front of me. She was wearing shorts and a pink tube top that left her shoulders bare. I was a little afraid of her, but I needed to know, so I tapped her shoulder. She wheeled around, angry, and then not angry. "Oh, it's you, Laz."

"What's g-going on?"

She grinned sarcastically. "My family just moved in, and now we're getting booted out."

"What are you t-t-talking about?"

"Jet City is going to be demolished. One hundred twenty-five high-class townhomes are going to be built right here."

"T-Townhomes?" I said, not believing. "B-Behind a d-driving range?"

"They're tearing down the driving range, too." Her smile broadened. "You get it double. You lose your home and your job."

There was a roaring in my ears. "D-does it s-say when?"

"Somebody said three months."

From across the roadway, Garrett called her name.

"Got to go," she said, and she wiggled her fingers as a good-bye wave.

I headed down the gravel road to our trailer, where no one was home. After dropping my backpack on my bed, I walked to work. There was another **PROPOSED LAND ACTION** sign in the parking lot of the range. No one was crowded around it, so I was able to read everything. When I stepped into the golf shop, Mr. Matsui looked up. "You saw?"

"Is it t-true we have to b-be out in three months?"

He shook his head. "Who told you that? Summer is more like it."

The roaring in my ears lessened. Summer meant there'd be time for Mom to find a new place, time for me to finish high school. Then I thought of my job. "Is the d-driving range g-going to stay open?"

"That's the plan. You can work here until they tear it down."

"What about y-you?"

"Weighing my options, as the rich guys say." He smiled. "Chances are, I'll be here to the bitter end, or close to it."

His phone rang. As he answered, I grabbed the keys to the John Deere and headed out.

It was so noisy driving up and down the range that I couldn't think, which was okay. On one pass, a golf ball whacked the metal cage protecting me, making me jump. A guy on the range pointed at me with his club, a big smile on his face, while next to him his buddy laughed.

After I'd picked up the range, I drove to the far back fence. Golf balls get caught in the net there, and the only way to retrieve them is by hand with a ball shagger.

I'd walked almost the entire fence line when I spotted Garrett and Dustin Browner heading down the gravel road toward their hangout. Dustin had been in the juvenile jail up on Capitol Hill. I tried to remember what he'd done. Stolen a car?

"That looks like fun, Laz," Garrett said as he neared me.

"Laugh a m-minute," I answered, working quickly.

"You missed some," Dustin said, pointing behind me. "There's one there and another one there. And two more there." He snorted. "You kind of suck at your job."

I kept going forward.

"You'll see your brother tonight, right?" Garrett said after a while.

"Yeah. Why?"

"Have him call me. Tell him I've got something for him."

"Why don't you c-call him yourself?"

Garrett looked at the sky. "Because his phone is off or else his battery is dead. So just give him my message. Okay?"

I could feel my chest tighten, as if it were in a vise. I picked up a couple more balls and then faced him.

"N-No," I said.

Garrett looked confused. "What do you mean, *no?*"

"I m-mean, you want to sell d-drugs—that's your b-business. But k-keep my b-brother out of it."

"You're joking," Garrett said, smiling in disbelief.

Instead of answering, I turned and headed back to the John Deere.

"K-k-k-keep m-m-my b-b-b-b-brother out-out-out of-of-of it-it-it," Dustin called after me, and they both laughed.

FOUR

I WORKED UNTIL EIGHT. When I returned to the trailer, Mom was sitting at the kitchen table, smoking for the first time in months. Curtis, drinking a beer, sat across from her, two empties in front of him.

"You see the sign?" Mom asked.

I nodded.

Curtis took a swig of his beer. "America. Land where the rich get richer and the poor get poorer."

Mom stubbed out her cigarette and lit a new one.

"Mr. Matsui says nothing will happen until summer," I said.

Mom blew out a stream of smoke. "I hope he's right. Old Mr. Hastings says Christmas, but he's always doom and gloom. Maybe they expect us to move into a stable with Baby Jesus and the donkeys." She paused. "There's an information meeting Friday at the community center."

Curtis checked the time on his cell. "Where's Antonio?"

"I d-don't know. I've been at work."

Curtis hated it when Antonio was out late on school nights. Mom had never been strict about things like that.

Right then we heard Antonio's footsteps on the metal stairs leading up to the trailer. "Where you been?" Curtis asked once Antonio stepped inside.

"Just hanging," Antonio mumbled.

"Did you see the sign about the townhomes?" Curtis asked.

Antonio nodded. "Yeah. I saw it. It sucks." He turned toward Mom. "Is there something I could microwave? I'm starving."

Mom stood. "I'll do it for you. How about you, Laz? You must be hungry, too."

Ten minutes later, as Curtis was watching a football game in the main room, Antonio and I were eating enchiladas, rice, and beans. As we ate, I thought about Garrett. Antonio would get his message somehow, but it wasn't going to be from me.

"Classes go okay?" Mom asked.

"Fine," Antonio said.

She looked to me.

I explained—my voice low so Curtis wouldn't hear—that I was worried I wouldn't be able to learn anything from the new algebra teacher.

"I can help you," Antonio said. "If you want."

"That'd be g-great," I said. "Thanks."

I finished eating, cleaned up, and then went to my room to listen to the Mariners game. Antonio stayed in the living room to watch football with Curtis, which only half surprised me. Some days they got along; some days they didn't. It was a flip of the coin.

That night, I could hear the two of them shouting at the

refs and groaning over botched plays. It was ten thirty before the last game ended and the television went silent. I rolled onto my side and tried to sleep. Only then did I realize I hadn't told anyone about Laurelhurst.

FIVE

CURTIS TOOK OVERTIME whenever he could, which is why he was still at work the next night when Mom put dinner together. As I helped her, I told her about the training program with Mr. Thurman and then the chance to play for the team. "Their coach wants b-both m-me and Antonio to try out."

Antonio must have been listening from the front room. "He doesn't want me," he called. "He doesn't even know who I am."

"Yeah, he d-does," I shouted back.

"Why does he need to meet me?" Mom asked, ignoring Antonio.

"There are p-papers you need to sign."

Mom sighed. "Papers and more papers. All right. Tell him to come by Saturday morning at ten. You've got his phone number, right?"

"I've got it," I said.

All week, I stressed about Mr. Thurman. What would he think of Mom, of Curtis, of the trailer, of Jet City? Mom never once mentioned Mr. Thurman; I think she forgot all about him.

The only thing she and Curtis talked about was the meeting with the developers who wanted to knock down Jet City.

When Friday night came, Curtis was stuck working late at a job along I-5, north of Everett. Antonio wasn't home either, which was typical. "Come to the meeting with me, Laz," Mom said after we'd eaten the tomato soup and grilled cheese she'd made for dinner. Her voice was flat, and she had dark circles under her eyes.

All the chairs in the gym at the community center were taken, so we stood along the back wall. Mr. Leskov went to the microphone, motioned with his hands to quiet everybody, and then introduced a woman—her name was Heather something—who took his place at the lectern.

She had on black high heels, a dark blue skirt, a white blouse, and a blue jacket. She wore a gold necklace and a bunch of gold bracelets. Her teeth were bright white, her lipstick bright red, her short hair perfect.

After Leskov darkened the room, she showed a PowerPoint presentation explaining what would happen, trying to make it seem like closing Jet City was a great break for everyone because her company was going to pay relocation costs.

"But where are we supposed to go?" a man shouted from the darkened room.

She clicked ahead a few slides. "There are many possibilities," she said, and then she clicked and clicked, showing trailer parks in Kenmore, Everett, and even Mount Vernon, which is sixty miles away — almost halfway to Canada. "Remember the saying: when a window closes, a door opens. It sounds silly, but it's true."

The PowerPoint ended; the lights came back on. "There are brochures on the back table near the exit," the woman said. "In them, you'll find a list of all the mobile home parks I just showed you, plus a few more."

"What about Seattle?" a voice called out.

The muscles in her face tightened, but she kept smiling. "There are some mobile home parks just outside Seattle, and they are listed in the brochure, but they all have waiting lists. Construction will begin on July first, so you will need to be in your new homes by the end of June."

Shouts came from around the room. "This is our home" . . . "I work here, not in Everett" . . . "Why don't *you* move to Mount Vernon?"

Mr. Leskov took the microphone and tried to restore order, but the shouting only grew louder. Mom gave my elbow a pull, saying, "This is going nowhere." On the way out the door, she grabbed a brochure.

In the night air, she lit a cigarette.

"At least they're going to pay for moving," I said as we walked to Jet City.

Mom took a drag and blew out a stream of smoke. "Laz, don't let that woman in there fool you with her pretty clothes and her fancy words. Their money won't cover half of what moving will cost, if we can even find a place. She doesn't care about us. Nobody cares about us but us."

SIX

WHEN I GOT UP Saturday morning, Antonio was gone, off to his morning job at Home Depot. Mom was sitting on the sofa with Curtis, the brochure from the meeting in front of them. I could tell they'd been calling trailer parks. I could see lines drawn through some of the names.

"Morning," I said.

"Morning," Mom replied, looking up and giving me a smile.

In the kitchen, I poured cereal into a bowl and stuck two pieces of bread in the toaster. Mom and Curtis were taking turns calling, but I could only hear half the conversation, so not much made sense.

I was certain Mom had forgotten about Mr. Thurman, so after eating, I stepped into the living room to remind her.

"Who?" she asked.

"The m-man from Laurelhurst. Remember? He's c-coming this morning at t-ten."

Mom punched in another number. "Yeah, I remember now. But he can't take long. We've got to be in Kenmore by eleven."

A gold SUV pulled up in front of the trailer at ten on the dot. I opened the front door as Mr. Thurman was getting out, recognizing him right away. You don't forget a man who tells you that you've got a golden arm. He came inside and shook hands with Curtis. Standing side by side, the two of them made our trailer seem even smaller.

Mom had him sit down in the chair across from the sofa. Mr. Thurman started talking about what a warm September it was, when Mom cut him off. "Sorry, but we've got to leave soon, so —"

"Okay," Mr. Thurman said. "I'll make this short."

It took him just a few minutes to explain the fall training program. When he finished, Mom nodded. "Okay, all that sounds good. Give me the forms and I'll fill them out."

Mr. Thurman started to hand a manila envelope to Mom, but Curtis raised his hands. "Hold on a second. You wouldn't be breaking any rules having these workouts, would you? I played high school football, and there were strict regulations about out-of-season practices."

I felt my face flush. He was calling Mr. Thurman a cheater.

If Mr. Thurman was angry, he didn't show it. "Good question. And the answer is no. The program is run by the YMCA, not Laurelhurst. It's a regular eight-week class like all the others the Y offers. They'll be no Laurelhurst coaches there."

Curtis wouldn't let it drop. "But all the kids just *happen* to play on the Laurelhurst team. Come on. We all—"

Mom jumped in. "Curtis, Kenmore at eleven. Remember?" Then her eyes went to me. "Laz, you want to do this, right?"

I nodded.

She turned back to Mr. Thurman. "If you leave those papers, I'll fill them out and get them back to you."

Mr. Thurman handed Mom the envelope. "Our first session is Tuesday. Laz can bring the forms with him then."

"You got forms in there for my son, Antonio?" Curtis asked.

Mr. Thurman stood. "Yes. Laz mentioned Antonio, so you'll find two sets of paperwork in there."

As soon as Mr. Thurman had driven away, Mom turned on Curtis. "What was that all about?" she asked, puzzled.

"What was what all about?"

"Hassling the man like that? He's doing the boys a favor."

Curtis snorted. "Timmi, he didn't come here to help Antonio or Laz. He's here because he thinks they can help *him*. I just wanted him to know that I know his game."

Mom started to say more, then stopped. She picked up her purse and handed Mr. Thurman's envelope to me. "Fill out everything you can, and I'll do the rest when we get back. Do Antonio's form, too. Okay?" She turned to Curtis. "The Corolla is almost out of gas. We should take your truck."

SEVEN

I GOT GOOD NEWS that night: Antonio agreed to give Laurelhurst baseball a try. Mom told me when I showed her where she needed to sign the forms. "He said no at first, but then Curtis asked him to give it at least one shot, and Antonio said he would." A little smile came to her face. "I know. I was surprised, too."

I was glad Antonio was going with me. Really glad. But later, when I was in my room, an unexpected sadness came over me. Curtis wasn't ever going to win Father of the Year, but he tried to point the way. Sometimes Antonio listened; sometimes he didn't. Either way, Antonio had a dad—something I'd never have.

When school let out Tuesday, I got my duffle bag from my locker and hustled to the bus stop. There were seven minutes between the final bell and the bus's arrival—plenty of time.

But as the minutes ticked away, I worried. Where was Antonio? Right as the bus pulled up, he bounded down the school stairs. "Hurry," I yelled, standing half on and half off the bus so the driver couldn't shut the door and drive away.

Twenty minutes later the bus pulled to a stop at Sandpoint Way and we got off. What struck me first about Laurelhurst were the trees. They were everywhere, lining every street. Some were red and orange. Others were tall evergreens. The trees at North Central High were the same tree, over and over. Laurelhurst trees were different kinds, and they glowed in the late-afternoon light.

"Do you know where this field is?" Antonio asked as the bus rolled away.

I checked the map I'd printed from a library computer and pointed. "Two blocks that way."

When we reached the diamond, about a dozen guys were loosening up on the infield. Mr. Thurman must have been looking out for us, because he waved and smiled as soon as we stepped onto the field.

"Laz! Antonio! Come on and meet the other guys."

I handed him the envelope with the completed forms. He took it and tossed it into a box with other envelopes. Next he introduced us to the Laurelhurst players, explaining that North Central High was dropping baseball, so we were going to try out for their team.

We warmed up, Antonio and I, by playing catch. Talk filled the air around us, but the only sound between us was the smack of a baseball hitting leather.

We'd made about twenty throws when a whistle blew and the workout began. Mr. Thurman had four stations set up around the diamond, with adults running each of them. The other kids knew the names of each of the men, but I called them all Coach. Antonio did the same.

We rotated through in small groups. Fielding. Throwing. Hitting. Base running. At every station Antonio and I stuck together. That ended when Mr. Thurman separated pitchers from position players. While I was in the outfield playing long catch with Kevin Griffith, the kid who had been the Seattle Marauders pitcher, Antonio waited his turn to hit off the pitching machine.

I kept peeking over. I wanted Antonio to show Mr. Thurman that he was a player. Wasn't he ever going to get his turn?

And then he was up.

It went as I'd hoped: he drove the ball hard, smacking line drives to all fields.

Near the end of practice, I was called to pitch live batting practice. Twice Mr. Thurman told me not to throw hard. "Even ninety percent is too much. Don't risk injury."

For the first three batters, I tossed up slow fastballs, if there is such a thing. Then Ian Thurman stepped into the box. He was my last batter, and he got seven pitches. I threw the first five the way I was told, and he blasted line drives into the gaps. I would have been okay with that if he hadn't grinned after every hit. When my sixth pitch was roped 350 feet to dead center, I stepped off the mound and looked hard at him. I wanted him to know what was coming. He gave me a nod. I climbed onto the mound, went into my motion, and came with everything I had. He swung from the heels . . . and missed.

The next kid stepped to the plate, and I went back to throwing watermelons.

Finally, a whistle blew and the workout was over. "Thursday. Same time." Mr. Thurman called out. "And remember—there are a lot of good teams in the state. The one that wins that championship will be the one that works the hardest. So be here."

EIGHT

ANTONIO AND I REACHED THE BUS STOP just in time to see the bus pull away. Who knew how long it would be before the next one? Plopping down on his duffle bag, Antonio looked straight ahead.

Mr. Thurman's gold Lexus SUV pulled to a stop across the street. The driver's window lowered, and Mr. Thurman called out. "Can I give you boys a ride?"

"That's okay," I called back.

"It's no problem. Buses don't come too often around here."

I looked at Antonio, and he shrugged. We grabbed our stuff and hurried across the street.

This is how dumb I can be. I was surprised to see Ian in the front passenger seat. Where else would he be?

As Mr. Thurman drove toward Jet City, he asked questions about the workout. Was it too long? Not long enough? What would make it better? Ian had his iPhone out, thumbs flying. Antonio said nothing, leaving me—the stutterer—to do the talking.

As we headed north on Aurora Avenue and neared Jet City,

my stomach knotted. I didn't want Ian to see Jet City, didn't want him to go to school the next day and say — *Those two guys from North Central? You're not going to believe this, but they live in a trailer.*

Mr. Thurman pulled to a stop at a red light by the driving range. Without warning, Antonio threw open the door. "This is good right here," he said, grabbing me by the elbow and yanking me.

"Hold on. Are you sure?" Mr. Thurman said, but by then we were both on the street. I managed a *thank you* before Antonio slammed the car door shut. The light turned green, and the Lexus drove off.

"Couldn't take it any longer," Antonio said.

That night, everyone was home at dinnertime, which didn't happen often. Mom bought bean salad and French bread to go with the macaroni and cheese she had made. "We made the news," she said as she spooned the gooey pasta onto the plates.

"How?" Antonio asked.

"There's an organization — Keep Seattle Affordable — that is trying to save Jet City."

"A bunch of do-gooders against a multimillion-dollar developer," Curtis grumbled. "Who do you think will win that battle?"

"At least they're trying," Mom said.

The bean salad and bread made their way around the table.

"How did the practice go?" Curtis asked as he piled food onto his plate.

"It was g-great," I said. "I learned a l-lot."

Curtis looked to Antonio. "So you're going to keep going?"

Antonio shook his head. "Laz can do what he wants, but I'm never going back there."

My eyes went wide. "I thought you l-liked it," I said.

"Yeah? Well, you thought wrong," he said.

"Why didn't you like it?" Curtis asked.

"Because I didn't."

Curtis kept after him. "Because they've got more money? Is that why?"

Antonio shrugged. "Money is part of it."

Curtis kept after him. "What's the rest?"

Antonio filled his mouth with food. "I don't know," he mumbled. "I just know I'm not going back."

"Come on, Antonio," Curtis snapped. "You've got to do better than that."

Antonio's eyes went to Mom.

"Curtis," she said quietly. "You asked him to go once, and he did. Now he's telling you he didn't like it. So . . ." Her voice trailed off.

Curtis opened his hands. "So I'm just supposed to go along?"

Mom nodded. "Yeah. You are."

"And that's it?"

"That's it."

Curtis sat back in his chair. I was sure he was going to go after Antonio, or Mom, or both, but he didn't. "All right," he said, his voice calm but his eyes angry. "You don't want to play baseball, don't play baseball." Then he dug his fork into the mac and cheese and got back to eating.

There wasn't much talk after that. When dinner was finished, I went to my room and Antonio went to his. I tried to read, but I could hear Mom and Curtis arguing in the kitchen. The argument lasted about ten minutes, and then the trailer went silent and stayed silent.

Later that night, Antonio knocked on my door and stepped inside. "You're okay without me playing, right?"

"N-Not really. I don't g-get it. You could b-be a g-good player. Really g-good. And you know what I th-think about G-Ga—"

"This has nothing to do with Garrett," he said, interrupting. "I'm just done with baseball."

I shrugged. "All r-right. That's it."

We were both quiet for a moment; then he nodded toward the main room, where Curtis was watching TV. "What do you think of him?"

"He's okay." I paused. "And Mom's happier since he m-moved in. She l-likes him a lot."

Antonio's face broke into a smile. "I guess I'm proof of that."

He stood in the doorway a little longer, his eyes way off somewhere. Finally he looked at me. "You show those rich kids the kind of ball we play in North Central. Okay?"

NINE

WHEN I GOT HOME from school the next day, Mom was sitting at the kitchen table, her hand bandaged.

"Are you all r-right?" I asked.

"I cut myself at work. Careless. I'll be fine, but they sent me home."

"Can I h-help with something? Dinner?"

"No, but stick around. I've got news I want you and Antonio to hear at the same time. I texted him. He'll be home in a few minutes. I texted you, too, but your phone is dead."

She had a pamphlet open in front of her. When she caught me trying to look at it, she turned it over. "Go recharge that phone of yours. There's no point in having one if you don't keep it charged."

I hadn't forgotten; I'd charged it a day earlier. My phone just didn't hold a charge for long. Neither did Antonio's, but I didn't tell Mom that. We couldn't afford new ones, so what we had was what we had.

I'd just finished plugging my phone into the charger when I

heard Antonio come through the front door. Back in the kitchen, Mom was waving both hands in front of her face. "Antonio, I'm not going to die. It's just a cut. Relax." She pointed to the chairs at the kitchen table. "Now sit down, both of you."

We sat.

Mom took a deep breath and exhaled. "They've found us a place. Magic Lantern Trailer Park up in Marysville. If we take the spot, we get a two-year lease and the townhomes developer pays our moving expenses and our first month's fees. "

She slid the pamphlet she'd hidden from me to the middle of the table.

In the photos, the trailer park looked old and tired, but so did Jet City. "Marysville is a l-long way, isn't it?" I asked.

"Twenty-five miles north."

Antonio flipped through the pamphlet. "We'd have to change schools."

Mom nodded. "It would mean changes for all of us."

Antonio dropped the pamphlet on the table. "Have you signed?"

"Not yet. We have until January first, and if we do sign, we won't move until April. So nothing will happen right away."

I felt as if the walls of the trailer were closing in on me. April was in the middle of baseball season. I'd just be settling in at Laurelhurst and I'd have to leave.

Mom's eyes moved from Antonio to me, but neither of us spoke. Finally she opened her hands. "Look, I hope something else comes through, but this is a whole lot better than being homeless."

Other pamphlets were stacked up on the far side of the table. Antonio reached for one and held it up. "I know this place. Woodacres Apartments. It's just across Aurora, five blocks from here. A girl from Jet City is moving there with her mom. Why can't we go there?"

Mom shook her head. "They turned us down."

"How come?"

"They only have one-bedroom apartments, and the manager allows three people per unit and no more. With so many families from Jet City scrambling for a new place, he can pick and choose."

Antonio tilted his head. "Couldn't we lie?"

Mom shook her head. "Wouldn't work."

"Why not?" Antonio persisted.

"Because to qualify for the relocation money, I had to fill out a form. The developers gave that form to the manager at Woodacres. All four of our names are there in black and white."

Antonio's chin dropped. "If Curtis hadn't moved—

"Stop," Mom said firmly. "Not another word."

After dinner, I walked in a light rain to the community center. I had reading to do for history and English, and ten algebra problems. But before I tackled my homework, I used one of Mr. Leskov's ancient computers to look up the Marysville baseball team.

They hadn't had a winning season in seven years. Worse, they played all their games in Snohomish or Skagit County. There was a good chance the Marysville coach wouldn't let me join the team—not in April. But even if he did, what would it matter? No major-league scout would drive hours to see an unknown pitcher on a bad team.

TEN

THURSDAY CAME UP RAINY, WINDY, AND COLD. I thought the workout at Laurelhurst would be cancelled, but no message from Mr. Thurman came through on my cell, and the charge was good. I almost skipped anyway. Since I'd be moving to Marysville, what was the point?

Because I didn't have anything better to do, I went. The rain stopped during the bus ride, but when I reached the field, it was empty—the workout had been canceled. I was headed back to the bus stop when Mr. Thurman called my name.

"I thought you might be here," he said as he walked across the parking lot toward the field. "I must have your number wrong; I kept getting an error message."

I gave him my number and he made the correction. "Where's your brother?"

I told him Antonio wouldn't be coming anymore. I thought he'd ask why, but he didn't. Instead, he looked up at the sky. "Since we're both here and it's not raining, why don't we work on a few things."

I'd been leading with my shoulder, but he wanted me to lead with my hip. "If you bring your hip back at an angle," he explained, "you can throw your leg forward as you release the ball. You'll get more velocity and put less strain on your arm."

Once I got the feel for the new motion, he had me repeat it. "Burn it into your muscle memory. Then, in a game, it'll come automatically."

Slowly, I could feel both my control and my velocity improve.

Black clouds rolled in from the southwest, bringing back the rain. When I slipped after a pitch, Mr. Thurman waved his hands. "That's it, Laz."

I packed my stuff and started toward the bus stop, but again he offered me a ride.

There'd been an accident near Evergreen Washelli Cemetery, so traffic on Aurora Avenue crawled. As we inched along, Mr. Thurman talked about how excited he was for the upcoming season. "The head coach at Laurelhurst is retiring after this season. Coach Vereen. All three of my boys played for him. He's won everything except the state championship. We made it to the quarterfinals last year, and the core players are back. With the extra pitching you'll bring . . ." He looked over at me. "If ever a man deserved to go out a champion, it's Pop Vereen. It would be the perfect ending to a great career—"

Drops of sweat were rolling down my spine.

"Mr. Thurman, I need t-t-to t-tell you s-something."

His eyebrows went up. "So, tell me."

"The p-property where I live—Jet City—it's been s-sold."

He nodded. "I know. I read in the newspaper about the townhomes. It's rotten. It really is. They shouldn't be able to take people's homes like that."

I swallowed, then plunged forward. "They found a new place for my f-family in M-Marysville."

"What do you mean they found a place? Who found a place?"

"The d-developers. They're going to p-pay to move our t-trailer out there."

"And when is this move going to happen?"

"A-April."

"April," he repeated.

I nodded. "So I won't b-be able to p-pitch for Laurelhurst."

There was a long silence. "And this is definite?"

"Not t-totally. My m-mom has until January f-first to decide, but there's really n-no place else."

We were past the accident, and traffic loosened. Both Mr. Thurman and I stayed silent until he reached Jet City. When he pulled to a stop at the entrance, I got out and then turned back to thank him. He leaned toward me. "Laz, I need to check a few things, but don't totally give up on Laurelhurst, and keep coming to the workouts."

After that, on Tuesdays and Thursdays, I took the bus to Laurelhurst once school let out. At every session Mr. Thurman taught me something. The grip for a changeup. The pickoff move to first. The way to field a bunt. He knew everything.

In fifth grade, Mrs. Fleetwood had taught us about irony.

Firemen having their houses burned down. Indy drivers getting a ticket for driving too slow. Cops getting robbed. Things like that. I always thought her examples were funny. Now I'd become one of those examples. For years, I'd been on teams, but hadn't had a real coach. Now I had a coach, but no team.

ELEVEN

IT WAS THE WEEK OF HALLOWEEN. After the workout, I'd gotten a ride back to Jet City from Mr. Thurman, which I was glad to take because I had a long algebra assignment.

When I stepped inside the trailer, Curtis was glaring at Antonio, his arms folded across his chest. Mom was standing by the sofa, her hands on her hips. "Laz, did you know about this?" she snapped, waving a piece of paper at me.

"Know w-what?"

"He doesn't know," Antonio said, "and I'm not going to flunk anything. It's still early in the semester. I got time."

"Tomorrow," Curtis said. "You'll go to your teachers tomorrow and come up with a plan to make up this missing work. Understood?"

Antonio rolled his eyes.

"Understood?" Curtis barked.

"Yes," Antonio said, annoyed.

"And no more hanging out at night. Not on weekdays, not on weekends. Never."

Antonio looked at the ceiling. "So, I'm supposed to spend my life in this trailer? I can't have friends?"

Curtis was breathing through his nose like a bull. He was about to answer, but Mom put her hand up, stopping him.

"Antonio," she said, "this is not a prison. Get your grades up and keep them up, and the rest will take care of itself." She paused. "Now I'm going to put some dinner together, and we're all going to sit down and eat, and there's going to be no arguing."

Mom microwaved two frozen pizzas, and they tasted terrible. The crusts were rubbery and the cheese was like Jell-O, but nobody complained.

When we'd finished eating, Antonio looked at me. "You got homework tonight?"

"Yeah."

"Community center sound okay?"

"Sounds great."

Mom and Curtis exchanged a glance.

Mr. Leskov had the back room set up as a study area. We found an empty table and got to work. Antonio took notes from a text on American history, but whenever he saw me struggling with a math problem, he helped.

On the walk back to the trailer, there was no moon and half the streetlights weren't working. It was so dark that Antonio's voice seemed to come out of the night. "Whenever I almost like Curtis, he does something to make me hate him. The guy always has something to say, even when it's none of his business."

Antonio was making it easy for me to slam Curtis. And most of me wanted to. But every once in a while I'd seen Antonio look at Curtis in a way that was different and good. And I'd seen Curtis look back at Antonio in the same way.

"He's t-trying to b-be a real d-dad," I said. "That's all."

Antonio shook his head. "If he wants to be a real dad, then why doesn't he marry Mom?"

"M-Maybe he will s-someday."

"Yeah? Well, he sure isn't in a hurry."

TWELVE

AFTER THAT, ON SCHOOL NIGHTS Antonio and I went to the community center to study. In the beginning, he stayed until closing, working hard to catch up on his missing assignments. Once he'd caught up—which didn't take him long—he'd knock off his homework and then go hang out with Garrett and Jasmine and the rest of them.

After he'd left, Suja would come and sit next to me, shoulder to shoulder, our heads nearly touching as we studied. One night, after she'd helped me solve substitution problems that had seemed impossible, we walked back to Jet City together. The trees were rustling in the wind; the moon was low in the sky. I was thinking about taking her hand or putting my arm around her when Antonio appeared out of the darkness.

That had become standard procedure. He'd hang around our trailer when he knew I'd be coming along, and then we'd go into the trailer together. Mom and Curtis just assumed that we'd been studying together the whole time. I didn't like it, but I'd gone along.

Suja quickly said hello to Antonio and goodbye to me before heading to her trailer.

"Hey, hey," Antonio said, grinning as he watched her go. "Got something going? About time, Bro."

"I'm n-not doing this anymore," I said, my voice hard.

"What are you talking about?" he asked, confused.

"Pretending we've b-been studying together. I'm not doing it."

He shook his head. "Come on. Is this about Suja? Next time I'll wait till you split up."

"This is n-not about Suja."

"Then what's the problem? Going in together just makes things a little easier for me."

"Maybe I d-don't want to m-make things easier f-for you."

He frowned. "Because?"

"You know why. I've t-told you."

He shrugged. "All right. You go home when you go home and I'll go home when I go home." His smile came back, but it was mocking. "Mom and Curtis won't even notice. You'll see."

You take a stand, and you think something should happen, but Antonio turned out to be right. When I stepped inside the trailer the next few nights, Mom and Curtis were snuggled together on the sofa, binge watching episodes of *The Wire*. They didn't notice that I'd come in alone. After Friday, it didn't matter, because a letter came from the school stating that Antonio was passing all his classes.

Mom read it before Curtis had come home from work. She waved the piece of paper around, smiling, and then hugged Antonio. "Don't do this to us again," she said. "You hear me?"

"I won't. I promise." He paused. "Can I ask a favor?"

"You can ask."

"Back off a little?"

She stared at him. "You going to keep your grades up?"

Antonio nodded.

"All right. I'll cut you some slack."

"Thanks." He paused. "Curtis, too?"

She nodded. "I'll talk to him."

THIRTEEN

MOM MAKES A BIG DEAL about birthdays. When November 14 came around — my birthday — she bought a fancy cake and Ben & Jerry's ice cream. She baked a ham for dinner and made us all wear party hats, even Curtis, as if I were turning nine instead of nineteen. As we ate, she took pictures and threatened to post them on Twitter.

I got great presents. Mom gave me a fifty-dollar gift certificate to Baseball Express; Curtis got me a new Mariners cap; and Antonio gave me a poster of Ken Griffey, Jr. After dinner and cake, we watched *Back to the Future* on Curtis's television.

That was a good day, but it was about the only good one. Nobody mentioned Marysville, but we all could see that Jet City was dying. One day a trailer would be there; the next day it'd be gone.

The driving range was falling apart, too. I had to make an **OUT OF ORDER** sign and then tape it above one of the drinking fountains. "The owners aren't going to pay for any repairs," Mr. Matsui said. When three floodlights went dark along the netting on the west side, they stayed dark.

The only good things those days were my workouts at Laurelhurst. Mr. Thurman worked with me on my technique, teaching me how to get more power from my legs and my core. "You don't want to be arm-y," he explained. "That puts a strain on your shoulder and leads to injury. It sounds weird, but you want to throw the ball with your legs." He took everything slow with me, the way I like it. Repeat. Repeat. Repeat.

Thanksgiving came, and, for the first time in a long time, Mom cooked a turkey. After dinner, she insisted that we play Monopoly at the kitchen table. "We're going to be a regular family," she said, and we were.

The sessions at Laurelhurst were supposed to continue one week past Thanksgiving, but on Sunday night a storm blew in from Hawaii. The Pineapple Express, the weather guys call it. Rain poured down Monday and Tuesday, closing all fields citywide. I had some hope that Thursday's session wouldn't be canceled, but the rain returned on Wednesday afternoon.

Wednesday night I got an email from the YMCA, letting me know that Thursday's class had been canceled and wouldn't be rescheduled. The last sentence read *The YMCA thanks you for your participation, and we hope to see you again!*

So that was it—the end of my time practicing with the Laurelhurst guys.

FOURTEEN

IN THE WINTER, HARDCORE GOLFERS still go to the driving range, but most players stick their clubs in the garage. Fewer guys hitting meant fewer hours of work for me.

When I showed up at the driving range on the first Saturday of December, I was actually glad to see that crows had strewn garbage all over the parking lot. Cleaning up the mess meant an extra hour of pay.

Once I'd made the lot presentable, Mr. Matsui had me write "30% off" on the tags of the golf shirts and "50% off" on the top of the boxes of shoes. After that, I power washed the hitting stalls before heading onto the range to pick up golf balls.

With the bad weather, Garrett and Antonio and the rest of them had moved inside the deserted maintenance shack. As I rode the John Deere, I could see the glow of cigarettes, but I couldn't make out any faces. I did see two addicts trudge to the shed, but only two. Maybe Garrett was smalltime, after all.

I had swept half the range when Mr. Matsui waved me in. When I drove the cart to the shed and started unloading the golf balls, he stopped me. "Do that later, Laz. You've got a visitor."

A visitor?

I left the cart and walked into the golf shop.

Mr. Thurman was waiting for me in Mr. Matsui's office. He stuck his hand out. "Hey, Laz. Good to see you."

"Is something wrong?" I asked. What was he doing at the driving range?

He shook his head. "No, no. I knew you worked here, and I've taken a few lessons from Len. I thought I'd stop by on the chance that I could borrow his office so we could have a talk—" He stopped. "Why don't we both sit down."

I sat, and he took a chair across from me.

Mr. Thurman leaned toward me, his elbows on his knees. "Is the move to Marysville still in the cards?"

I nodded. "My m-mom signs on January first."

Through the wall, I heard the familiar *thwack* as golfers hit balls out into the range. Mr. Thurman cleared his throat. "I told you I had an idea. Well, here it is. Instead of moving to Marysville, I'd like you to enroll at Laurelhurst High and live with my family. Ian's older brothers are both away at college, so we have plenty of room. And if you live with us, you could play baseball for Laurelhurst. Your school credits will transfer, so that won't be a problem." He stopped. "I know it's sudden, but what do you think?"

I felt like I was twenty feet underwater, and he was shouting at me from a boat bobbing on the surface.

"I don't know. I'd have t-t-to talk with—"

He interrupted. "Your parents. I mean, your mom and her

114

friend. Of course you would. And I'll talk to them, too. I'll answer any questions they might have. I didn't want to bother bringing it to them before I'd checked it with you."

His words were clear, but the meaning stayed strange.

"Why would you d-do this for me? You don't know me."

"I know you better than you think. You're hard-working. You're talented. You're coachable. You deserve a shot at the next level, and I know that's what you want. You'll have a better chance of making a name for yourself at Laurelhurst than you'll ever have in Marysville."

He paused, waiting for me to answer, but no words came. He waited some more, and then clapped his hands and stood. "Okay. You think it over. If you like the idea, and your mom likes the idea, we'll make it happen."

FIFTEEN

THAT NIGHT, EVERYBODY WAS HOME for dinner. Mom cooked hamburgers and french fries. As we were eating, she asked about the driving range. "You still getting your regular hours?"

Instead of answering, I told her about Mr. Thurman's offer. Mom's eyes narrowed as I explained, but I didn't stop. "If I do m-move in with them," I said, looking around the table, "you c-could all move into Woodacres instead of having to go to M-Marysville."

Everyone had stopped eating. Antonio and Curtis exchanged glances—I could tell they thought it was a good idea. But Mom's face was stony. Finally, she folded her hands in front of her and stared into my eyes. "You can tell Mr. Laurelhurst that we don't need his help, thank you very much." She looked around the table and then said to no one in particular. "They're taking my house from me; now they're trying to take my son."

"But M-Mom, playing at Laurelhurst would be g-good—"

"Stop, Laz," she said, cutting me off. "This is not up for discussion. The answer is no."

Curtis leaned back in his chair. "Timmi, I think you're

missing part of the picture. The top players from Laurelhurst get drafted by major-league teams. If Laz pitches well for them, he could be one of them."

Mom's jaw dropped and her eyes went wide. "Laz could get drafted by a major-league team? Are you hallucinating?"

Antonio jumped in. "Mom, Laz is good. Really, really good. Way better than anybody knows."

"If he's so good," Mom replied, "then why does North Central lose all the time?"

"Because the team sucks," Antonio said. "And the coach sucks, and everything about the baseball program at North Central sucks. Laurelhurst is the exact opposite. He'd rock for them."

Mom leaned back in her chair and fixed her eyes on Antonio. "So you want your brother to move in with this Mr. Thurman?"

Even though I'd been on him about Garrett, he stepped up for me.

"Yeah," Antonio said, looking right back at her. "I do."

Mom's eyes turned to Curtis. "And you agree?"

"I think it should be Laz's call."

Mom faced me. "Okay, let me ask you this. Say you live with this Mr. Thurman and we move into Woodacres. Where are you going to go when the school year ends if this major-league fantasy doesn't pan out? Woodacres won't let four people live in the apartment. That's not going to change. There won't be a place for you."

"I've g-got some m-money saved. I'll find a p-place."

Mom shook her head. "You'll find a place. Where? Under the Ballard Bridge?"

"Timmi," Curtis said, his voice not much more than a whisper. "You've got to let him live his own life."

Mom took a deep breath, exhaled slowly. "You're sure you want to roll the dice on this? Because you can't unroll them."

SIXTEEN

AFTER THAT, MY BODY was in Jet City, but my mind was living for spring. Christmas break drifted into the New Year. On January first, Curtis and Mom signed a lease for a one-bedroom at Woodacres, with a move-in date of April 1.

Finals week came in late January. On Friday, after I'd finished my last test, I walked outside the main entrance and looked around. You go to a school for three and a half years, and on your last day you want to say goodbye to someone. For me, that someone was Suja.

I stayed at the top of the stairs for a few minutes, hoping to see her, but then gave up. As I started toward home I heard her call my name. "Laz, wait—"

A few seconds later she was standing next to me. "This is it, right? Your last day?"

"Yeah."

"I'm going to miss you."

"I'll miss you, t-too."

"I hope Laurelhurst works. I really do."

I smiled. "I do too."

Her eyes clouded. "What are you going to do about algebra?"

I'd been worried about that. Laurelhurst's classes were sure to be harder, and I needed a passing grade to stay eligible.

"I'll m-manage."

"If you want, we could get together for a study session. Saturday or Sunday morning? Whichever works."

I felt my face flush and hoped she didn't notice. "That'd be g-great."

Just then Tessa, one of Suja's friends, called to her from across the lawn. "Are you coming? Because we're leaving."

"I've got to go," Suja said, and then she leaned forward and hugged me.

"Suja!" Tessa called.

"Okay!" Suja shouted back. She took a few quick steps and then turned back to me. "Do you like doughnuts?"

The next morning, Mom helped me pack up two boxes of stuff, and we loaded them into the back of Curtis's pickup. As Mom and Curtis headed down the walkway, I stayed behind to say goodbye to Antonio. "You d-don't think I'm d-deserting you, do you?" I asked once we were alone.

He shook his head. "No, no. This is your chance. Go for it. Besides, you're not moving to the moon. We'll see each other."

Curtis closed the back of the pickup with a bang. "Let's go, Laz," he called.

Antonio gave me a soft punch on the shoulder. I did the same to him and then walked to the pickup.

• • •

The Thurmans lived on Latimer Place. Curtis used the GPS on his phone, but he still had trouble finding the house. "Do any of these streets just go straight?" Mom said, irritated.

Eventually we found it. Mrs. Thurman had the door open and was smiling as we walked up the porch steps. "Welcome!" she said in a happy voice. "Come in! Come in! My husband and son are meeting with a coach from Arizona State, but I expect them any minute."

She had us sit on a sofa that must have been fifteen feet long. Plates loaded with fruit and cheese and crackers were on a glass-and-wood coffee table. "Can I get you something to drink? Tea? Coffee? A soda?"

"A glass of water will be fine," Mom said, so we all had water.

Mrs. Thurman sat across from us on a matching sofa that was about twice the size of ours. Mom was wearing jeans and a Seahawks shirt; Mrs. Thurman was dressed in a skirt and white blouse and wore a pearl necklace and pearl earrings. I was afraid to eat the crackers, because crumbs would get on the sofa, but both Mom and Curtis ate.

For the first few minutes Mom and Mrs. Thurman — "Please, call me *Catherine*" — talked about how gray and cold January had been. Things went quiet, and then Mrs. Thurman told Mom that Laurelhurst was a great school and that I'd get a wonderful education. Mom replied that North Central was great, too. Mrs. Thurman said she was sure it was, and then the room fell silent again. Finally, Mrs. Thurman stood. "How about if we get Laz settled in his room."

After Curtis and I went to the pickup to get my boxes, Mrs. Thurman led us through a gleaming kitchen to a door leading downstairs. Mom and Mrs. Thurman went first. When we were halfway down, Curtis smiled and whispered. "Be careful on these steps, Laz. You fall down, break your arm, can't pitch, and they'll kick your butt onto the street."

A basement room sounds dark and gloomy, and the room was dark, but it was also twice the size of my room in the trailer. It had a gigantic bed, a chest of drawers, a huge closet, and it connected to a bathroom Mrs. Thurman said I wouldn't have to share with anyone.

"This is really n-nice," I said.

Mrs. Thurman beamed. "I'm glad you like it."

Mom's face was expressionless. Had I hurt her feelings? I wanted to tell her that I liked my old room—my real room— better, but how could I say that with Mrs. Thurman standing there?

"We need to go," Mom said, her voice a little shaky. She paused and then reached out and took Mrs. Thurman's hand. "Thank you for giving my son this opportunity. He won't cause you any trouble. He's a good son, and a good young man."

"I'm sure he is," Mrs. Thurman answered. "And don't worry, we'll take care of him."

Mom nodded and then went up the stairs, not stopping until she'd reached the Thurmans' porch. When I caught up to her, she reached up, pulled my head down, and kissed me on the forehead. "Don't be a stranger," she said.

Mrs. Thurman was right behind me. She waited, and then held out a business card to my mom. "Our phone numbers are on there. Please feel free to call at any time."

"Thank you," Mom said as she took the card. Then she went down the porch stairs to Curtis's truck.

Curtis lingered behind for a moment. "You and me? We're okay? Right?" he asked.

I nodded. "We're okay."

A minute later the pickup turned a corner and was gone.

Back inside, I sat again on the long sofa. Mrs. Thurman disappeared into the kitchen and came back with a glass filled with ice and a bottle of Coke. "I'm sure you want something other than water." She put the glass down on a coaster, poured the Coke into it, and then put the bottle on another coaster. "So tell me about yourself," she said, returning to her own sofa and folding her hands on her lap.

I did okay. I didn't stutter much, probably because I didn't say much. What was there to say? I go to school. I have a mom and a brother. I work at a driving range. I suck at school, especially math. I pitch.

When I'd finished, she picked up a key from the table and held it in front of her. "This is to the front door. But before I give it to you, I need to tell you our expectations. I'm sure none of this needs saying, but better to be clear in the beginning than to have confusion later on."

I nodded. "Yes, ma'am."

She was right. She didn't need to tell me. No loud music, no parties, no smoking, no drinking, no drugs, no girls in my bedroom. "Of course you can have friends over," she said, handing me the key. "Just keep everything within reason."

SEVENTEEN

I WENT DOWN TO MY ROOM and unpacked. Once that was finished, I didn't know what to do. I sure wasn't heading back upstairs to sit on that sofa. I wanted to go outside into the air so I could breathe, but where could I go? Better to stay put.

I lay down on the giant bed. It was quiet, too quiet. I missed the noise of Jet City—the people yelling, the music playing, the cars rolling over the gravel, the constant roar of traffic from Aurora Avenue. I felt a lump form in my throat. Then I got mad at myself.

Time to man up.

Upstairs, the front door opened and closed. I heard Mr. Thurman's muffled voice and his wife's answers. After that came footsteps on the stairs, followed by a knock on my door.

"Sorry I wasn't here earlier, Laz. Everything just took longer." He glanced around the room. "You look settled. How about if I show you the yard and the practice area?"

I pulled on my sweatshirt and followed him down a hallway to a door that opened onto the yard. "Ian is over at a buddy's house," he said as we walked. "You'll see him later. I hope you two will become good friends."

"I hope s-so t-too," I said, knowing it wouldn't happen.

The Thurmans' backyard was like a park, or actually two parks, because there were two separate levels. On the upper level was a deck that looked out over Lake Washington. Furniture was covered in waterproof cloth and pushed up against the house. The top level also had a flower garden, though nothing was in bloom—not in late January.

I followed Mr. Thurman (he wanted me to call him Bill, another thing that wasn't happening) down a stone stairway to the lower level of the yard, which was so big it could have held three single-wide trailers. Tall green hedges separated the Thurmans' lawn from the neighbor's yard. Tucked up against the hedge was a screened batting practice area.

Mr. Thurman spotted me eyeing it. "I had that built by a sports construction company," he said. "I used to pitch to Ian every day when he was young, but I can't do that anymore." He patted his right shoulder. "Rotator cuff. That's why we've got the pitching machine."

The whole setup was incredible. Not just the mound and the batter's box and the netting, but that he and Ian had practiced every day. No wonder Ian was such a good hitter.

"This is a-amazing," I said.

"Feel free to use this anytime. And if you need a workout

partner and I'm around, just ask. I'm an investment banker. That means I work on East Coast time. I start at six or earlier most mornings, but I'm home most afternoons. There's nothing I enjoy more than tossing around a baseball."

EIGHTEEN

MR. THURMAN LOOKED EAGER to coach me right then, but I had to work. Even though he offered me a ride to the driving range, I turned him down. I needed to learn the buses.

I made my transfer, but the trip still took forty minutes. Mr. Matsui had me clean the range and then wash the pro shop windows. The owners had hired some guy to paint **EVERYTHING MUST GO!** in bright red letters across the top of the largest window, as if it were great news. Once the windows were clean, I drove the John Deere back and forth, back and forth in a steady rain.

Then it was two buses back to the Thurmans'. When I stepped onto the porch, I took out the key, then put it back in my pocket and knocked. Mrs. Thurman opened the door and frowned, a gentle frown, somehow. "You live here now, Laz," she said. "You don't have to knock."

I nodded, and then started to step inside, but she stopped me. "I didn't mention this earlier, but we're a no-shoes household."

"No p-problem," I answered. As I took off my beat-up shoes,

I remembered how Mom and Curtis and I had tromped around inside the house earlier in the day, and I winced.

Inside, Mr. Thurman was standing at the doorway leading downstairs. "Ian is in his game room," he said eagerly. "I'll show you."

I followed him down the stairs. At the bottom he turned left, away from my room, walked down a hallway, and threw open a door. "Ian," he called out, "say hello to Laz."

My eyes must have been spinning—there was so much to take in. A pool table stood in the center of the room. To my left were a table and chairs, a small refrigerator, and a microwave. To my right were a foosball table and a pinball machine. On the opposite wall was a huge TV, twice the size of Curtis's. It was like being at the community center, only all this belonged to one guy.

Ian was sitting on the sofa in front of an Xbox, working a joystick. He half looked around when he heard us come in. Then he hit the pause button and stood. "Hey, Laz. Good to see you."

"Yeah," I said. "G-Good to s-see you."

We stood looking at each other until Mr. Thurman spoke. "Laz, a little advice: Ian is very good at pool, so I wouldn't gamble with him. In fact, I wouldn't gamble with him in anything. Foosball, darts, video games, golf, or bowling on the Wii—he beats me at everything every time."

Mr. Thurman grinned; I smiled; Ian looked bored. More silence. Again it was Mr. Thurman who spoke. "Well, I'll leave you. Oh, last thing, Laz. Food. With all the different schedules, it's pretty much every man for himself. That refrigerator will always be stocked with food. Help yourself. Same thing with the refrigerator upstairs. We have fresh fruit, vegetables, juice, nuts, yogurt—all the nutritious stuff. And in the freezer you'll find pizza, burritos—good things like that. So when you get hungry, eat. The microwave down here is pretty basic, but it works. Sunday we do try to eat together. Mostly that doesn't happen either, but sometimes it does. Catherine will let you know."

NINETEEN

ONCE HIS FATHER LEFT, Ian turned back to his game. "Let me finish, and then you can play."

"Sure," I said, even though I didn't want to.

I watched as he worked the controls. The main guy was a Special Forces type. Navy Seal, I think. He was chasing a bad dude across an airfield. The bad guy stole the plane, flew for a while, strafing people who were shooting SAMs at him from the ground. Finally the bad dude landed on a beach. He raced across the sand, getting shot at some more before breaking into what looked like a drug lab. There was another shootout, and this time the Navy Seal guy shot him right between the eyes.

Ian handed me the controls. "You try. The guy in camouflage with the Nazi hair is a terrorist. He steals, maims, murders —all the good stuff. Your job is to kill him before he blows up a passenger jet."

I took the controls. Ten seconds in, the terrorist guy hijacked a car and threw the owner over a cliff. The guy bounced off a bunch of rocks, leaving his brains behind. Seconds later, I was in a Hummer, chasing him, but I made some mistake, because the Hummer went off the road and into the woods. Somehow I came out on the main road again, with the pyscho-terrorist, now on a Harley, right in front of me. I forced him off the road and into a tree. The Harley was totaled, but the guy got up, blood pouring down his face, and took off running. I chased after him. I thought—*I'm doing okay*—when I turned up a pathway and a bunch of his terrorist buddies jumped out of a cave and shot me a zillion times. The word *WASTED!* filled the screen as an evil chuckle came through the speakers.

Ian snickered. "That was fast."

I handed back the controls. "I d-don't play much."

"What do you have? PlayStation, Xbox? Wii?"

"N-nothing."

He leaned back. "Nothing? No wonder you suck."

I wanted to take him out to his fancy batting cage, stick a bat in his hand, and strike him out on three pitches, but I kept my mouth shut.

He switched to *Grand Theft Auto*. "You live near Aurora Avenue, right? I mean, where you used to live," he said, his eyes on the screen.

"Yeah."

He laughed. "My mom is kind of freaked about that."

I felt myself straighten. "W-Why?"

"There are prostitutes working around there, right?"

"I g-guess."

"You ever see them? Prostitutes, I mean."

Did I ever see them? A half dozen worked out of trailers in Jet City. "Yeah, I've s-seen them."

He paused. "You ever — you know?"

"N-No."

"You ever think about it?"

"Sure."

"So why didn't you? If they were right there."

"I d-don't know."

"Scared?"

"Not scared. I j-just haven't."

"How about drugs? There are dealers there, too, right?"

I felt my blood pounding in my head. "I d-don't know."

He paused the game and then looked from the screen to me. "Come on, Laz. There's a guy there, he calls himself G-Man. Drives a black Subaru. Your brother or half brother or whatever he is hangs out with him. You must know him. This G-Man guy sells pills."

"Yeah, ok-kay. I know who h-he is. B-But my b-brother doesn't s-sell anything." I stood. "Look, I've g-g-got s-stuff to d-do."

He grabbed my arm. "Wait. I've got a proposition. Sometimes on Friday night one of us goes up there and buys from that G-Man guy. We cut his pills in half, wash them down with a beer or two, and then chill. No big deal. Once a month. Maybe twice. No more than that."

He stopped talking and looked at me, as if he expected me to say something.

When I stayed silent, he screwed up his face. "The thing is

—none of us likes going into Jet City. No offense, it's your home and all, but that place is sketchy. So I was thinking that I could give you money and you could buy from G-man. You could keep twenty bucks for yourself, and it would be work out for everybody." He paused. "What do you say?"

I shook my head. "N-No."

"Why not?"

"J-J-Just n-no."

He sat still for a minute; then his eyes returned to the screen. "All right."

I started for the door.

"Hey, Laz, you won't say anything about this to my dad, will you?"

I shook my head. "Don't w-worry."

Back in my new room, I lay down on my bed and stared at the ceiling. Ian was an idiot. He could choose either a major-league baseball or a college scholarship, but he'd lose both if he got caught doing drugs. Then another thought came, and I felt numb.

Kids at Laurelhurst High—which was five miles from Jet City—knew about Garrett. I suck at math, but I know that if you draw a circle with a radius of five miles, you get an area that's more than seventy-five square miles.

What if the wrong guys inside that circle found about Garrett and came after him? What if Antonio was hanging out with Garrett when those wrong guys showed up?

TWENTY

MONDAY. MY FIRST DAY as a student at Laurelhurst High.

When I got up, the house was silent. Mr. Thurman was off doing his investment job, whatever that was. Ian had a free first period, so he was still sacked out in his room upstairs. Mrs. Thurman had gone to her gym or was out running. I ate a breakfast burrito and slipped out the front door.

The walk took about fifteen minutes. As I neared Laurelhurst, I expected the sidewalks to crowd up like they did around North Central, but it never happened, not even on the final block. Instead, the streets filled with cars, creating a traffic jam around the school.

Before heading up the main stairway, I took a few deep breaths, preparing myself to be the unknown new guy. I was surprised when a burly kid came up beside me. "Hey, I'm Hadley Welsh. You're our new pitcher, right? The kid from North Central High?"

"Yeah, I g-guess. But how d-did you know?"

"Ian told us. I'm your catcher." His cell pinged. He read a

text and looked up. "Got to go, Laz. That's your name, right? Cool name, by the way. See you around."

Nobody else actually spoke to me, but some guys—baseball players, probably—nodded in my direction. I tried to nod back without looking like an idiot.

My first three classes—English, Spanish, history—were about the same as classes at North Central. Maybe the kids were a little less rowdy, the teachers a little more relaxed. Definitely everybody was better dressed. Fourth period was algebra. *Here goes nothing,* I thought as I pushed open the door and found a seat in the third row by the window.

The teacher was Mr. Marsh, an older guy with wild gray eyebrows and tiny ears. I was the only new kid in the class; he knew everyone else from the first semester. When the period ended, he asked me to stay behind. "I heard from your counselor at North Central that math isn't your strong point," he said once we were alone.

"You t-talked to my c-counselor?"

"You bet I did. And I talked to your former math teacher. I want you to start on the right foot. 'Well begun is half done' —that's my motto."

"I s-stink at m-math," I said, trying to make a joke.

Mr. Marsh narrowed those eyebrows and wagged a finger at me. "I'm a great teacher, and we have a great peer-tutoring program. You don't stink at math anymore."

He had me fill out a form for after-school tutoring in the library. "I'll give this to Ms. Cramer, our librarian," he said when I handed the form back to him. "She'll be looking for you."

"When d-does this start?" I asked.

Those bushy eyebrows again furrowed. "Today."

When I left, I made my way to the cafeteria, where I filled my tray with pizza and salad. I qualified for free lunch; moving to Laurelhurst High hadn't changed that. At North Central, kid after kid scanned their card under a reader, and a computerized voice said, "Thank you."

But as I worked my way up the line at Laurelhurst, I didn't see a scanner and I didn't hear a single computerized "Thank you." I broke into a sweat when I reached the front of the line and showed my card to the lunch lady. What if she didn't know what it was? She took it, then reached down under the cash register to pull out the card reader. After she scanned my card, the machine made a whirring noise followed by a full volume "*Thank you.*" I might as well have hung a sign around my neck reading **POOR KID**.

I carried my tray to a corner and found a chair that faced the wall. I'd taken a couple bites of pizza when Hadley Welsh came up and nodded at the chair across from me.

"Okay?"

"S-sure."

He looked like a linebacker, and he ate like one, too, polishing off two pieces of pizza and a fistful of french fries in a couple of minutes. It wasn't until he started on his apple that he spoke.

"You struck me out in the summer. Do you remember?"

"No."

"I didn't figure you would, because you struck out just about everybody. That's why the guys are so pumped to have you here. Or at least most of them are." He stopped to wipe his mouth with his sleeve. "Some kids think your transferring here is cheating."

"Ch-Cheating?"

He scrunched his face. "Not cheating, exactly. Just iffy. New pitcher coming to a new school for one semester. Kevin Griffith, our number one starter, has friends who want him to stay number one. I get it. He won a ton of games last year and the year before. The problem is that Jesuit High keeps bombing him in the state tournament. I mean, they totally lit him up two years straight. Actually, he kind of sucks against all the good teams." Hadley paused. "This is Coach Vereen's last year—you know about him, right? He's a god around here. A living legend and all that crap. All the other coaches call him Pop because he's been around forever."

I nodded. "What's he l-like?"

"He's okay as long as you don't cross him. Get on his bad side, and there's no getting back." Hadley stretched his arms above his head and smiled. "So, Laz, my new best friend forever, here's all you need to do. Pitch Laurelhurst to its first state title so dear old Pop Vereen can retire a champion. Do that, and you'll be everybody's best friend forever."

"Ha, ha," I said.

He wagged a finger in front of my face. "No joke."

TWENTY-ONE

MY AFTERNOON CLASSES LOOKED EASY: visual arts and then PE with Coach Vereen. I'd thought it was a fluke that I'd been assigned to his class, but ten guys from the baseball team— including Hadley and Ian—were also there.

Everybody had talked about how old Vereen was, so I expected him to be beaten down and bent over. The man in the front of the gym was at least six foot three and well over two hundred pounds. He had wiry gray hair, a hawk's nose, and dark brown eyes.

After the warm-up exercises were over, Coach Vereen led the baseball players to the wrestling room, where he passed out notebooks—green for infielders, blue for outfielders, and red for pitchers. Mine contained a series of exercises to increase leg strength, arm strength, flexibility, and agility—along with directions and pictures of how to do each properly.

In a Marine sergeant voice, Coach Vereen gave us a pep talk about how preparation today leads to winning tomorrow, and then the guys got to work—all except Ian and two of his friends—Martin Moran and Andrew Comette. The three of them worked hard when Vereen was watching, but when he returned to the main gym, they stopped. "Are they always like that?" I asked Hadley, motioning toward them.

Hadley shook his head. "They used to work harder than anyone. Especially Ian. But this is their fourth year of hearing Vereen say the same things. It gets old."

Near the end of class, Coach Vereen came over, watched me for a while, and then tweaked the way I was doing a core exercise. "Just like that. Good. Really good." Then he paused and lowered his voice. "Don't worry about anything, kid. I'll ease you in. I don't expect you to be Cy Young."

The school day was over, but my day wasn't. I took the slip of paper Mr. Marsh had given me and headed to the library. The librarian, Ms. Cramer, led me to a back room. "I've assigned you to Jesus Ramirez."

Ramirez was short—maybe five foot two. He had a long, braided ponytail and wore a Pokémon Go T-shirt and black sweatpants. "Cool problems," he said when I showed him my math assignment.

He talked loud and he laughed even louder, but he explained the math step by step. If I asked him to show me something twice, or even three times, he did.

It was nearly five before I returned to the Thurmans' house. I used my key to get in, closed the door quietly, took off my shoes, and headed toward the stairs leading to the basement. I'd almost reached them when Mrs. Thurman called my name, stopping me.

"I've got something for you," she said, and then she handed me an Apple laptop.

"This is f-for m-me?" I asked, confused.

"We bought it for Ian when he started high school. We thought he could take it to his classes, but it has a fourteen-inch screen, which makes it too heavy. We got him a MacBook Air, so this one has just been sitting in a closet."

"I c-can't—"

"Laz, it's silly to have it sit unused. So please, just take it. Our WiFi password is STATECHAMPIONS. All caps, one word." A smile came to her eyes. "A household with dreams."

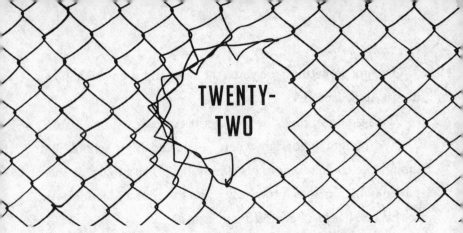

TWENTY-TWO

THAT SUNDAY, I WASN'T SCHEDULED to work at the driving range until one, so I arranged a noon meeting with Suja at Krispy Kreme. I didn't really need math help—Jesus Ramirez was keeping my head above water—but I wanted to be with her.

We each ordered a mocha and a maple bar. I pulled out my algebra book, and she went over stuff that I understood, though it didn't hurt having it explained again. "How did the week go?" she asked when we finished.

I gave her a quick summary, leaving out Jesus. When I finished, she looked at me quizzically. "So . . . when you're in that big house, what exactly do you *do?*"

"Pretty much I j-just hole up in the b-basement. There's a microwave and a kitchen down there, so I make my own m-meals. You wouldn't believe the f-food they have."

A little smile played on her lips. "Sounds like you're sort of a pet rat."

I was confused. "What d-d you m-mean?"

The smile got larger. "They're keeping you down in the basement until they want you to come out and play. Right?"

I felt a touch of anger. "It's n-not like that."

She lowered her head. "Okay, I'm sorry. Don't get mad." She paused. "What about their kid? What's he like?"

"He's got a g-girlfriend named Mariah; and he's g-got a b-bunch of buddies. I won't see m-much of him."

"He's not going to be your new bro?"

I shook my head. "Not even c-close."

She paused. "How about your old bro? You keeping up with Antonio?"

"I haven't t-talked to him since I m-moved. I've been k-kind of busy," I said.

She dropped her eyes. "I know you won't want to hear this, but every day this week I've seen him driving Garrett's Subaru in and out of Jet City."

"So?" I asked, not understanding what she was trying to tell me.

"So, Garrett loves that car. He won't even let people lean against it."

I felt as if I were in a math class staring at a problem I didn't understand. I shook my head. "I don't g-get what you're s-saying."

She leaned forward and lowered her voice. "Okay, maybe Garrett's just being a good guy, lending his car to his friend. That's possible. But maybe he's got your brother out there doing things that are risky, things that Garrett doesn't want to do himself." She paused. "Antonio likes flashy stuff, right? Maybe it's sort of a deal they've got going. You see what I mean?"

143

She stopped, and her words hung in the air. My heart was pounding so hard and so fast I thought it would come through my chest.

"I've got to g-get g-going. I'm s-supposed to be at work right now."

Suja frowned. Then she stood and squirmed into her backpack. "I need to go, too." She paused. "You want to meet next week?" Her voice was cheerful, trying to smooth away the tension.

"Yeah, I d-do," I said. "And Suja, th-thanks for t-telling me about Antonio. I always want to know even if I d-don't w-want to know. That d-doesn't m-make sense, b-but—"

She smiled. "I get it, and I'll do it." Then she held up her phone. "I've got Garrett in my contact list. I don't know how or why, and it sort of freaks me out that he's got my number. But you ever need it, just ask."

That afternoon, as I drove the John Deere back and forth, my mind went in circles. I tried to tell myself that there was really nothing there. A guy lets his friend drive his car? Big deal. The other stuff? Suja was just guessing—she'd said so herself. But what if her guess was right? What then?

Mom had called earlier in the week, telling me to come by. I finished work at five, signed out with Mr. Matsui, and then headed along Aurora until I reached Jet City.

I'd walked the gravel path to our trailer thousands of times, but never before as a visitor. I noticed things I'd never noticed before: how rutted the road was, how close together the trailers were, how many windows had sheets instead of curtains, how the cars and trucks were parked helter-skelter, how toys were strewn about the side yards.

At the front door, I knocked, even though I still had a key. It was strange to have keys to two houses and not belong at either. Mom opened the door, grabbed my arm, and pulled me into the living room.

"Sit down, sit down," she said once she'd let me go. "Curtis and Antonio are making a dump run. When they get back, we'll all go out to dinner."

While we waited, she peppered me with questions. What was Mr. Thurman like? Mrs. Thurman? The kids at Laurelhurst? The teachers? The coaches? Was everyone treating me okay? Was I happy?

The pickup pulled into the driveway. Antonio and Curtis came in and asked the same sort of questions Mom had asked, only fewer of them. "Let's go eat," Antonio finally said.

We all piled into the Corolla. "Did Antonio tell you?" Curtis asked as he was driving.

"Tell m-me what?"

"Tell him, Antonio," Mom said.

Antonio groaned. "Could we not do this?"

"He made the honor roll," Mom said.

"From flunking everything to honors," Curtis said, looking

over his shoulder at Antonio. "That shows what you can do when you try."

Antonio looked sideways at me and shook his head.

"Way to go," I said. "That's g-great."

We went to the Ram restaurant at Northgate. The Ram has at least fifteen televisions mounted on the walls, and most were tuned to the Golden State Warriors game. People cheered and groaned as they watched.

We got a booth and ordered. Mom had toured the apartment at Woodacres, and while we were waiting for the food to come, she told me about the new appliances in the kitchen, the tile in the bathroom, the double-paned windows that would keep out drafts. "But the best thing is that there's a walk-in closet that can work as a bedroom for Antonio."

The food came. Antonio and I had both ordered cheeseburgers, and we got to work on them. Across from us, Curtis was pointing out to my mom the great plays Steph Curry was making. Mom burrowed in right next to him, her eyes on the big screen.

Looking back, that was my chance. I could have said something to Antonio about Garrett. The restaurant was so loud that he would have been the only one to hear. But I didn't. This was one of the few times Mom and Curtis and Antonio and I were all happy and together. I didn't want make it all go sour.

With a minute left in the game, Steph Curry drained a long three-pointer to seal the win for Golden State. Curtis reached across the table and gave Antonio a fist bump.

"That man can shoot," Curtis said.

"Sure can," Antonio said as he stuffed the last fries into his mouth.

Then Antonio gave me a fist bump, too.

TWENTY-THREE

BASEBALL TRYOUTS were the last week of February. At North Central, Mr. Kellogg had coached the team by himself. Coach Vereen had two assistant coaches and three parent volunteers. I was hoping Mr. Thurman would be one of the volunteers, but he wasn't. "That off-season program and the summer team?" Hadley explained. "Because of those, he can't be connected to the school program, or he'd being breaking some rule."

I stayed nervous until Vereen separated the four pitchers from the other guys. Two—identical twins named Marc Robosky and Andrew Robosky—were tall, skinny sophomores. You could see in their eyes that all they wanted was to make the team.

That left Kevin Griffith as my only competition for number one starter. Kevin was a good pitcher, but when we threw side by side, my fastball was faster and had more movement. If I could see that, Coach Vereen had to see it, too.

But as the week passed, I started to think he didn't. When Vereen wanted a pitcher to demonstrate a fielding technique, he chose Griffith. When he wanted live batting practice, Griffith pitched first. And when we played practice games, the starters backed up Griffith while I had second-stringers and guys from the freshman team behind me.

You ask me, you ask Hadley, you ask anybody, and they'll tell you that I outpitched Griffith during tryouts, but at the team meeting before the opener, Coach Vereen announced that Griffith would start the opener. The guys congratulated him. I smiled, but it felt like a fist to the gut.

When the meeting ended, Coach Vereen called me to his office and had me sit in a chair across from him. He put his elbows on his desk and leaned forward. "You understand, don't you? Why you're not starting?"

"Not r-really," I said, my voice shaky. "I outpitched him."

I was certain he'd be angry, but he nodded in agreement. "I know you did. But this is Kevin's fourth year in the program. Making him watch you throw the first pitch in his senior year wouldn't be right. We play twenty games, not counting the play-offs. You'll get your chance."

PART
THREE

ONE

WE OPENED TUESDAY AFTERNOON at home against the Sumas Warriors. Laurelhurst was my team, but as I sat at the end of the bench, chomping on sunflower seeds, I found myself pulling for the Sumas guys.

They were poor. No other way to say it. They wore T-shirts instead of jerseys, blue jeans instead of baseball pants, tennis shoes instead of baseball cleats. Looking at them was like looking at my North Central team. I didn't really want Sumas to beat us; I just wanted them to do okay.

And they did, for three innings. They banged out a couple of hits off Kevin in the second and scored a run. Their pitcher gave up two in the bottom of the second, but it was still 2–1 when we came to bat in the bottom of the fourth.

But that was the end of them doing okay.

A couple of walks and an error brought Ian to the plate with the bases loaded. When the Sumas pitcher guided a fast-ball down the middle, Ian swung so hard he about came out of his shoes. The ball soared high in the afternoon air, clearing the fence by twenty feet. The guys on the bench pounded one another in awe.

After that, the hits and runs kept coming. In the bottom of the fourth, Jay Massine, our third baseman, smashed a two-run triple to left center, pushing the lead to 11–1. The ten-run mercy rule kicked in, ending the game. When we went down the line high-fiving the Warriors and saying "Good game," only a couple of them had their heads up.

And my team? "Jack the Giant Killer" is a great story, but when the Giant grinds Jack into the dust? We quietly high-fived one another and headed home.

Mr. Thurman stopped and bought fish and chips for Ian and me at Ivar's. He was amped, congratulating Ian on his big game, talking up the team. I ate and smiled along, but when your uniform is spotless, you aren't part of anything.

Back in my basement room, I closed the door and replayed the game in my head. Kevin Griffith had given up only a couple of hits.

Competition.

I'd never had any at North Central High. From the day I took the mound in my freshman year, I'd been the number one pitcher.

Things would be different at Laurelhurst. Sure, I'd been better than Griffith at tryouts, but if I didn't outperform him in the games, he'd start the big games against the top teams and I'd get the leftovers.

TWO

MY FIRST CHANCE CAME that Friday against the Mount Vernon Bulldogs on their field. The team bus rumbled up I-5 in the HOV lane toward Mount Vernon, passing first through Everett, where the big Boeing plant is, and then Marysville. I stared out the window, looking for a trailer park, thinking I saw one, but then realizing it was just a place that sold used RVs.

By the time we reached the field, rain was falling and a cold wind was blowing down from Canada. I'd read online that Mount Vernon had been picked to win the Skagit Valley league. I'd need good stuff to beat them, but during warm-ups, I struggled to get loose. When Coach Vereen saw that my fastball had no zip, he told me to keep the ball low. "Trust your defense."

I nodded, but because of my poor warm-up, I treated Mount Vernon's first two hitters as if each were Babe Ruth, walking them both. That brought up their three-hitter, a guy who looked like a heavyweight wrestler. The cleanup hitter, loosening in the on-deck circle, was even bigger.

Hadley called time and jogged out to the mound. "Hey, Laz," he said, "you're forgetting something."

"What?"

He filled his lungs with air and then exhaled. "Breathe. Remember how to do that?"

I forced myself to smile. "I remember."

As he returned to his position behind home plate, I took a few deep breaths, and my heart stopped beating like a woodpecker hammering on a tree.

The hitter was crowding the plate—there was no way he could get the barrel of the bat on an inside fastball. I went into my stretch, looked back at the runner at second, and delivered —a two-seam fastball that moved in on his hands. He swung and caught the ball on the fists, lifting a wounded duck into no man's land in short right. The ball hit the chalk and danced away from our right fielder, Martin Moran. By the time Martin got the ball back into the infield, two runs had scored and the Mount Vernon hitter was clapping his hands at second base, his eyes shining.

I peeked over at Coach Vereen. He had his cap off and was running his hands through his hair. I wanted to shout over at him not to worry. I'd made a good pitch—the hitter had been lucky.

It took only four pitches to strike out the cleanup hitter. The number-five batter hit a little dribbler to first for the second out, and I finished the inning with another strikeout, this one on three pitches.

On the bench, guys were laughing and loose. At first I didn't get it. At North Central, trailing by two runs felt like trailing by twenty. But these guys—I still had trouble thinking of them as *my guys*—had scored eleven runs against Sumas, and they expected to do the same against Mount Vernon.

And they . . . we . . . did come back—chipping away at the lead by scoring a run in the second on an error, and then another in the third to tie it. I mowed down the hitters by keeping the ball low and pounding the strike zone.

In the top of the fifth, the Mount Vernon starter tired. After every pitch, he walked to the back of the mound to regroup. When he hit two guys in a row, their coach took him out. The reliever looked like a sixth-grader—chubby face, scared eyes.

Hadley ripped a screaming liner into right center field for a double, the first of five straight hits. When I took the mound in the bottom of the fifth, we were leading 9–2.

I set them down one-two-three by letting my fielders do the work. Hadley caught a foul pop for the first out; Comette gobbled up a grounder behind second and made a great throw for the second out; Ian settled under a lazy fly ball to end the inning.

When I returned to the bench, Coach Vereen patted me on the back. "That's it for today, Laz. Nice job."

I protested. "I'm not tired. I can finish."

He waved that off. "Long season, and the twins need work."

Marc Robosky gave up a run in the sixth, and his brother gave up two in the seventh, making the final 9–5.

After the *Good game* stuff ended, I heard a shout. "Laz! Over here!"

Antonio was up the third base line. I jogged over to him.

"Did you just g-get here?" I asked.

"You kidding? My only bro is pitching his first game for a hotshot team? I was here from the start."

I gave him a look.

"Okay, maybe I missed a few innings. But I made it, right?" He paused and nodded toward the parking lot. "I got wheels. I'll take you home."

Vereen's rule was that we had to go to games on the team bus, but the ride back was optional.

"Sure," I said. "As long as we get something to eat."

THREE

ANTONIO HAD GARRETT'S SUBARU, not Mom's Corolla or Curtis's pickup. We drove south on I-5 toward Seattle, my stomach in a knot. "How about Riley's?" he asked when we reached Seattle. "I haven't had barbecue since the last time we were there."

"Sure," I said, glad to get out of that car.

Riley's mainly serves takeout, but they have a few picnic tables that look out over Lake Washington. Across the lake the city lights of Kirkland gleamed. I tried to pay for my meal, but Antonio wouldn't let me. "Stars never pay for their meals," he joked. His wallet was thick with more money than he made working at Home Depot.

We sat eating barbecued beef sandwiches and sweet potato fries and drinking Mountain Dew. A gas heater on a post made it almost too warm.

After a few minutes he put his drink down, wiped his mouth, and leaned back. "Did you sign up for College Bound when you were in middle school?"

"I d-don't think so. What is it?"

"Mrs. Elizabeth had my entire class sign up. She said that if your family has no money, you get good grades, and you don't get arrested, the state will pay your tuition at college."

"Really?"

"Yeah, really. Nobody believed her, but she wasn't blowing smoke. A woman from Central Washington University found out about me making the honor roll. She called Mom and told her that if I keep my grades up, I can go there for free."

"That's g-great, Antonio. That's fantastic."

He shook his head and smiled. "Me getting a scholarship? Pretty wild. Mom is crazy excited. So is Curtis."

"N-Nothing w-wild about it. You're s-smart. You know you are."

He looked out over the water. "I went on Google Maps. Central Washington University is over the mountains. You ever been over the mountains?"

I laughed. "How would I ever g-get over the m-mountains?"

"It's supposed to be all wheat farms and apple trees over there."

"So what? You'd b-be in classes, not p-picking apples." I reached across and punched him on the shoulder. "It's g-great."

"It hasn't happened yet."

We stopped talking and concentrated on our food. He was finished and I was nearly done when his cell vibrated. He flipped it open, read the text, tapped a reply, and then looked down at my plate. I quickly finished the little that was left.

Back in the Subaru, Antonio cranked up the volume on the stereo as he drove — fast — toward Laurelhurst.

The text had been from Garrett. I knew it, and Antonio knew I knew it. Talking about going to college and then running errands for a drug dealer — it made no sense. I switched off the music.

"That was from G-Garrett, wasn't it?"

He turned his head toward me. "What?"

"The t-text. It was from G-Garrett. Right?"

"Yeah. So?" I could hear a challenge in his voice.

"D-Don't be stupid. The guy is using you."

He snorted. "First you tell me I'm smart, and now you tell me I'm stupid. Which is it?"

"B-Both," I said.

"Yeah? Well, I'm not both. Okay? I do the easy stuff. Only the easy stuff. No risk."

"How d-do you know?"

"Because I know."

The car filled with uneasy silence. Antonio reached forward and hit the play button. The music came back on, full volume until he pulled into the Thurmans' driveway.

"Thanks f-for coming to m-my game," I said in a cold voice as I got out of the Subaru.

"No problem," he said, his voice distant.

I was about to walk away when he leaned toward me. "You got baseball, Laz. That's where you can be you. I don't have that.

I can't be me at school and I can't be me at home. So I hang out at the back fence."

Suja, or somebody like her, would have known what to say. And maybe what they said would have worked, would have kept all the bad things that happened from ever coming down the pike. But I'm not Suja, and nothing right came to me, nothing at all. I nodded, closed the door, and then tapped the window twice. Antonio gave me a smile and a thumbs-up before he drove off, the taillights of Garrett's Subaru slowly disappearing in the darkness.

FOUR

WHEN I WOKE THE NEXT MORNING, I opened the laptop Mrs. Thurman had given me and navigated to the high school section of the *Seattle Times,* hoping there'd be something about me. The headline read **Laurelhurst Throttles Mount Vernon**. It was followed by a paragraph detailing Ian's extra base hits and RBI. I skimmed all that, but I read the last sentence over and over: "After a shaky start, transfer Laz Weathers settled down and picked up the win."

At school, I was a three-hour star. All morning I got high-fives. About halfway through lunch, my phone vibrated—a text from Suja. **Rock star!**

I must have smiled, because Hadley said, "Something good?"

"A girl from my old school. She read about my game."

"She's in love," he said, batting his eyes at me. "And you are, too. How sweet."

"Sh-shut up," I said, smiling, and went back to eating.

"Text back, Romeo. You know she's staring at her phone right now, heart aflutter."

"Give me a b-break."

He was about to razz me more, then stopped, which is why I liked him.

A bunch of times that afternoon I pulled out my phone and looked at Suja's message. I wanted to write a great reply, but nothing came. At two o'clock I gave up, typed **Thanks**, and hit send.

When school ended, I headed to the baseball field for practice. Two TV trucks had pulled up onto the field, and a handful of cameramen and reporters milled around. I sidled over to where Hadley was standing. "What's g-going on?"

"Ian is announcing his decision."

"What decision?"

"His choice for college."

"They send r-reporters out for that?"

"For Ian they do. He's a five-star recruit. Local news will carry it, and it'll be on 247Sports, Facebook, maybe even ESPN."

Ian was standing at the front of the pitcher's mound, Coach Vereen on one side and a young guy in a gray suit on the other. The cameraman was halfway between home and the mound. The smiling guy handed Ian a maroon and gold Arizona State sweatshirt and baseball cap. Ian pulled the sweatshirt over his head, stuck the cap on his head, and then everybody started shaking hands. Mr. Thurman and Mrs. Thurman stood behind the cameraman, arm in arm. Mr. Thurman looked like he was wiping away tears.

"He'll get drafted in June by a major-league team, too," Hadley said quietly. "If he gets picked in the first round, that's millions of dollars in bonus money. The Thurmans are rich, but nobody turns down millions."

FIVE

AT THE END OF MONDAY'S PRACTICE, Coach Vereen named Kevin as the starter for Tuesday's game. I expected it. We'd both given up a couple runs early, we'd both settled down, we'd both won, and I was the newcomer. As I left the field, Hadley trotted to catch up with me. "Be ready," he said in a soft voice.

"Why? You heard Vereen."

"Means nothing. We're playing Eastside Catholic. They beat Kevin's brains out last year. First sign of trouble, and Vereen will yank him."

Before Tuesday's game, Kevin and I warmed up side by side.

The ball was flowing out of my hand, but he was tight. You could see it in the jerky way he moved. When your muscles are tense, you can't throw—Mr. Thurman had drilled that into me. Kevin's fastball had nothing, and the more pitches he threw, the more nothing it got.

The umpire shouted, "Play ball!" Kevin looked over at me as if he'd just been called for the long walk to his execution. I gave him a pat on the back. "Go g-get 'em."

He pursed his lips. "They're toast."

I found a place on the bench next to one of the parent volunteers who had the scorebook in his hands. "I could d-do that for you."

He eyed me, unsure. "You know how to score?"

"Sure."

"Okay. Force out at second, second baseman to shortstop. Runner safe at first."

"Fielder's choice. F-Four-six."

He handed me the scorebook. "It's yours."

Hadley had predicted that Kevin would struggle, and he was right. When the leadoff hitter smacked Kevin's first pitch into center field for a single, my breathing grew more rapid. Ten feet from me, Coach Vereen clapped his hands. "Easy, Kevin. Don't force it."

The next hitter stepped in. Kevin pawed at the dirt, went into his stretch, delivered. From the bench I could tell that he was guiding the ball, afraid to let it fly. The bat zipped across the plate, sending a line shot over third base. By the time Evan Peterson tracked down the ball and fired it back to the infield, runners were at second and third. Coach Vereen strode toward me, snatched the scorebook from my hand. "Get out there and get ready. Now!"

As I hustled to the bullpen area by third base, Vereen walked slowly to the mound. He talked to Kevin for a while and then walked slowly back to the bench—buying time for me to get loose.

Whatever Vereen said didn't help. Kevin's first two pitches to Eastside's three-hitter were way outside. The third pitch was a batting practice fastball, right down the middle. The hitter crushed it, sending a towering drive down the left field line. The ball landed far past where the chalk line ended, but the home plate umpire made his call loud and clear.

"Foul ball!"

The batter, who had already neared first, threw his head back and returned to home plate. Boos cascaded down from the Eastside Catholic fans.

Coach Vereen had seen enough. He held up four fingers to Kevin. The intentional walk loaded the bases with nobody out. Vereen looked out to me. I nodded to let him know I was ready.

A minute later Kevin handed me the ball. Coach Vereen put his hand on my shoulder. "It's just the first inning. Don't worry about a run or two scoring. Just keep the bleeding to a minimum. We'll fight back."

"Yes, s-sir," I croaked, my throat as dry as dust.

It was the first time in my life that I'd been a relief pitcher, and it felt totally unfair. Eastside Catholic's best hitter was stepping to the plate with runners on every base—and I hadn't put a single one of them there. It was like having to take a test in a class you'd didn't know you were in.

I took a deep breath and peered in. Hadley flashed the sign —fastball, low. The things Mr. Thurman had made me repeat and repeat and repeat? They all happened without me thinking about any of them.

Simple wind-up.

Shoulder and leg turn.

Drive toward home.

Release.

Then, when I needed her most, Lady Luck smiled on me. The batter swung, sending a one-hopper right to me. I fielded it cleanly and made a chest-high throw to home plate. Hadley stepped on the dish and then fired down to first for the double play.

The guys on our bench exploded, and so did the kids and parents up in the stands. The last voice I heard was Mr. Thurman's. "Stay focused, Laz. One more batter."

He was right: if you celebrate too early, you'll wind up not celebrating at all. Against the five-hitter, I worked the ball in and out, up and down, finally fanning him on a fastball at the letters. As I walked off the field, more cheers rained down.

I sat on the bench with a towel draped over my head. I needed to stay in the zone. That's why, as the rest of my team and all the parents and kids in the bleachers jumped to their feet when Ian drove a two-run double into right center, I remained seated, alone in my world.

Back on the mound, I didn't worry about anything but the catcher's glove. Hadley had me move the ball around, high and low, inside and out. I threw mainly straight fastballs, but sometimes I'd try a two-seamer. When I did, I lost some velocity, but the ball seemed to sink at the last minute. If the batter hit the pitch, it was on the ground.

Eastside Catholic's pitcher, after his rocky first inning, matched me. Innings rolled by, but the score stayed the same. Laurelhurst 2, Eastside Catholic 0.

And then it was the seventh inning—Eastside's last at bat. I saw one of the twins—I couldn't tell which one—warming up along the sideline, but that was for show. Vereen wasn't bringing him in.

This was my game.

No reason to hold back, I thought as the first hitter stepped up. But then I remembered that Mr. Thurman had told me that was the *wrong* way to think. I slowed everything down. The easier I threw, the faster my pitches would be.

The leadoff batter went down on three pitches, swinging late on each. I struck out the next hitter looking. With two out, everybody on the bench and in the stands rose and cheered. I could feel the hairs on the back of my neck rise. I wanted to strike out the last guy, finish in style. The first pitch was a fastball inside. He tried to bunt, but instead hit a pop-up just behind home plate. Hadley was out of his crouch in a flash. I don't know how he found the ball, but he did. At the last second he dived . . . and caught it.

It was such an unexpected end to the game that no one moved for a few seconds. Then the guys were on me, slapping me on the back, grinning as they danced me back to the dugout.

"Do you know what you just did?" Mr. Thurman said, coming over to the bench as I was packing up my gear. "Do you?"

SIX

I'D PITCHED A PERFECT GAME.

Sort of.

Eastside Catholic had had three base runners in the first inning, but they weren't my base runners, they were Kevin's. I hadn't given up anything.

Seven innings, no hits, no walks, no errors.

No nothing.

The *Seattle Times* ran an article in the prep section the next morning with the headline

Better than Perfect!

The writer, Clay Pearson, made a big deal that—because of the double play in the first inning—I'd gotten twenty-one outs while facing twenty batters. He wrote that it was the first time in Washington prep baseball history that it had happened.

Before I made it to school, I'd gotten texts from my mom and Antonio and Suja—and pretty much anyone who had my number. When I did step inside Laurelhurst, my teammates were all over me, congratulating me by razzing me.

And then things got crazier.

After practice, I went back to the Thurmans' house and down to my room to finish replying to texts and emails. I was half done when Mr. Thurman pounded on my door. I opened up, and he shoved a telephone into my face. "It's a guy from ESPN. He wants to interview you for *SportsCenter*."

I took the phone. The man introduced himself, but I didn't take in his name. Then the questions came.

Did I realize what I was doing while the game was going on?

How does it feel to be better than perfect?

What's next?

I was so nervous, I was sure my answers made no sense. The ESPN man didn't care. "Perfect, kid. Short and sweet."

"C-Could we r-redo it?" I asked.

"Why?"

"I s-stuttered. I know I d-did."

"Just makes you more human." He paused. "No guarantees, but watch the nine o'clock *SportsCenter*."

At nine o'clock I was downstairs sitting in front of the TV with Mr. and Mrs. Thurman. Ian wasn't there, and his parents didn't mention him, so neither did I. "Call your mom," Mrs. Thurman said. "She'll want to see."

"What if I'm n-not on?" I said.

"Call her."

I went into my room and texted her.

We'll be watching, she texted back, with about twenty smiley faces after her words.

When I returned to the living room, *SportsCenter* had started. NCAA basketball. NBA scores. NHL scores. Baseball scores. Golf. As one segment followed the other, I felt foolish to have texted my mom. I could picture her and Curtis and Antonio stuck watching hockey highlights.

The man had warned me.

No guarantees.

And then, in the last minute, my photo and the words *Better than Perfect* popped up in the left-hand corner of the screen.

The anchor guy briefly explained what I'd done, and then my voice—though it didn't sound like me—was on national TV.

Twenty seconds and two questions later, a commercial for Gatorade came on. Mrs. Thurman clapped her hands together. Mr. Thurman patted me on the back. My cell rang.

I looked at the screen—Antonio.

The Thurmans left, giving me a wave as they headed upstairs.

"Whoa—you actually answered?" Antonio said when he heard my voice.

"Why w-w-wouldn't I?"

"National star. I figured you'd forget all about us."

I started to speak, but he'd handed the phone to my mom.

"I'm so proud of you," she said.

Then there was more fumbling, and Curtis's voice followed. "It's great that you're doing great."

I thanked him, and then it was Mom again, and then Antonio.

"We'd better cut this connection," he said. "The Yankees will be calling to offer you ten million dollars. And when they do, say yes, Bro. Say yes."

SEVEN

AT PRACTICE THE NEXT DAY, Ian worked harder at the plate and in the field than I'd ever seen him do. In a base-running drill, he barreled right into shortstop Andrew Comette, his best friend, bowling Andrew over.

"That's because of you," Hadley said, nodding toward Ian.

"Me?"

"Sure. This team has been the *Ian Thurman Show* for three years. You show up and you're on ESPN within a couple of weeks. He's never been on ESPN, and nobody has ever called him better than perfect."

Halfway through practice, Coach Vereen came down the sideline where Kevin and I were throwing. He watched for a while, chewing on his lower lip. Finally he told us to huddle around him.

"I want you to know what your roles will be going forward." He looked first at me. "Laz, you'll be our number one starter." He turned to Kevin. "Laz's pitch count gets high, you're in. Laz can't find home plate, you're in. You'll be pitching, and pitching a lot." He paused. "Any questions?"

Neither of us said anything. When Vereen headed back to the infield, I turned to Kevin. "I-I-I'm—"

He waved me off. "It's okay. I saw this coming. I'm actually kind of glad. Eastside Catholic, Blanchet, Jesuit, Gonzaga—you can have them. I'm tired of being the guy who gets the blame when we lose. Been there, done that."

On Friday afternoon, when I took the mound as Laurelhurst's number one starting pitcher, the guys—even Kevin's friends—totally accepted it. Coach Vereen hadn't handed me the job; I'd earned it.

We were playing Skyline at their field in our last non-league game. They'd come in second in their league the year before and, like us, had won their first three games of the new season.

As I warmed up, the name Johnny Vander Meer jumped into my head. He's the only major-league pitcher to throw back-to-back no-hitters. I thought how wild it would be if I could match him, in a high school way.

I was still thinking about Vander Meer as Skyline's leadoff batter stepped to the plate. My first pitch was a fastball on the outside corner. In a blink, the guy pushed a bunt toward second. I froze for an instant before coming off the mound. The ball slid past my glove, and by the time our second baseman, Jared Bronzan, fielded it, the runner was across the bag.

Bronzan tossed me the ball, and I stepped back onto the mound, feeling shaky. If I hadn't been in fantasyland, I'd have made the play.

Skyline's number two hitter was skinny. No power, but probably pesky. As I went into my stretch, I checked the runner at first. He had that *I'm-going-to-steal* look. I dropped my eyes, then wheeled and rushed a throw to Sam Huffman at first.

The throw was in the dirt. Huffman tried to short-hop the ball, but it got by him. The runner raced toward second, looked back to the see the ball rolling along the chainlink fence, and kept going, taking third. Coach Vereen stepped out from the bench. "Come on, Weathers! Let's go!"

I nodded, my chest tight. You read about athletes who get what they want and then immediately have a letdown. I couldn't let that happen.

I looked toward home plate. The hitter was rhythmically swinging his bat back and forth. I checked third and delivered —fastball, right down the middle. The batter's swing was late; all he could manage was a weak ground ball to second. But as Bronzan threw him out, the runner on third trotted home.

Skyline 1–0.

Huffman walked the ball to me. "No big deal," he said, dropping the ball into my glove. "We'll score ten."

I retired the next two batters, striking out the first and getting the second on a pop fly. Coach Vereen clapped his hands. "Let's get it back."

And we did. Andrew Comette worked a leadoff walk. He stayed at first as Bronzan struck out, bringing Ian to the plate.

In the first three games, Ian had been impatient in the early innings, swinging at bad pitches. This time he laid off pitches that missed the plate. With the count in his favor at 3-0, the Skyline pitcher had to come in with a strike.

Ian's bat whipped through the zone, catching the ball solid. It rocketed out of the park, gone in seconds. Guys on the bench erupted, whooping and hollering.

Ian wasn't done. In his second at bat, he cleared the bases with a double into left-center, driving in three. He lined out in the fourth inning, a bullet that almost took the third baseman's glove off. In the sixth, he hit what looked like a routine fly ball to left field, but the ball kept carrying and carrying until it dropped over the fence—a three-run homer.

Ian's totals: three for four with eight RBI.

After my shaky start, I settled down and pitched four innings, giving up a bloop single to right in the third and an infield single in the fourth. Kevin finished up with three solid innings of his own. The only hard-hit ball came with two outs in the seventh. The Skyline hitter ripped a fastball into right center, but Ian ran it down and made a backhand catch to end the game. As he trotted in, he gave me a look that said *I'm still the star of this team.*

I didn't care.

I'd gone 3–0 in the preseason, with an earned run average under one. My name had been in the paper, and my face had been on *SportsCenter*.

EIGHT

I MET SUJA on Saturday morning. We got maple bars and mochas and then went over my algebra. The whole time we worked, she seemed about to explode.

"T-Tell me," I said when we'd finished.

"Tell you what?"

"Come on. I c-can see it in your face. What happened?"

"Whitman College. I got in—with a full scholarship."

All week at Laurelhurst I'd heard kids talking about receiving acceptance letters from WSU and Western Washington and other colleges, some that I'd never heard of. Whitman was one of those. "That's great, Suja. It's f-fantastic." I paused. "Where is it?"

She talked for five minutes straight. Whitman was in Walla Walla, way out in eastern Washington, but even though it was in the boonies, it was almost as good as Stanford. She was going to study chemistry or environmental science or be premed. She stopped. "I've been talking too much, haven't I?"

"No, I w-want to hear."

She exhaled. "Well, you heard."

She took the first sip of her mocha—which must have been cold—and then asked me how I was doing. I had nothing much to tell, so I was done quickly. At the table close to us, a little boy spilled his Coke into his sister's lap. She started crying, his mom snapped at him, and then he started crying. Suja leaned forward and whispered, "I don't think I ever want kids."

We watched as the mom cleaned up the mess and quieted the kids. "How's J-Jet City?" I asked once peace had been restored.

She shrugged. "Closing down little by little. Every day or two, somebody leaves. My parents signed a lease at a trailer park out in Bothell, but we won't move until school ends. Your mom and her friend and Antonio are going to Woodacres, right?"

"Yeah. April first."

"How about you? Are you going to move back with your mom when school ends?"

"I can't. W-Woodacres won't let four people s-stay in a unit. B-But I wouldn't g-go anyway. C-Curtis is Antonio's d-dad, not mine."

"So where are you going to live? What are you going to do?"

"I don't know f-for sure, but I'll f-figure s-something out."

Her mouth dropped open. "You amaze me. You really do. If I didn't know where I'd be living, I'd be in a panic."

"I've got s-some ideas."

Her cell vibrated. She jumped up, went to a quiet corner, and talked for a few minutes. "That was my mom," she said when she came back. "My grandparents are calling from Delhi in twenty minutes, so she wants me home. Sorry."

Half an hour later I was driving the John Deere back and forth across the driving range. I'd shrugged off Suja's questions when she was across the table from me, but with nothing else to think about, that's what I thought about.

Where *was* I going to live?

What *was* I going to do?

The Thurmans would let me stay in their basement for a few weeks or maybe even a few months after school ended. But living downstairs, taking their charity—I couldn't do that for long. I'd heard about guys fishing or working in canneries up in Alaska, but I didn't even know how or where to apply for that kind of job, and I'd never been on a boat in my life. Recruiters for the army and navy had come to Laurelhurst. I'd missed the meeting, but I'd taken the pamphlets. I could try to enlist, but I'd have to take a test, and I didn't know if I could pass.

What I did know was baseball, which is why my mind kept coming back to the June draft. *If I could just get picked.* That would solve everything. I didn't care what team or what round. I'd sign for whatever money they offered; I'd play in whatever town they sent me to. I'd sleep on the team bus or in the dugout if that's what I needed to do.

NINE

METRO LEAGUE PLAY STARTED in early March with games against two south Seattle schools, Garfield on Tuesday afternoon and Cleveland on Friday night.

I watched the Garfield hitters closely in batting practice.

Their power guys had long swings; they wouldn't be able to catch up to a fastball like mine. "No changeups or off-speed pitches," I told Hadley before the game. "Nothing but heat until they prove they can hit it."

Andrew Comette beat out a bunt to open the game. He took off on the first pitch to the next batter, stealing second on a close play. He went to third on a groundout and scored when Ian ripped a single past the pitcher's ear to drive him home.

Taking the mound with a lead, even if it's only one run, makes pitching easier. I struck out the first guy on a high fastball. The number-two hitter nubbed a grounder toward third. Jay Massine backed away from it, hoping it would go foul, but it rolled to a stop right on the chalk.

As I went into my stretch, the runner took a big lead off first. I looked toward home plate, then wheeled and fired to first.

This time I remembered what Mr. Thurman had taught me and didn't hurry my throw. The runner had started toward second, tried to come back to first, tripped, and ended up on his knees. Huffman put the tag on him for the second out. When the next guy popped up to first, I had what I'd wanted—a dominant first inning.

As I neared the bench, Mr. Thurman moved down next to the fence and motioned me over. "The man in the Mariners cap?" he said in his gravelly voice, nodding toward an older guy with a gut who was sitting behind home plate, notepad in hand. "That's Tommy Zeller, a Mariner scout. He's here to evaluate Ian, but he's not going to close his eyes when you're pitching."

My eyes were on the field during the top of the second, but I didn't see anything. When the guys around me grabbed their gloves and headed out to play in the field, autopilot kicked in. I picked up my glove and trotted to the mound.

Tommy Zeller's presence worked like a shot of adrenaline. My pitches had more velocity and better movement. I struck out the leadoff hitter on three heaters. Their second batter chopped a ball off home plate and beat the throw to first, but a pop-up and strikeout followed, and another inning was over. As I walked off the mound, I saw Tommy Zeller writing in his notebook.

On the bench, I stared at the ground. I didn't look up even when guys around me cheered. If we'd scored, I didn't want to know. I wanted to pitch as if I were on the mound in a tie game in the World Series.

As the innings rolled by, my fastball kept its velocity and

movement. The Garfield hitters were free swingers, but they weren't making solid contact. A bloop single in the third, an infield hit in the fourth. That was it.

In the fifth, I felt stronger than I had in the first. Hadley put his mitt in the middle of the plate and I poured fastball after fastball into it. Three strikeouts, two swinging and one looking. Six more outs and I'd have a complete game shutout.

But as I returned to the bench, Coach Vereen clapped his hands and gave me two thumbs up. "Great pitching, Laz. You're done for today. Kevin will finish up."

I started to argue, but he gave me a look, and I stopped. Kevin gave up a run in the sixth but shut Garfield down one-two-three in the seventh. The final was 8–1.

As I packed up my duffle, Tommy Zeller was laughing with Ian and Andrew Comette and Jay Massine. I held back, not wanting to shove in where I wasn't wanted. But then Zeller turned from them and walked toward me. "Hey, kid, come over here."

He introduced himself, opened his wallet, pulled out a business card, and handed it to me. It had a Mariner logo on the front and his name and email address on the back. "Whenever you pitch, send me your stats. Runs, hits, walks, strikeouts. If you pitch great, tell me what was working for you. If you stink up the joint, tell me what went wrong. Just keep it short. I don't read novels."

On the drive back to Laurelhurst, Mr. Thurman talked about how great Ian had hit and how great I had pitched. I guess I said some things, but I don't remember what.

I couldn't settle down that evening. I was starving, but I only ate a few bites of the chicken teriyaki I microwaved downstairs. Back in my room, I read a short story for English and did math homework, which killed some time. I turned on the Mariners game, listened for thirty minutes, and flicked it off.

I fell asleep right away, but woke up at two, staring at the ceiling. I'd made a good first impression on Tommy Zeller, but that was all. I had more to do.

Lots more.

TEN

OUR NEXT GAME WAS FRIDAY at five. Late Thursday it started to rain, and it kept raining Friday morning. At noon an announcement came over the intercom: the game had been rescheduled for Saturday afternoon. Five minutes after the announcement, the sun came out.

I arranged a tutoring session with Jesus Ramirez. He helped me edit my history paper, and we didn't call it quits until it was done. Then I walked to the Thurmans' house under a perfectly clear sky.

Mr. Thurman and Ian were eating in the kitchen when I stepped inside. "Join us, Laz," Mr. Thurman called.

The food was takeout from a Thai restaurant. Ian wolfed it down. "I'm going to watch the Dubs–Clips over at Martin's," he said as he wiped his mouth and stood up to leave. His father caught his eye, and he turned to me. "You can come if you want."

I shook my head. "Thanks, b-but I've got stuff to do."

As he left, his father called to him. "Don't be out too late. Game tomorrow at noon. You hear me?"

"Yeah, yeah," Ian said, not looking back. "I hear you."

I studied, watched the last quarter of the Warriors–Clippers game in the downstairs TV palace, and turned off my lights a little before eleven. I woke up when I heard the hum of machinery as the garage door opened. Seconds later, the SUV's headlights lit up my room as Ian pulled into the garage.

I checked the time on my cell—3:12.

Saturday morning came up windy and cold, terrible weather for baseball. For breakfast I had orange juice, a bowl of yogurt with cantaloupe, some mango slices, and a cinnamon bagel with blackberry jam. I still wasn't used to the food the Thurmans just *had*.

Once I'd finished, I went outside to the batting cage, stretched, threw a couple of dozen balls into the screen, then stretched some more. Mrs. Thurman came out and said hello before heading off on her morning run. When I returned to the house, Mr. Thurman was eating breakfast and reading the newspaper. "Ian up yet?" he asked me.

"I d-don't know," I said.

Ian didn't come down until it was time to leave for the game. His face was gray; his eyes were bloodshot; he moved like an old man.

"What time did you get in last night?" his father asked as we got into the car.

Ian shrugged. "I don't know exactly. Not too late."

As soon as we got to the field, I knew that Cleveland would be more of a challenge than Garfield. The coach ran their warm-up with precision. And their power guys had quicker, shorter swings than Garfield's hitters.

Because of the cold weather, my fastball didn't have its usual jump. I couldn't overpower the Cleveland hitters, so in the early innings I changed speeds and worked both sides of the plate. I wasn't striking anybody out, but I was getting through the innings.

To my eye, Cleveland's pitcher—a stocky guy who looked like a young Russell Westbrook—was just okay. Every inning, he walked some guys or gave up some hits. The table was set, but nobody could deliver the clutch hit.

Twice Ian batted with runners in scoring position—striking out in the first and popping up in the third, his bat slow both times. Martin Moran and Andrew Comette were both green in the face and sluggish in the field. It didn't take Einstein to figure out who'd been partying with Ian.

The game was scoreless in the top of the fourth. I got a couple of quick outs but then gave up a single. I hit the next batter when a fastball slipped out of my hand. That brought up Cleveland's cleanup hitter, a guy about thirty pounds overweight.

I worked the count to two strikes, then threw a fastball off the outside corner. The guy put a good swing on the ball, but he caught it on the end of the bat, sending a line drive to straight-away center. It should have been an easy out, but Ian backed up a few steps and then—realizing he'd misjudged the ball—raced in. He took half a dozen steps, lost his balance, tripped, and fell on his face as the ball bounded past him. Ian lay on the ground for a couple of beats before he got back to his feet and chased after the ball. By the time he tracked it down, both runners had scored and the hitter was puffing his way around third.

Bronzan was in short center ready to make the relay home. Had Ian made a decent throw, we would have at least gotten the guy out at the plate, but Ian's throw sailed over Bronzan's head. The Cleveland guy staggered home, scoring standing up. His teammates were laughing and shouting. If you were going to pick the most unlikely player on either team to hit an inside-the-park home run—and that's how it was scored—you'd have picked him.

Cleveland 3–Laurelhurst 0.

Hadley carried the ball back to me and dropped it into my glove. "Shake it off," he said.

I was calm on the outside, but inside I was seething. Sure, things happen in baseball. But your best fielder—a future major-leaguer—misjudging an easy fly ball, then falling down, and then making a terrible throw? Dawit at North Central had never made a play that bad. Not even close.

In the fifth, Comette let a ground ball get by him, allowing another run to score. I lost it then, walking two guys in a row. When the count went to 2-0 on the next batter, Coach Vereen yanked me. Kevin Griffith allowed both of those guys to score, pushing the lead to 6–0.

And our guys? We didn't mount any kind of a threat until the seventh. Then, with the bases loaded, Ian grounded into a double play—pitcher to catcher to first—to end the game. He didn't even bother to run it out. The Cleveland players mobbed their pitcher: it was their first win over Laurelhurst in a decade.

Guys on my team packed up fast and left fast. I got in the back seat of Mr. Thurman's SUV; Ian slumped down in the passenger seat.

Mr. Thurman backed up the car and pulled into traffic. "I'm not stupid," he said once we were out on the street. "I know when someone is hung over from booze or drugs or both. Understand one thing. You get caught, Coach Vereen will kick you off the team. Guaranteed. That happens, and you can kiss your Arizona State scholarship goodbye. And as far as getting drafted by a major-league team? You think they'd waste a pick on an eighteen-year-old with a substance abuse problem?"

"I had a bad game. That doesn't mean I was drinking or doing drugs," Ian growled.

"Now you're lying, which makes it worse."

Ian slumped down further. "What's the point of talking if you don't believe what I say?"

They both stayed silent after that. When we reached the Thurmans' house, I went downstairs to my room, booted up the laptop, and forced myself to type an email to Tommy Zeller. I wrote about the cold and the wind and Ian's misplayed fly ball. I read it over and knew it was wrong. I deleted and started again.

We *lost 6–0. I pitched four innings, walked three, struck out three —just didn't have it. Laz Weathers.*

I hit send and then sat staring at the screen.

ELEVEN

IT WAS ONLY TWO THIRTY. I still had time to put in some hours at the range, and driving the John Deere would be a lot better than moping around the Thurmans' basement. I used the back door to slip out and then caught the 45 and RapidRide E to the driving range.

As I walked down the steep driveway from Aurora, I saw Mr. Matsui staring at the front of the pro shop. The words **EAT THE RICH** had been spray-painted on the wall. "Nice, isn't it?" he said when he saw me. "Though the thought isn't all bad." He paused. "I've got some paint. Cover this up before you do anything else today, okay?"

"The s-s-security c-c-camera catch anything?"

"The owners took them away. If somebody burned the place down, they'd be happy."

I painted over the graffiti, but the words still peeked through. When I asked about a second coat, Mr. Matsui shook his head. "That's good enough. Pick up the range and power wash the stalls, and then get out of here and do something fun."

As I drove the John Deere near the back fence, I got a good

look into Jet City. I didn't see Garrett's Subaru or Garrett or Antonio or anybody.

When I finished work, I decided to go see my mom. Maybe Antonio would be there, too. It was after six when I walked through the entrance to Jet City. Bulbs had gone out on the neon sign over the manager's trailer, so **JET CITY** now read: **J T CI Y**.

I knew something was wrong the instant I saw our trailer. No lights were on, and the shades had been pulled down. The flowerpots along the side were missing. Then I understood. It was two weeks early, but they'd moved.

I walked up the steps to the front door of the trailer. The welcome mat—in shreds—was still there, a bad joke.

I turned the handle on the door, pushed, and it banged opened. No reason to lock it. I flicked on the light for the main room. A bare bulb hung down, giving off a brutal light.

My footsteps echoed as I wandered through the empty trailer. The rug was dirty; the kitchen linoleum was coming up; the wood paneling was warped. Why hadn't I noticed those things before, when the trailer was my home?

I forced myself to go through each room and see everything. Only then did I return to the front door, switch off the light, and leave. I was on the gravel path heading out of Jet City when Garrett's black Subaru pulled up next to me.

The passenger window rolled down, and Antonio hung his arm out. "Hey, Laz. What's up?"

"How c-come nobody t-told me about the move?"

"I sent you a text, and Mom called you."

I took out my phone and flipped it open. Dead battery. Again.

"M-My fault. Sorry."

"Did you beat Cleveland last night?"

I shook my head. "We p-played today, and we lost six to nothing."

"What? That other kid pitch?"

"No, I pitched."

His face screwed up in disbelief. "Cleveland scored six? They suck. And how come your guys didn't score a dozen? I thought that Ian kid hit a home run every time he stepped to the plate."

"T-Today Mighty C-Casey struck out." I paused. "I was going to the new p-place to see Mom. You want to go with m-me? I don't even know which unit it is."

He looked to Garrett. "An hour?"

"No problem," Garrett replied. "Just don't be late."

TWELVE

"SO H-HOW IS IT?" I asked Antonio as we walked toward Aurora Avenue.

"Woodacres? It sucks."

"M-Mom said it was g-great."

He grimaced. "Yeah, well, she wants it to be great. That huge closet isn't so huge once you stick a bed in it. And with you not there, it feels off." He paused and forced himself to smile. "But change is good, right? That's what everybody says."

"Is Mom g-going to s-sell the trailer?"

He snorted. "She's going to try, but nobody will buy it. It'd cost more to move it than it's worth."

We'd reached Aurora Avenue. The roar of the cars put a temporary end to our conversation. When the light turned green, we hustled across.

"You g-getting along okay with C-Curtis?" I asked once we'd walked far enough from Aurora to hear each other again.

"Trying."

He pointed down the street toward a driveway. "You see that blue light? The apartment is at the end of that road on the right. Number Four-C. I don't see Curtis's pickup out front, so it'll just be Mom."

"Aren't you c-coming? At least for a while?"

"I don't think so."

I swallowed. "Come on, Antonio. I n-never see you. And it would b-be just the three of us, l-like the old d-days."

He looked toward the apartment, and then he stood there for a long moment. Finally he shook his head. "I spend enough time in there." And then he was gone, headed back to Jet City.

Mom must have seen me from the window, because she opened the door to the apartment before I knocked. She hugged me and then gave me a tour. The apartment had real walls and a real roof and a real plumbing system. The stove and the micro-wave and the refrigerator looked new, but Antonio's room was so small she couldn't open the door all the way. "Once we save some money, we're going to replace this bed with a chair that folds out for sleeping. That'll give your brother some room. Right now, he looks for any reason to stay away . . ." Her voice trailed off.

We ate dinner together: a take-and-bake extra-large sausage pizza from Papa John's. We were sitting at the same old kitchen table with the same old plates and the same old knives and forks and glasses. I could almost pretend we were in Jet City, before Curtis and before the townhomes and before everything. Mom told me a funny story about an old man whose whole family had practically moved into her hospital, sleeping on the sofa and in the chairs, watching TV day and night, eating the old guy's food, even asking for seconds. I told her about my baseball games, leaving out the loss against Cleveland. She drank only one glass of wine and didn't smoke a single cigarette.

We'd just finished eating when the pickup pulled into the driveway. "See you found your way, Laz," Curtis said as he stepped inside. He motioned with his head toward the main room. "A lot nicer than that trailer, isn't it?"

"It's g-great," I said.

"Do I smell pizza?" he asked.

Mom stood and went to the oven. "There's lots left."

He got a beer from the refrigerator and then sat and stretched his arms high above his head. Mom put the pizza in front of him. "I am starved," he said as he picked up a piece and bit into it.

As he ate, he complained about working in Windermere, a rich neighborhood near Laurelhurst. "Those people don't want me to trim the limbs hanging over the electric lines, but they'll go ballistic if they lose their power in a storm."

At Jet City, the trailer had been Mom's and Antonio's and mine. Curtis had been the outsider, the one who never quite fit. But Woodacres was his home. I was the outsider.

When Curtis finished eating, Mom wanted us all to watch *Skyfall*, a James Bond movie. I lied and said I needed to get back to Laurelhurst. "I'm going to p-play some v-video g-games with Ian and other g-guys on the team."

"So you have friends?" Mom asked.

"Oh, yeah," I said.

Curtis drove me back to the Thurmans'. He knew that I'd pitched well against Garfield, but he hadn't heard about the Cleveland game. "Those baseball scouts find talent in the Dominican Republic. If they can do that, they'll find you in Seattle, Washington, U.S. of A. You'll see."

THIRTEEN

THAT SUNDAY, MRS. THURMAN, Mr. Thurman, Ian, and I all had dinner in the dining room. When I'd first moved in, Mrs. Thurman said they did that most Sundays, but this was the first time.

She cooked salmon with brown rice, Brussels sprouts, salad, and great bread from a bakery. I told her how tremendous it all tasted, which was true. "Wait until the Copper River salmon comes in," she said. "That's even better."

As we ate, Mr. Thurman talked about a geography book he was reading. I asked a couple of questions, and so did Mrs. Thurman. Then he asked me if I was ready for midterms. Through all of it, Ian said nothing.

Toward the end of the meal Mr. Thurman turned in his chair to face him. "Son, I apologize for what I said in the car yesterday. I want you to know that I *do* believe you."

Ian kept his eyes on his plate. "Forget it."

"Does that mean my apology has been accepted?"

Ian looked up. "Yeah. Sure."

A few minutes later Ian stood. "That was great, Mom. I've

got lots of homework." He looked at his dad and nodded, and Mr. Thurman nodded back.

I finished my dinner quickly. If I were in Jet City, I would have done the dishes, but here I just put my dirty plate in the dishwasher and beat it down to the basement. It felt good to be alone. Before taking out my history book, I checked the sports scores on the Internet.

I hadn't been reading long when I heard footsteps, followed by a knock on my door. I opened up.

Ian.

"You want to shoot some pool?" he asked.

He broke, sinking one and leaving himself an easy second shot. "So, you got anything going for next year?" he asked as he lined it up. "College recruiters or major-league scouts?"

He took his shot, missed, then looked at me.

"Tommy Z-Zeller," I said, keeping my voice level. "The Mariner g-guy who s-scouted you. He asked m-me to send him updates."

I stepped to the table, took my shot, missed.

"Anybody else?" he asked, moving in.

I shook my head.

"Colleges?"

"I'm not r-really interested in c-college."

He smacked the six ball into the corner pocket. "So, if nothing happens for you, will you move back in with your mom and your brother?"

"I g-guess," I said, not wanting to explain.

"You don't sound like you want to."

"I d-don't," I admitted.

He snorted. "My dad wouldn't care if you stayed here forever. He likes you a thousand times more than he likes me. My mom will want you out, though. Not right away, but by the end of summer."

"I won't s-stay that long."

He held the pool cue upright. "You don't like it here?"

"I didn't s-say that."

"But you don't. And you don't like Laurelhurst High."

I nodded toward the pool table. "How about we j-just play?"

He looked at me for a long moment, then returned his attention to the table. After he'd knocked in the eight ball to win the game, he turned back to me. "All right. Here's the deal. My dad was right. I did get wasted Friday night. A bunch of us did. We drank some beers, supplemented with a little oxy from that G-man guy up at Jet City that you pretend you don't know. We got loaded, and it cost us the game. But you knew that, right?"

He paused, waiting for me to answer. What could I say?

"It won't happen again," he went on, waving his cue stick around. "That's a promise. Partly it's for you, because I get how much this season matters to you. But mainly I'm doing this for me. I'm tired of living here, tired of my dad, even though this time he was right. If a team picks me in the first round, I'm set for life. But if I get booted off the team, I'll be playing for some community college and living at home. I couldn't stand that. So it's all clean living from here on out. And what I do, the other guys will do."

His eyes spun back to the pool table. He broke, pocketing two balls. Then I watched as he cleared the table, setting up each succeeding shot like a pro, knocking in the eight ball to end the game. I never got a shot.

FOURTEEN

I WANTED TO BELIEVE IAN, but I wasn't one hundred percent convinced. Guys at North Central were always saying things like *Starting tomorrow, I'm going to come to school every day,* and then two days later they'd be cutting class again.

Our next game was in West Seattle. Technically, West Seattle is part of Seattle, but the neighborhood is separate from the rest of the city. From Alki Point, the Space Needle and downtown seem miles away.

The team bus got stuck in traffic on I-5 through downtown and then got stuck again on the West Seattle Bridge. Rain was predicted, so we'd hardly warmed up when the umpire screamed "Play ball!"

It didn't matter that nobody was loose. Ian tripled in a run in the top of the first, and he scored one pitch later with a headfirst slide after a wild pitch bounded ten feet from the catcher. In the bottom of the first, Andrew Comette came busting in on a little dribbler, fielded it barehanded, and—all in one motion—fired to first for the out.

That's how the game went—heads-up baseball from the first

pitch to the last. I had good stuff, not my best, but the defense sucked up every hard-hit ball.

The score was 10–0 after four innings. The mercy rule ended the game, and I was sitting in the back seat of Mr. Thurman's SUV heading to Seattle when the sky opened and sheets of rain poured down.

Friday's home game against Chief Sealth was a rerun of Tuesday's game, only without the rain. Ian hit a home run in the first and pushed the score to 6–0 with a two-run double in the third. I kept the ball on the corners, throwing loose and free. I hit 92 on the speed gun, and my pitches darted just before they reached the plate. When Kevin replaced me in the fifth, we were up 7–1, the one run coming on a walk followed by an opposite field double that was fair by six inches. Kevin pitched a scoreless fifth, and the twins pitched the final two innings, with both giving up a couple of runs. The final was 10–5.

When I got back to my room, I wrote to Tommy Zeller, laying out for him my totals for the two games. *Eight innings. One run. Four hits. Twelve strikeouts. Three walks. Fastball in the low nineties.* I admired those numbers for a while.

Then I hit send.

FIFTEEN

LAURELHURST HIGH was the New York Yankees of the Metro League. All the other city schools circled our game on their calendar. Over the next weeks, Roosevelt, Ballard, Rainier Beach, and the rest of them came at us with everything they had, turning every game into a big game.

The thing about baseball is that talent doesn't always translate into wins. A guy can hit a ball on the screws, absolutely crush it, and have it turn into a double play. The next guy up can be completely fooled, throw his bat at a pitch, and hit a flare down the line that ends up a triple.

To win, you need to focus. That takes leadership. Our leader was Ian. He kept the promise he made to me after the Cleveland game. He was all business at practice, pushing himself to get stronger, faster, quicker. His hands flashed through the hitting zone; his hips turned in perfect unison with his shoulders. He must have popped out sometimes, but it seemed as if he hit the ball hard every single at bat.

I was becoming more and more of a pitcher, just like Mr. Thurman wanted, and not just a thrower. I still got my share of strikeouts, especially in the early innings. Once we had a lead, I pitched to contact. Guys hit ground balls and pop flies, but only once or twice in a game would anybody square up anything. The wins kept coming. After every game I emailed my stats to Tommy Zeller.

Antonio had said I had baseball to hang on to, and he was right. If I could have stayed on the baseball diamond all the time, my life would have been as clear as a blue sky in summer. But when I wasn't practicing or playing, everything turned murky. I kept wondering where my home was. Not in Laurelhurst. Not at Woodacres. Not anywhere. And my family, too. My mom would always be my mom, but Curtis had changed things between us. No sense in pretending that he hadn't. And Antonio? For years, we'd been half brothers and best friends. Now we were half brothers and sort of friends. Was a day coming when we'd just be half brothers—two guys who called each other every couple of years to say hello and then goodbye?

When May came, that early loss to Cleveland remained the single blemish on our record. Cleveland, though, had lost two league games, one to Ballard and one to Sealth. So technically, we were ahead by a game in the standings, but if they beat us a second time and then won out, they'd hold the tiebreaker. Cleveland, not Laurelhurst, would represent Seattle in the state playoffs.

We had to win the rematch.

The game was on a Friday night at their park. Their starting pitcher was the same stocky Russell Westbrook look-alike who'd shut us down in the first game. Throughout the warm-ups he had a cockiness to him—cap a little off-center, walk a little too loose, grin a little too big. The message came through loud and clear: *I shut you down last time, and I'm going to do it again.*

It rankled. Guys on my team wanted to make him eat that smile. But he mowed us down in the top of the first, even getting Ian to strike out on a pitch in the dirt.

The way he breezed through the first inning pumped Cleveland up. I struck out the first guy looking and got the second on a tapper right back to me. My first pitch to the three-hitter was a fastball on the inside corner, right where I wanted it. But he turned on it, sending a hard line drive down the third base line. It was only 275 feet to the fence, and the ball just cleared it, but there was nothing lucky about it. If it hadn't gone over the fence, it might have gone right through it—that's how hard he hit it.

I was stunned, and then I heard Hadley's voice as he walked out toward the mound to toss me a new ball. "First inning, Laz. Lots of time." I nodded, took some deep breaths, and then struck out their cleanup hitter.

They had only one run, but I could see the fire in the eyes of every player on Cleveland's team. Powered by the confidence that came from that home run, their pitcher got tougher. We put a runner on base in every inning, and sometimes two runners, but the clutch hit wouldn't come.

The score remained 1–0 through three innings . . . four

innings . . . five innings. In the top of the sixth, we loaded the bases with two out. I could feel a clutch hit coming, but Hadley bounced out to second.

Their crowd—maybe fifty people—went crazy, clapping and stomping the metal bleachers, sounding like one thousand. The Cleveland players fed off that excitement. We were down, and they were ready to knock us out.

I felt strong when I took the mound for the bottom of the sixth, but I took extra time between pitches. I wanted to slow the adrenaline rush the Cleveland guys were feeling, make them wait. I tuned out the shouting from the stands, focused on Hadley's glove—and I got them: one-two-three. A clean inning.

Top of the seventh.

Our last at bat.

The season on the line.

I didn't have to look at the lineup card to know that Ian was batting fourth. If somebody could get on and bring him to the plate, he'd have a chance to work his magic. The Cleveland pitcher had been in trouble most of the game. We just had to keep hammering at the door, hoping it would open.

But Evan Peterson, leading off, popped up to shortstop on the first pitch. The second out came when Andrew Comette fanned with a wild swing at an eye-level fastball. The Cleveland fans rose to their feet as Jared Bronzan, our last chance, stepped to the plate.

Jared isn't a great hitter, but he's a battler. The Cleveland pitcher got ahead in the count, but Jared stayed alive by fouling off two nasty fastballs, barely making contact on the second. The next pitch was probably outside, but too close to take. Jared swung, sending a nubber past the pitcher toward second base. His swing got him moving toward first, and he turned on the jets, running faster than I'd ever seen him run.

Cleveland's second baseman raced in, fielded the ball, and, in one motion, threw to first. Jared's foot came down as the ball smacked into the first baseman's glove. The umpire paused. "Safe!" he screamed, throwing his arms out. A cascade of boos came down from the Cleveland side while the small group of parents and kids on our side cheered.

Ian.

The Cleveland coach trotted out. He had a couple of pitchers warming up, but they looked young and scared. He wasn't making a change.

I was certain—probably because that's how it always happens in the movies—that the count would go to 3-2, that Ian would foul a couple off, and only then whatever was going to happen would happen. Instead, Ian swung at the first pitch, sending a towering fly ball down the third-base line. It cleared the fence by twenty feet, but was it fair?

I couldn't tell. Nobody on either bench could. The foul pole extends just ten feet above the fence. The only person who had a clear view was the home plate umpire. I held my breath, waiting for his call.

Nothing.

And then he twirled his index finger in the air—the signal for a home run. We'd taken the lead, 2–1!

When I took the mound in the bottom of the seventh, I was the one with the adrenaline racing through my bloodstream. The Cleveland hitters looked dejected. I needed to pour strikes over the plate. And that's what I did. I struck out the side, never giving them even a sliver of hope.

SIXTEEN

PACKING UP MY STUFF, I composed my email to Tommy Zeller in my head, when a young black man—thin face, short beard, rangy build of a wide receiver—called out. "Laz Weathers, got a minute?"

He strode over and stuck a hand out for me to shake. "I'm Clay Pearson of the *Seattle Times*. I wrote the 'Better than Perfect' article."

"Thanks f-for writing that," I said, "and g-good to m-meet you."

I glanced toward Mr. Thurman's SUV. He had the hatch open, and Ian was already heading across the parking lot.

Clay Pearson followed my eyes. "This won't take long. I heard some of your life story from Curtis Driver. He's your stepdad, right?"

"Not really. It's c-complicated."

"No? Well, anyway, he works tree service with my dad. Curtis told my father how you lost your team and your home. You're even losing your job, right? But instead of quitting, you fought back. It's a good story. Number one pitcher for the city champions, headed to the state playoffs, maybe a major-league pitcher someday."

My face went red. "I'm just hoping for a ch-chance in the minor l-leagues."

He nodded. "Sure. Here's the deal. I'll take you out for pizza, interview you, write up your story, and submit it to my editor. If she likes it, the *Times* prints it. If she doesn't like it, you're out an hour or two of time, but you got a free pizza. Interested?"

My throat tightened. "I'm not g-good at t-talking."

"Doesn't matter, because I am good at writing."

"I d-don't know," I said.

"Look, kid, you just said you want to get drafted. Publicity can only help. So think it over. Give me your number, and I'll call in a couple of days for your answer. Fair enough?"

In the SUV, Mr. Thurman did most of the talking, as usual. "Gutsy calls by the umpires. Two in a row against the home team. You don't see that every day. And a clutch hit, Ian. File that in the memory bank."

Then Mr. Thurman looked over his shoulder at me. "You pitched great, Laz. Fantastic. And that last inning. Wow! Talk about shutting the door."

Back in my room, I emailed Tommy Zeller. The numbers —*seven innings, one run, four hits, nine strikeouts, one walk*—spoke for themselves.

I showered, went into the game room, and turned on the Mariners. The M's reliever—just up from Tacoma—was getting rocked. He didn't have a clue where his pitches were going.

I thought about my own control. I'd had the ball on a string, putting it right where I wanted it, with movement.

After I'd been watching the game for ten minutes, Mr. Thurman came in and sat down in the big chair off to the side. "You okay with some company?"

In the eighth, the Mariners mounted a rally, but a double play killed the inning. "What did Clay Pearson want?" Mr. Thurman asked as the commercials came on.

For a second I was surprised that he knew Clay Pearson, but it made sense. Ian had been a top player for years—Clay Pearson would have interviewed him. Pearson had probably talked to Ian's older brothers, too.

I explained about the interview. When I finished, Mr. Thurman shook his head. "I don't think that would be a good idea."

"Why n-not?"

He frowned. "Look, there's nothing against the rules in what you're doing. Playing for Laurelhurst, I mean. And there's nothing wrong with my off-season program either. But there are haters out there—people who'd call us cheaters. Call *you* a cheater. You don't need that kind of attention. Better to stay under the radar, if you see what I mean."

"I g-guess so," I said.

There was a long silence.

"Have you arranged anything yet?"

"N-No. He's giving me a couple days to think about it."

"When he calls, just tell him you don't want any distractions."

The commercials ended; the Mariners game came back on. After the Astros banged out four straight hits to blow the game open, Mr. Thurman stood. "It's déjà vu all over again. I can't watch." When he reached the door, he turned back. "Great pitching today. That was special."

SEVENTEEN

I MET SUJA ON SUNDAY at Krispy Kreme. As soon as I saw her, I knew something was up. She was dressed in a long black skirt and blue blouse, and she was wearing lipstick and eye shadow. Ten seconds after I said hello, she pulled out her cell.

"G-Got something?" I asked.

Her eyes danced. "I'm meeting two women from Whitman College. Grads. They're going to tell me what to expect."

"Where are you meeting them?"

"Here. I didn't want them to see Jet City. They're coming in ten minutes." She reached across and took my hand. "I can't believe this is really happening."

As we ate, her eyes kept going to the entrance. We were about half done when she sat bolt upright. "There they are."

Two women in their thirties had just stepped inside the door. Their hair, their makeup, their shoes, their jackets, their skirts, their blouses—they looked like models in the Nordstrom catalog my mom sometimes gets in the mail. Suja leaned forward and gave them a tiny wave. They spotted her, smiled, and started toward our table.

"I'll s-see you n-next w-week," I said, getting up.

She reached out and grabbed my hand. "I hope I don't make a fool of myself," she whispered.

"You won't," I whispered back.

I crossed Aurora Avenue and walked down the roadway to the pro shop. The thwack of golf balls grew louder with each step. A decent number of cars were in the parking lot, which meant I still had work.

The pro shop looked about the same. Clubs, shoes, balls, clothes—the shelves weren't full, but they weren't empty either. It was hard to believe that soon a bulldozer would pulverize everything.

I started by picking up the litter in the parking lot. There was more trash than usual; I guess the golfers figured that since the place was being torn down, use of the garbage cans was optional. Once the lot was presentable, I straightened the clothes racks and made sure the shoes were correctly paired.

"Take a break," Mr. Matsui said to me when he saw me reaching for the keys to the John Deere. "You're making me feel guilty."

Why not? I thought. I bought a Coke from the vending machine, sat on one of the benches, and watched guys hit. A couple of them were really good, pounding long drives to the back fence or hitting iron shots that soared high and landed softly. Most were mediocre, hitting one or two good shots and then snap-hooking or slicing the next one.

I looked toward the ball-dispensing machine and then

looked again. Curtis? Was that who was punching numbers into the keypad? The balls clattered down the chute into the green basket. Curtis picked them up, turned toward me.

If I could have, I'd have sneaked off. But Curtis nodded in my direction, then carried his bucket and a couple of clubs down to where I sat.

"I didn't know you p-played g-golf," I said as he took the hitting stall in front of me.

He shook his head. "I don't. But when I have a bad day at work or when Antonio is rattling my chain, I come and take it out on these." He nodded toward the range balls. "I usually hit sixty-nine crooked balls, but when I do catch one on the sweet spot — that does make life better."

I sipped my Coke as he hacked away, and he was a hacker. After he topped four in a row, he leaned the club against a post. "I need a break," he said, and he came and sat next to me.

"Thanks for t-talking to C-Clay Pearson about me."

Curtis's eyebrows went up. "He got in touch with you, then? I didn't say anything to you, because I didn't want to get your hopes up and have jack come of it."

"I s-saw him after our last g-game."

"So when will the story be in the paper?"

"There's not g-going to be story," I said, and then I repeated all that Mr. Thurman had said.

Curtis snorted. "And you're going to do what he says?"

I shrugged. "I don't want to c-cause tr-trouble. He's been g-good to me. They all have."

Curtis looked up at the sky and then looked back at me. "Good to you? Laz, he's got you down in his basement like a servant. You don't think there's an empty room upstairs in that house? They're using you to get the title they can't win on their own." He paused for a moment. "Listen to me. Right now your job at the driving range is to wash the rich man's balls. You got no money, so you got no choice. But you don't want to be stuck in this kind of job for the rest of your life. Do what's good for you and don't worry about Thurman or your coach. They'll be fine. People like them always are."

He went back to the stall and smacked a drive that soared high and straight until it hit the back netting. He looked at me and smiled. "Every once in a while."

He had at least a dozen balls left, but he didn't hit them. "That's the one to quit on," he said, and he walked back to the parking lot.

EIGHTEEN

AFTER CURTIS LEFT, I got back to work. One of the arms on the Gator had stopped spinning, so collecting the golf balls took longer, giving me even more time to think. All these months, I'd thought that Mr. Thurman was looking out for me and that Curtis didn't care. Was it possible I had it backwards?

My eyes went to the back fence every time I made a turn. The area was deserted. I hated it when I saw Antonio with Garrett, waiting for customers, but I hated it when he wasn't there, too. Because if Antonio wasn't in Jet City, then where was he? And what was he doing?

I was nearly finished when a silver VW GTI came racing down Jet City's main road, flying toward the back fence so fast that I was sure the car would crash right through and drive onto the range. Just in time, though, the driver slammed on the brakes. The car skidded across the gravel, sending up a cloud of dirt and dust.

Immediately four guys jumped out of the GTI. They fanned out, calling for someone, but the John Deere's engine drowned out their words. One of them kicked open the shed door and pushed his way in. The others prowled the area, tossing the plastic chairs aside, tipping over the empty oil drums, eyes searching.

I knew in my gut that they were looking for Garrett. And *looking* wasn't the right word. They were *coming* for Garrett. If Antonio were with him, they'd be coming for him, too.

I'd heard about the drug cartels down in Mexico, had seen on TV how brutal they were. I wanted to believe that stuff that bad didn't happen in Seattle, but I couldn't be sure. Antonio could be heading to the back fence right that minute. He didn't know these guys were here, waiting. He'd walk right into their trap.

I flicked on the John Deere's warning lights and drove to the back fence. When I neared it, I cut the engine, sounded my horn, and held my cell phone up so the gang guys could see it. "I'm c-calling the police," I shouted through the metal cage that protected me from golf balls. "See. I'm c-calling them right now."

They stared at me as if I was a lunatic. I didn't care. I dialed 911 and put the phone to my ear.

Nothing.

Dead battery.

"Hello!" I screamed anyway. "I want to r-report—"

I didn't have to fake anything more.

All four guys raced back to the VW. Doors opened; door slammed shut; the engine roared to life; dust and dirt rose for a second time. They were gone.

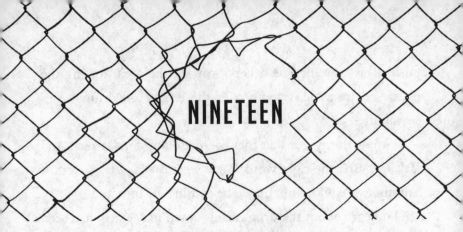

NINETEEN

I SAT, THE JOHN DEERE IDLING, until my pulse finally stopped singing in my ears. Then I turned around and finished picking up the range. I loaded the ball dispenser, checked out with Mr. Matsui, and headed to Woodacres.

Maybe Antonio would be home. I could get him alone and talk some sense into him. When I neared the driveway leading down to the apartment, I saw that it was filled with cars and trucks. From the roadway I could hear loud voices and occasional groans. Curtis had friends over and they were all watching baseball or maybe basketball.

I knew Antonio wouldn't be there, so I turned and headed back toward Aurora Avenue. I thought about stopping by the community center, but I wasn't a North Central kid anymore. There was nothing to do but catch the bus back to Laurelhurst.

When RapidRide E came, I took a window seat and looked out as the used-car dealerships and fast food restaurants flashed by. When the bus stopped near Woodland Park, the driver got off and a new driver got on. As the new guy was putting his gear away, I spotted the field lights at Lower Woodland. I didn't know who was playing, but a game was on, and that was good enough. I got off.

At a Kidd Valley across from the fields, I bought a burger, fries, and a milk shake before heading to the diamonds.

A girls' softball game—Roosevelt versus Ballard—was just starting on Field A. I found a seat in the bleachers directly behind home plate, ate my food, and watched.

Only I didn't watch. Not really. My eyes were on the field, but my mind was on Antonio. I needed to tell him . . . tell him what? That some guys had driven into Jet City, gotten out of their car, and searched for him, trashing everything in their way? What good would that do? He'd blown me off before; he'd just blow me off again.

Sometime in there I stopped worrying about Antonio and started watching the game. The Ballard pitcher was a tall blonde with a fluid delivery. She was like a machine, all business, dominating every hitter, every inning, the entire game, her eyes like lasers. The final score was 5–0. Roosevelt had one hit—a swinging bunt.

When the game ended, the pitcher's stone face immediately broke into a huge smile. She hugged teammate after teammate, her eyes glittering.

The field cleared and the benches emptied. I stayed in my spot above home plate, hoping another game would follow, but none did. When the wind came up and all the field lights went dark, I headed to the bus stop to finish the trip to Laurelhurst.

It was after nine when I slipped into the Thurmans' house, retreated to my room and plugged my cell phone into its charger. In about a minute the screen came back to life.

I had a text message from Clay Pearson, and it was short. **Yes/No?**

A feature article in the *Seattle Times* had to be good for me. I couldn't worry that it might be bad for Laurelhurst or Mr. Thurman or Coach Vereen.

I tapped **Yes.**

Seconds later another text came.

After Lincoln?

My thumbs moved on their own. **See you then**

TWENTY

LINCOLN HIGH WAS 5-11 on the year and next to last in the league. Tuesday night, just before game time, Clay Pearson settled into a seat behind home plate. Next to him was an older man wearing a San Francisco Giants warm-up jacket. He hunched forward in the same way Tommy Zeller had, and he had a flip notebook that was just like Zeller's.

I felt electric, and then, as quickly as that feeling came, it was gone. Because right behind Clay Pearson was Mr. Thurman. Twice, I'd started to tell him that I'd agreed to the interview, but I could never bring the words out.

The Lincoln guys played as if they were thinking about summer vacation and not the game. In the first inning, the shortstop booted an easy ground ball, and the left fielder misplayed a fly ball off Ian's bat into a two-run double.

With an early lead against a bad team, the smart thing would have been to keep the ball low, pitch to contact, and get a bunch of easy ground ball outs. But with a Giants scout watching, I needed to be great, not smart.

And I was.

From the very first pitch, my fastball was nasty, darting this way and that. Lincoln's leadoff batter fisted a slow roller right back to me. The other two hitters struck out swinging.

My second and third innings went the same way. Strikeouts and easy ground balls. I couldn't keep myself from peeking up into the stands. Sometimes I'd catch Mr. Thurman's eyes, sometimes Clay Pearson's, sometimes the Giants scout's.

Lincoln's pitcher held us down for a couple of innings. Then, in the fourth, Ian belted another two-run double and Jay followed with a two-run homer, making our lead 6–0.

Whenever we'd taken a big lead, Coach Vereen had pulled me and turned the game over to Kevin and the twins. But this time he let me stay in the game. I didn't get it. "You're pitching a no-hitter," Hadley said quietly. "He won't pull you as long as you keep it going—so keep it going."

That really got me pumped. I breezed through the fifth—pop-up, strikeout, groundout. I could feel the no-hitter . . . but then I got unlucky.

The leadoff batter in the sixth cued a ground ball toward third base. Jay raced in, trying for the bare-hand grab, but the ball had so much spin that fielding it was like trying to catch a lizard. By the time he picked up the ball, the runner had crossed first. Coach Vereen came out, patted me on the back, and brought in Kevin to finish up.

When the game ended, Clay Pearson called out as I was packing my duffle bag. Mr. Thurman was a few feet away, talking to Ian. He turned to me. "I'll talk to Clay for you, if you want," he said in a low voice.

I shook my head. "N-No. I've d-d-decided to d-do the interview."

Mr. Thurman tilted his head and eyed me. "But we discussed this, Laz. You said—"

"I changed my m-mind."

"Great game," Pearson said, coming up from the other side. "Hungry?"

I turned from Mr. Thurman. "Yeah. Starved."

TWENTY-ONE

WE WENT TO THE BALLARD PIZZA COMPANY. As we ate, Clay Pearson asked about the difference between Laurelhurst and North Central, and whether I missed my old school. When he was done with baseball, he asked about my family.

Mostly it was okay, but I didn't like his questions about my father. I had no answers, because I know nothing. The interview ended ten minutes after the pizza was gone.

"You think you can win it all?" he asked as we walked back to his car.

"I hope s-so," I said.

"So do I. Poor kid from a trailer park moves to a high-powered school and leads a bunch of rich kids to the state title they could never win on their own. It's the kind of story *Sports Illustrated* likes. Actually, it's the kind of story movie producers like. So how about we make a deal? You pitch Laurelhurst to the state title, I'll write another feature story, Steven Spielberg will turn it into a movie, and we'll both be rich and famous."

When I got back to the Thurmans', Mr. Thurman was sitting on the sofa, waiting for me. "Cleveland lost tonight," he said as soon as I'd stepped inside. "One more win, and we clinch a spot in the playoffs."

"That's g-great," I said, and I started for the stairway leading down to my room.

I didn't make it.

"How did the interview go?" he asked.

I turned back. "It w-went okay."

He pursed his lips. "Let's hope it stays okay, for you and the team." He started to say more, then stopped. "See you tomorrow, Laz. Great game."

We did clinch the title with a win on Friday night. It was May, but it felt like December. A cold wind was blowing from Puget Sound, carrying a misty rain. In the top of the first, O'Dea's starting pitcher gave up two hits and then walked Ian to load the bases. Jay Massine laced the first pitch he saw into left center for a bases-clearing double. Three more hits and another walk followed, staking me to a 7–0 lead before I had to throw a pitch.

When I took the mound, the wind was howling. The O'Dea batters swung at everything I threw, hitting pop-ups and ground balls when they weren't striking out. Their nine batter got a cheap hit—a slow grounder that died in the wet turf, and their cleanup batter almost took my head off with a line single to center field, but those two hits were all they got. We won 9–0, with one of the twins pitching the final two innings.

When the game ended, Coach Vereen announced that we were the Metro League champions. It was the first championship team I'd ever been on, but none of the guys even pretended to be excited. They let out a little cheer, then packed up and went home. From the first day of practice, they'd expected to take the league. All that mattered was taking the state.

Anything less was failure.

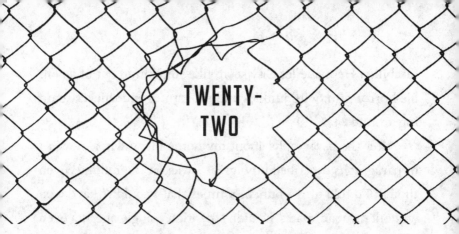

TWENTY-TWO

SATURDAY MORNING I WOKE UP at six fifteen. I slipped upstairs, took out three eggs and a couple of slices of Swiss cheese, and set to work cooking an omelet. I kept quiet, hoping to eat, clean up, and get back downstairs without waking anyone. I was halfway through my omelet when Mr. Thurman came into the room. "Got to go," he said as he dropped the *Seattle Times* on the counter. "Pearson's article is in there."

Once he left, I pulled out the sports section. The headline jumped out at me:

Lazarus Rising

As I read, my head swam. Clay Pearson had interviewed not just me but some of my North Central teachers and my mom, too. She'd told him how I'd nearly died as a newborn. "My boy has always been a fighter. He's my Superhero."

That was the worst, but lots of other places were bad. Pearson wrote that we were almost homeless; that I never knew my father; that I had a speech impediment and a learning disability. He made Jet City seem like something out of a zombie horror film, with junkies and prostitutes and thieves roaming around 24/7.

After the paragraphs about my home life, a whole new set of paragraphs described how great I was on the mound. Even though I'd told him a bunch of times that I couldn't have won without my teammates, he didn't mention a single one, not even Ian. I'd been starving thirty minutes earlier, but by the time I finished reading, I wanted to puke.

I managed a few more bites, then scraped what was left of my omelet into the compost bin, put my plate and silverware in the dishwasher, and went back to my room. I had an hour to kill before it would be time to leave to see Suja and then head to work.

I'd barely closed the door when I got a one-word text from Antonio: **SuperBro!** Seconds later came a phone call from my mom. She told me how proud she was and how she was glad other people would know that I was the one who was making Laurelhurst so good. I tried to explain that nobody does it alone, but she wasn't hearing it. "Curtis says you're the man, and he knows baseball. I didn't want you to go to that school, but I was wrong." She paused. "You stop by here when you finish work. You're having dinner with us tonight."

I left early for the bus stop. When the bus pulled up, I climbed aboard and leaned my head against the window. I wanted to ride to the end of the line, wherever that was, but I got off at the stop near the Krispy Kreme. I hoped Suja hadn't seen the article, but she held up a newspaper and waved it around as soon as she saw me. "You're famous!" she half yelled as I neared her, and she looked around, as if other people might recognize me and ask for my autograph.

"D-Don't," I whispered.

"And that's cool about how you got your name. You never told me that."

"Please."

"Oh, all right," she said, lowering her voice. "But I don't see why you're being so modest."

We got our regular orders and, since the sun was shining, took them outside. Before she could talk more about me, I asked about her day with the women from Whitman. The excitement drained from her eyes.

"I don't think I'll go."

"Why n-not?"

"The other kids are all going to be rich, like those women. They'll have expensive clothes and jewelry. I'll be trailer trash to them."

"They won't know whether you're rich or p-poor."

"They'll know, Laz."

"So what? You're smart. You'll do g-great."

"Let's talk about something else."

"Okay."

She swirled her plastic spoon around in her mocha. "I have a favor, Laz. You're going to think it's pretty random—"

"Okay, what?" I asked.

"Take me to the Senior Ball."

"The Senior B-Ball," I repeated.

"I told you it was random. But we're seniors now, remember?"

"At Laurelhurst?"

Her eyes went wide. "Are you crazy? North Central. And it's not for some sex thing. We'd just go as friends." She paused. "I didn't say that right, but you know what I mean."

My face went red. I wanted to answer, but nothing came out. She waited, then drank off the rest of her mocha and stood. "Okay. I get it. You don't want to. Forget I asked."

"No," I said, reaching out and taking her hand. "I want to g-go with you. I really do. When is it?"

She sat back down and went into business mode. "June. The Saturday before graduation. They'll be six of us. We'll rent a shuttle van and hire a driver from that company that takes people to the airport. Maybe we'll eat at that barbecue place — you know the one I mean — or maybe someplace else. I'll work on that. And nobody spends money on clothes. We're going as ourselves and as friends. We'll hang out and say goodbye to North Central. That's it."

TWENTY-THREE

AFTER WE SEPARATED, I headed to the driving range. I'd been away only one week, but in that week the pro shop had gone from okay to a total wreck. Red signs shouting **75% OFF!** and **EVERYTHING MUST GO!** were slapped on the walls, the shelves, the windows. And almost everything *was* gone. Clubs, bags, balls, carts, gloves, towels, tees—wiped out. The clothes racks were bare except for XXL or XXS. The same with the shoes.

Mr. Matsui looked up as I entered. "Hey, Laz," he said, the usual spark in his voice missing. He opened his hands and gestured to the store. "An ad ran in the Monday *Times*. It was crazy for three days, but then things settled down, mainly because nothing much is left. The locusts got it all."

"Should I straighten things up?" I asked.

He shrugged. "Don't bother. Just pick up the range and then use the shag bags to get the balls that are caught up in the nets."

I walked to the corner shed where the John Deere was parked. On the way, I passed the two ball dispensing machines, one of which had an **OUT OF ORDER** sign taped to it. The John Deere had a **FOR SALE** sign on the driver's side door.

After starting it up, I headed onto the range, driving slowly. The one functioning arm caught the balls and spit them into the baskets. Every once in a while a golf ball would smack the metal cage, jolting me. Mostly it was driving back and forth.

When I reached the back fence, I parked the John Deere and used the shag bags to collect the balls that had rolled into the netting. As I worked, the screen doors of the abandoned trailers in Jet City slapped open and closed in the wind. Antonio wasn't hanging out at the back fence. No VWs came flying down the road.

When I finished, it was almost five. "Your mom called," Mr. Matsui said as I put the keys back. "She asked me to remind you to stop by."

I pulled my cell out of my back pocket. The screen read **four missed calls**. The John Deere had been so loud I hadn't heard the rings. I hit the callback button.

"Just finished work," I said when my mom answered. "I'll b-be there in fifteen minutes."

Antonio let me in. "Mom's going crazy over this," he warned me, smiling. A second later, she was standing in front of me, shaking the *Seattle Times* in my face. "This is wonderful, Laz! Your picture in the paper and an entire article all about you."

Curtis came out from the kitchen holding a Budweiser, which he tipped in my direction. Mom took both my hands and squeezed. "I am *so* proud of you." She looked around. "We all are."

Ten minutes later we sat down to eat. Mom had bought two

rotisserie chickens at Central Market, and mashed potatoes and grilled vegetables and salads to go with them.

As we ate, we talked some about Antonio and some about Curtis and some about my mom, but mainly the conversation was about me. Antonio said that the kids at North Central were following my games. "The teachers, too. It's like North Central wins whenever you win."

I was in a glow the whole time. Everybody was. It was as if, for one evening, we had become the family we wanted to be. When we finished eating, we watched *Hoosiers* on the big TV. I kept expecting Antonio to say he had to leave, but he stayed and cheered for the Hickory Huskers just like the rest of us.

"I should h-head b-back," I said once the movie ended.

"Curtis can give you a ride," Mom said, "but hold on for a second."

She went to the closet and came out holding a box that she handed to me. "From all of us."

I felt almost dizzy when I looked inside. A brand-new burgundy-colored Rawlings glove.

"It's b-beautiful," I said, feeling the leather.

"Thank Curtis," she said. "He saw your glove in the newspaper photo and said you needed a new one."

Curtis slapped me lightly on the back. "If you play like a champion, you should look like one, too."

I didn't want to go back to Laurelhurst, but it was time. I hugged my mom, knuckle-bumped Antonio, and climbed into the pickup.

On the drive to the Thurmans', Curtis told me to nuke my glove in the microwave to break it in. "There's leather oil in the bottom of the box. Rub it in and then stick the glove in the microwave for twenty seconds. That's how the major-leaguers do it now. Go online if you don't believe me."

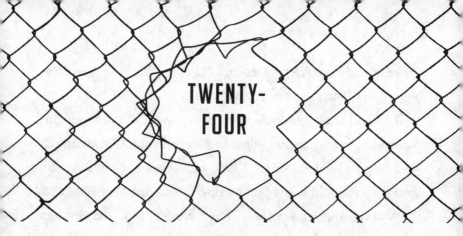

TWENTY-FOUR

I KNEW I'D GET RAZZED at school, but I hadn't even reached the campus when it started. "Hey, there's my Superhero," Jay Massine called out from a passing car.

Just about every player on the team said something, and kids who weren't on the team got in shots, too. "Yankees call yet?" . . . "How much for an autograph?" . . . "If you need an agent . . ." I felt like a boxer being worn down by jabs.

Even Hadley got in his dig. I saw him at lunch at our regular table. "Next game, let's try that Satchel Page thing. You know, have all the infielders and outfielders sit on the bench and then strike out the side with nobody playing defense. What do you say?"

"L-lay off," I said.

He snorted. "I'm guessing everybody has been giving you crap?"

"You g-got it."

He shrugged. "You kind of deserve it."

"I d-didn't say it the way it c-came out."

"It didn't sound much like you." He paused, and when he

spoke again, his voice was serious. "I got to warn you. Vereen is big on that *'There's no I in TEAM'* stuff."

I leaned back and looked at the ceiling. "What about the p-press conference for Ian when he s-signed with Arizona State?"

Hadley rolled his eyes. "Come on. The Thurmans are different. You should know that by now. So are the Comettes and the Morans and a few others. Their parents fund the Booster Club. That's uniforms, equipment, buses, field maintenance — everything that makes the Laurelhurst program one of the best in the state. Tell Vereen you're sorry and flow with whatever he decides."

"He won't k-kick me off the t-team, will he?"

Hadley shook his head. "Not as long as he thinks you might be his ticket to the state championship."

Coach Vereen didn't speak to me during gym class, and he didn't say anything at practice. But once practice ended, he had me stay behind and then made me wait five long minutes before he finally came over.

"Kevin will start the next game, and the twins will relieve. You're going to sit. While you're sitting, watch the effort your teammates put out. Maybe then you'll appreciate their part in your success."

My knees had turned to Jell-O. "Coach, I'm s-sorry. I d-didn't m-mean it t-to c-c-c-c . . ." The word stuck, but it didn't matter. I was talking to his back.

TWENTY-FIVE

OUR NEXT GAME WAS AT HOME against Broadview High. Before the first pitch, I moved to the end of the bench, away from everyone. I was staring at my shoes and had my cap down over my forehead when I heard a man's voice behind me. "Not pitching today, kid?"

I turned. It was the man with the Giants jacket, the one who'd sat next to Clay Pearson.

I stood. "No, sir. Coach is r-resting m-me."

The man pulled on one of his huge ears. "That's too bad. You got a DVD?"

"DVD?"

"Of your highlights. You got one?"

"N-No."

He handed me a card. "Put a DVD together and send it to me. And do it fast. We're working on our draft board right now, and we've got almost nothing on you."

He started to walk away. "I'll probably p-pitch—"

He turned back, waving me off. "This is my last day in the Great Northwest. Send me that DVD."

As Kevin cruised through the early innings, I studied the man's business card. It had the San Francisco Giants colors and logo on one side. On the other was the name Ralph Somerset, with an email address.

Coach Vereen had tape of all the games, but how could I ask him to put together a DVD for me? He'd have done it before the *Seattle Times* article, but now? I stuck the business card in my pocket and tried to watch the game, but my mind kept going back to that DVD. I had to get one. But how?

Kevin pitched five innings, his fastball sharp and his changeup even sharper. After he came out, each of the twins worked a solid inning. The final score was 7–1. It had been a methodical destruction — solid pitching, hitting, defense — and the team hadn't needed me at all. If Kevin kept pitching like that, why would Vereen ever put in the North Central kid with the big mouth?

TWENTY-SIX

I WAS DOWN IN MY BASEMENT ROOM a couple of hours later when Mr. Thurman knocked on my door. "Laz, I need you upstairs for a few minutes."

I followed him to the kitchen. He sat, shoulders slumped, at the table, so I took the seat across from him and waited.

"I just got a call from Mr. Chavez. You know him, right? Laurelhurst's principal?"

"S-Sort of."

He waved off my answer. "Doesn't matter. What matters is that the WIAA contacted him. They want to interview you, Coach Vereen, and me. Maybe others, but probably just us."

I looked to Mr. Thurman. "Why?"

He folded his hands together and leaned forward. "I warned you that an article in the *Times* would set off alarm bells."

"What will they ask m-me?"

"These investigations are always about academics and money. Are you going to class? Are you getting paid?"

"But I d-do go to c-class and I'm not g-getting paid."

"I know that and you know that. Now we just have to

convince them." He tapped the table with his index finger. "Here's the thing. Tell the truth. Don't keep anything back, whatever they ask. If you hide anything and they find out about it later, it'll be ten times worse."

Silence followed.

"When will they t-talk to me?" I asked.

"Tomorrow."

"T-T-Tomorrow?"

"They need to get this settled before the state tournament. If they decide you shouldn't have played, then we forfeit every game you pitched. We're out, and Cleveland is in."

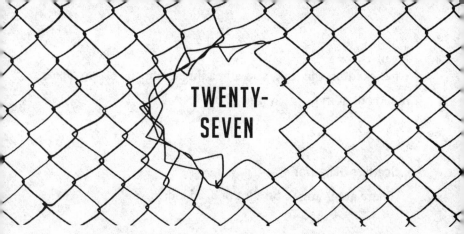

TWENTY-SEVEN

I RETURNED TO THE BASEMENT, feeling both guilty and angry. I didn't want to foul things up for Laurelhurst, but what had I done wrong? Mr. Kellogg, Mr. Thurman, Coach Vereen—all of them had said I wasn't breaking any rules. So why *not* get my name in the paper?

My mind went in circles for about ten minutes. Then I forced myself to do my homework, reading a section of *The Jungle Book* and then working on algebra problems. I nailed the first eight, but I'd need to see Jesus Ramirez for help with the last two.

That was all the schoolwork I had, so I opened the laptop and checked my email. Second from the top I saw Suja's name. The subject heading read *Senior Ball Schedule*.

I read quickly. Shuttle van picks kids up in Jet City at six thirty . . . Dinner at seven . . . Dance eight thirty to eleven . . . Game Kingdom in Ballard until two . . . Shuttle drops people off at their homes by three. I was about to log off when below Suja's name I saw a final sentence.

Laz—Don't be mad at me ☹ *but you need to read this.*

I clicked on the link, and a headline from the *Seattle Times* jumped out at me.

Seattle's Gang War
"There are going to be a lot of dead kids"

I wanted to skim over it, but I read every word. The writer had interviewed a detective who said there'd been a dozen shootings and three deaths since January. The detective described all the stupid reasons people were getting shot: graffiti crossed out, girls dating guys from rival gangs, cars or music or hair or clothes being dissed. But the number one reason? Drugs. "If a gang thinks somebody is infringing on their turf, we end up with teenagers in body bags."

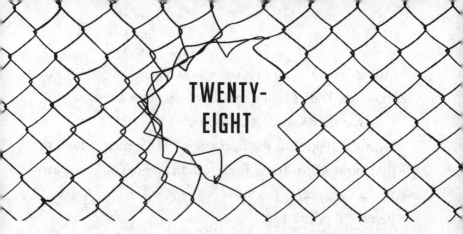

TWENTY-EIGHT

AT THE START OF FIRST PERIOD the next morning, I was called to the office. Mr. Chavez introduced Mrs. Dunne, a tall woman with reddish-brown hair who smiled as she shook my hand. Mr. Chavez then repeated what Mr. Thurman had told me.

"I'm ready," I said when he finished.

"Good," Mrs. Dunne said. "So am I. Before we start, though, I want you to know that I left a message on your mother's phone last night, but I haven't gotten a reply. We could do this another day if you'd like."

"I'm nineteen. I d-don't need my m-mother."

Mrs. Dunne looked over to Mr. Chavez.

"I'm observing classrooms today," he said, "so you're welcome to use my office for as long as you need."

Once he'd left, Mrs. Dunne took her phone out and laid it on the table. "I'm going to record this. Okay? Just so we have an accurate record."

"Sure," I said, but the setup made me feel as if I'd committed a crime.

She had written her questions on a yellow legal pad placed

next to her phone. The first set was about playing for North Central High. Did I like my coach? My teammates? My school? Why had the team folded? All easy stuff.

Then she flipped to the next page. "The closest school to North Central is Broadview, but you didn't try out for their baseball team. Why not?"

"Because they're b-bad."

"And Laurelhurst is good?"

"Yeah."

"And you wanted to win."

"Yeah. I m-mean, everybody wants to win."

"But not everybody changes schools."

"I w-wouldn't have ch-changed if North Central h-had a team."

"Okay." She paused. "Who first approached you about playing for Laurelhurst?"

"My North Central c-coach, Mr. Kellogg."

"And then?"

"Then Mr. Thurman called m-me and invited me to the off-season workouts that he ran."

"Did Mr. Thurman ask anybody else from North Central's baseball team to join Laurelhurst?"

"My brother Antonio thought about p-playing."

"But did he ask him?"

"Not really. B-But he didn't stop him."

"And did you hear from Coach Vereen during this time?"

"No."

She tapped her pencil against the desk. "Okay. So Mr. Kellogg told you that you could attend North Central and play for Laurelhurst. But why move in with the Thurmans? Why not stay in your own home and continue at North Central?"

"It's c-complicated," I said.

"I've got time."

I didn't like telling Mrs. Dunne about my family and money and Jet City closing and the rules at Woodacres. I didn't like explaining that Curtis was Antonio's dad but not my dad. But I got the story out. "So when Mr. Thurman offered me a r-room in his house," I said, finishing up, "I t-took it."

"Do you pay any rent?"

My mouth went dry. "No."

"You have a job, right?"

"I work at a d-driving range."

"And your mom has a job. And your mom's significant other —he has a job."

"Yeah."

"But you never paid any rent?"

I shook my head. "Nobody ever m-mentioned it."

"How about board? Did you pay for board?"

I didn't answer; I was so nervous I couldn't remember what *board* was.

"Food. Meals," she explained. "Do you pay anything for those?"

"No," I answered, wishing I could get a glass of water.

"Did anyone connected to Laurelhurst High give you cash or a debit card for day-to-day expenses?"

"N-No."

"How about clothes? Shoes? Gear? Did anyone buy you any of those?"

"No, except—" I stopped.

"Go on."

"Well, I g-got a Laurelhurst sweatshirt and p-polo shirt and socks from the Booster Club. And a d-duffle bag."

"How about your mother or your mother's friend? Did you think they might have received money?"

"No."

"How can you be sure?"

"Because my m-mom would have told me. Besides, she would have n-never have taken it. She d-doesn't like any of this."

"And why is that?"

"She j-just d-doesn't."

"Were you promised a college scholarship?"

"No."

"How about professional baseball? Were you introduced to major-league scouts?"

That stopped me for a few seconds. "M-Maybe."

"What do you mean, *maybe?*"

My head was pounding. "There's a Mariners scout, Tommy Zeller. He's t-talked to me, but I can't r-remember whether he just came up to me or if Coach Vereen called me over."

"So Coach Vereen might have introduced you to Tommy Zeller."

"Or Mr. Thurman. Or n-neither or them. I d-don't remember. And there is another scout, from the San Francisco Giants, but I know he just came up to me."

"And how about Clay Pearson's *Seattle Times* article? Did Coach Vereen or Mr. Thurman arrange that for you?"

I snorted as I shook my head.

"Why the reaction?" she asked.

"Everybody here is t-ticked at me about that. They think I'm a g-glory hog."

"So how did it get arranged?"

"Curtis—the man my mom lives with—he knows Clay Pearson's father."

She looked at her watch. "Just a few more questions about school. Your grades are better here than at North Central. Why do you think that is?"

"The c-classes aren't as r-rowdy here, and the school g-got me a t-tutor. I m-meet with him two or three times a week. I n-never had a tutor at North Central."

"How much help does he give you with your schoolwork?"

That did it. I was tired of the way she kept hinting that I was dishonest. "I do my own work," I said. "I take all my t-tests. I write all my papers. I don't cheat in b-baseball and I d-don't cheat in school, and I d-don't care whether you b-believe me or not."

She sat back in her chair, and her face relaxed. "Laz, I'm

sorry. I truly am. I know you think I'm your enemy, but I'm not. I'm just gathering information."

"Are you d-done?"

"Yes, I'm done. And thank you. You've been very helpful. Now, do you have any questions for me?"

I thought for a moment. "Is the t-team going to be k-kicked out of the playoffs because of m-me?"

"Not my decision. I interview everyone, write a report, and submit it to a committee of school administrators. That committee decides what steps to take, if any." She paused. "Anything else?"

"Can I g-go?"

It felt as though Mrs. Dunne had been grilling me for hours, but it had been only one period. All the players on the team knew about the investigation—things like that never stay secret. Ian approached me between classes. "How was it?"

"I d-don't know."

"My dad is talking to her next. I wonder if she'll talk to all of us."

"I d-don't think s-so."

We stood, neither of us speaking for a moment. I had this urge to tell him I was sorry, but I stopped myself.

We won on Tuesday 10–4 and on Friday night 11–5. Kevin started both games, and Marc and Andrew finished them. As I sat on the bench, I spotted at least half a dozen parents filming the games. It was a bad joke. There must have been hours of film of me from earlier games. Getting a DVD should have been simple, but the way things were now, I couldn't ask anyone for anything.

After Friday's win we tried to celebrate the end of the regular season, but it was impossible. Mrs. Dunne's investigation was a black cloud hanging over us. We were either city champions headed to the state playoffs or a team of cheaters headed nowhere.

TWENTY-NINE

LAURELHURST'S SENIOR BALL was that Saturday night. Ian was taking his girlfriend, Mariah Darcy, who was a soccer and track star. The Laurelhurst ball was pretty much the flip of North Central's ball. It cost money with a capital M. A tuxedo, flowers, professional photographs, private limousine, dinner at Canlis restaurant, another meal at the Four Seasons Hotel after the dance.

Before Ian left, Mr. Thurman talked to him in the kitchen. I was in my room, but I didn't have to be there to know Ian was getting the "No Sex, No Drugs, No Alcohol" lecture.

Once Ian was gone, I slipped into the game room and called Antonio. The *Seattle Times* article Suja had sent me had been like a weight pressing down on my shoulders. I didn't have any great plan of what I was going to say to Antonio. I just wanted to talk to him, to make sure he was okay. All I got was dead air.

I took a couple of burritos from the refrigerator, micro-waved them, and turned on a Spurs–Rockets game. Halfway through the second burrito, my cell phone started vibrating.

When I opened it, I didn't recognize the number, but I answered anyway

"Hello."

"Is this Lazarus Weathers?"

"Yeah. This is L-Laz."

"Laz, this is Mrs. Dunne from the WIAA." She paused. "It's all good news. You're cleared to play. There are some irregularities regarding the off-season workouts that your coach will need to clean up, but nothing serious enough to force any forfeits."

I was so stunned I couldn't speak.

"Laz? Are you there? Did you hear me?"

"I-I-I'm here. I heard you. And thank you. Thank you."

THIRTY

MONDAY, COACH VEREEN called a team meeting during lunch. The guys had heard the news, but they still let out a cheer when he said we'd been cleared to participate in the playoffs.

"Our quarterfinal game will be at noon on Saturday, Husky Ballpark," he said when the cheering stopped. "After we win that game, we come back for the semifinals Saturday night. And after we take that, we play in the finals the next Friday at T-Mobile Park."

More cheers. Then Andrew Comette yelled, "Who do we play in the quarters?"

The room hushed in anticipation.

"Jesuit High."

There was a low murmur and lots of groans.

"Hey," Coach Vereen barked. "You want to be the best, you have to beat the best."

When the meeting ended, my eyes caught Coach Vereen's, and he made the slightest nod. I knew what it meant—I was starting against Jesuit High.

Jesuit checked all the boxes. Fergus Hart checked all the

boxes. Undefeated. Number one ranking. Best hitting team in the state. Best pitcher in the state. Defending champions.

Tommy Zeller was sure to be at the game. It had been so long since I'd been on the mound that he'd probably half forgotten me, but if I shut down Jesuit, if I beat Fergus Hart, he'd remember. And if I beat Fergus Hart, Coach Vereen would make me a dozen DVD's to send to the Giants and the Mariners and whoever else I wanted.

In the morning, when I climbed upstairs to the Thurmans' kitchen, the *Seattle Times* sports page was laid out on the counter, opened to page three. One look, and I knew why.

The *Times* had made its all-city baseball selections. Ian was Seattle's Player of the Year; a photo of him was at the top of the page. The words *Five Tool Player* were written to the side. I felt a stab of jealousy, and let it go. We weren't friends and never would be, but he'd promised to put baseball first, and he'd delivered. That matters.

My eyes scanned the rest of the list. More Laurelhurst names jumped out. Andrew, Jay, and Martin were first-team selections, and smaller photos of them were next to their names. I looked at the slot for first-team pitcher, and my stomach sank—they'd picked the stocky kid from Cleveland High. Then I saw a red circle around a listing at the bottom of the page.

SECOND TEAM: *Lazarus Weathers, Pitcher, Laurelhurst.*

That was a crazy day. Before school my mom sent me a text. **Wow! Just wow! Call me tonight! Love Mom.**

In the halls at school, most of the buzz was about Ian being Seattle Player of the Year, with some minor buzz about the other guys who had made first team. Second team was no big deal at Laurelhurst, so I was left alone. But Suja found out and texted me, and she must have given out my number at North Central, because I got texts from a bunch of old classmates and teammates. **North Central Rocks! . . . You're the man! . . . Laz Rising!** I even got a text from Mr. Leskov. **You strike three them, Laz!**

You can go stale if you practice too hard. Coach Vereen knew that. And with all the excitement over guys making the all-city team, nobody was ready for a serious practice. So once we'd stretched, Vereen let us play Wiffle ball: seniors versus everyone else. After an hour, Martin's mom showed up with Otter Pops and Oreos, and we stuffed our faces like a bunch of eight-year-olds at the end of a tee-ball game.

I was feeling great as I walked off the field after practice, and then I spotted Garrett's Subaru. The driver's door opened and Antonio stepped out. He gave me a hug. "They cheated you. You deserved first team," he said.

"No c-complaints," I answered.

We stood facing each other for a long moment. His eyes didn't have their normal shine; his voice didn't have its normal ease.

"Everything o-okay?" I asked.

He broke into a forced smile. "Sure. Everything's great. I just wanted to shake your hand and tell you I'm proud to be your brother."

"How about we d-do something right now? You and me? There's a pizza p-place on S-Sand Point Way. We could t-talk. We haven't really t-talked in—Antonio, I'm worried about y-you—"

"That sounds great, Laz," he said, interrupting. "It really does. Only I can't right now. Soon, though. Really soon. That's a promise."

PART
FOUR

ONE

PLAYOFF SATURDAY. In the car, Mr. Thurman talked about how we had to approach the quarterfinal game as if it were like any other. "Yeah, Dad," Ian said, about twenty times.

As we drove, a strange thought came to me. What if I couldn't pitch? Just couldn't get my arm to work? Stuff like that happens to players, even to major-leaguers. The Dodgers had a second basemen, Steve Sax, who one day couldn't throw the ball to first.

The fear lasted until I stepped onto the field. Then my heart slowed and the saliva came back to my mouth. I was pumped, but it was the right kind of pumped.

The field at Husky Ballpark was better than any field I'd ever played on. The outfield grass was greener; the infield dirt was finer; the chalk lines were whiter; the pitcher's mound was smoother. And it was beautiful. You could see Mount Rainier and Lake Washington and the 520 Bridge and Capitol Hill and the tops of downtown skyscrapers.

I stretched, ran in the outfield, played long catch with Ian. Mom and Curtis settled into seats five rows above our bench.

Mom waved, and I raised my new glove toward her. At first I didn't see Antonio, which made my stomach tighten. I'd called him twice more and gotten nothing, not even voice mail. I was afraid he was out doing stuff for Garrett, but then I spotted him, two seats from Curtis, and I relaxed. Next to him was Suja.

A few minutes before game time, Hadley and I walked down the first base line toward the bullpen. I looked over to where the Jesuit players were warming up. "Which one is Fergus Hart?"

Hadley nodded toward the bullpen on the third-base side. "The tall sidearmer with the stringy hair. He's got a whip for an arm. When you're in the box, it feels like the ball is coming right at you. You jump out of the way, and then the pitch angles back over the plate. I've faced him six times and he's struck me out six times. Ian and Jay and Martin haven't done much better. We've managed a few hits, but we haven't scored a run off him. I'm not sure we ever got a guy to third base."

As I loosened, I kept sneaking peeks at Fergus Hart. That's how I noticed Tommy Zeller and Clay Pearson standing along the third-base line. Two other men who looked like they might be scouts chatted with them. All had their eyes fixed on Fergus Hart.

Hart had pounded the catcher's glove in warm-ups, but when the game started, his first pitch flew over the head of Andrew Comette and smacked against the backstop with a sickening thud—the same thud a baseball makes when it hits a batter in the skull. Andrew went gray. After that wild first pitch,

Hart came back with a strike. Andrew took that pitch, and the next strike, before going down on a wild swing at a pitch in the dirt.

Hart followed the same pattern with Jared Bronzan. He unleashed a fastball that sailed behind Bronzan, he threw a couple of strikes, and then he got Jared to lunge at a fastball outside and hit a little dribbler to the first baseman.

Old-time pitchers like Don Drysdale threw at hitters on purpose. Was Hart's wildness fake?

I leaned forward as Ian took his stance in the batter's box. A wild pitch, this time at Ian's ankles, followed by two strikes, and then a ball that bounced ten feet in front of the plate. With the count two and two, Hart pulled his cap down, went into his wind-up, and fired a sidearm fastball that had Ian jumping back.

"Strike three!" the ump shouted.

As Hart walked back to his bench, he glanced over at our bench, a hint of a smile in his eyes.

I took my normal warm-up tosses. After the last one, the ball went around the infield and came back to me. I turned and faced home plate, when it hit me. I was in the playoffs at Husky Ballpark, pitching against Jesuit High, the best team in the state.

Me.

Laz Weathers.

The trailer kid from North Central.

The home plate ump clapped his hands. "Play ball!" he shouted, and that was the end of the dreaming.

I started Jesuit's leadoff hitter—a lefty—with a fastball on the inside corner for a strike and then came back with another fastball, this one off the plate. He reached for it and bounced what should have been an easy two-hopper to Jay Massine at third. Jay treated the ball as if it were drenched in oil. When he finally got a decent grip, he threw wildly past first. The ball hit off one of the pipes on the cyclone fence and bounded down the line. The batter cruised into third standing up.

Jay slapped his fist into his glove and kicked the dirt. "Forget it," I called over to him. He nodded, his face frozen in a scowl.

I looked around the infield. No chatter. Eyes down. The body language was loud and clear: *This is what we expected. We're going down. Again. Just like we always do.*

Vereen had the infield play back, so the next batter just needed to put the ball in play on the ground to drive in the run. I needed to strike him out, and I did, getting him to swing at a high fastball at the letters. That brought cheers from the stands and some chatter from the infielders.

Jesuit's three-hitter had a compact swing. He'd be tough to strike out, but if I could somehow strand that runner at third, I'd turn the momentum our way.

Then Jesuit's coach did the unexpected. On my first pitch, the batter pushed a bunt past me toward second—a suicide squeeze. Jared charged, fielded the ball, and made a good throw to first for the second out, but the runner on third scored standing up. The cleanup hitter hit a soft fly to left to end the inning.

Jesuit 1–Laurelhurst 0.

Nothing disastrous, but the bench stayed quiet. I wanted to yell at the guys, tell them that this was a new year and a new game and they had a new pitcher. But talk doesn't work. So I kept my mouth shut, and as the innings rolled by, I kept the ball down and Jesuit off the scoreboard.

Fergus Hart matched me, but our guys made him work, taking pitches, fouling off pitches. I pitched to contact, getting outs early in the count, needing only nine pitches in the second inning and just ten in the third.

After Ian had struck out, Coach Vereen took him down the base line and demonstrated how to keep the left shoulder in. It must have been the millionth time Ian had seen that move and heard that pep talk, but he watched as if it were all new. In his second at bat, he had a decent swing on a fastball, pulling off it just a little and flying out to deep right. Hadley nudged me. "That's the best at bat he's had against Hart." But a long out is still an out, and the score was still 1–0.

I don't remember much of what happened, that's how deep in the zone I was, though it was a different sort of zone than I'd ever been in before. I wasn't overpowering guys with my fastball; I was really and truly *pitching,* moving the ball in and out, up and down, changing speeds, using my head as much as my arm. And Tommy Zeller was behind home plate, watching.

More innings rolled by — the fourth . . . fifth . . . sixth.

We were taking better swings, hitting the ball harder. Twice we moved a runner to second base, but in the clutch, Fergus Hart came up with the pitch to shut us down.

And then it was the top of the seventh.

Three more outs and our season was over.

Hart walked slowly to the mound. After every warm-up pitch he stretched out his shoulder. All those tough innings had taken their toll.

Hadley led off, and he battled, fouling off two pitches and working the count to 3-2. Fergus threw a fastball near the outside part of the plate. Hadley took it. You could see the ump start to raise his arm, then flinch, then mutter, "Ball four."

The Jesuit bench roared in disbelief; the Jesuit fans booed loudly. It didn't change a thing—Hadley was on first and Peterson stepped to the plate.

Down one, final at bat.

A bunt?

Not something normally done, but facing Fergus Hart wasn't normal.

I looked to Vereen, and he flashed the signal. Jesuit's fielders on first and third crept in a few steps. The pitch.

Peterson squared, stuck his bat out, made contact. But instead of laying the ball down, he popped it up. "Back! Back! Back!" we all screamed as the third baseman caught the pop and fired a bullet to first, trying to double up Hadley.

"Safe!" the umpire screamed, and more angry shouts cascaded down from the Jesuit side.

Andrew Comette stepped in.

Jared Bronzan moved on deck.

Ian was in the hole.

Comette worked the count full, then fouled off three pitches before getting the second walk of the inning on a ball that bounced in front of the plate, moving Hadley to second.

Jared Bronzan took his spot in the batter's box.

Fergus was struggling to find the plate. The smart thing to do was to take a pitch, make him throw a strike. But Jared—and I'll never know why—swung at Hart's first offering, sending a two-hopper to the left of the third baseman, a tailor-made double-play ball. The third baseman fielded it and fired to second for the force. The second baseman made the pivot, but double-clutched before releasing his throw. Foot and ball arrived at first base at the same time. All eyes were on the ump. Both arms went wide. "Safe!" he shouted.

The state championship game was a week away, but this was the matchup of the season.

Game on the line.

Fergus Hart versus Ian Thurman.

Players, coaches, parents, and kids—everyone was standing. Ian took a couple of practice swings, pulling his left elbow in across his chest as a reminder to stay closed, and then stepped in. Hart went into his stretch, checked the runners, and delivered.

Sidearm fastball, velocity pumped up by adrenaline.

But the adrenaline was flowing for Ian, too. He didn't open up. His head stayed on the ball, his swing stayed compact and powerful. The ball jumped off the bat—a line shot to left center. The center fielder raced after it, but the ball was by him, rolling and rolling, all the way to the fence. Hadley trotted home with the tying run. Bronzan, off at the crack of the bat, flew around third and scored standing up. Ian, careful not to make a base-running blunder, stopped at second. He had his hands above his head and was looking to the sky as the cheers from the Laurelhurst fans washed over him. Hart struck out Jay Massine on three pitches, but the damage had been done.

Laurelhurst 2–Jesuit 1.

It was up to me to hold the lead.

I wasn't exactly dizzy as I walked to the mound, but I wasn't completely steady on my feet. A locomotive was rumbling in my head.

I didn't try to calm myself. No hope of that. I blocked everything out and focused on Hadley's glove. I didn't aim, I threw —free and easy, and pitch after pitch hit Hadley's target. My arm felt like a separate animal, not part of me. The first hitter went down swinging; the second took a called strike three. I fired two more strikes and, with everyone on both sides shouting, nailed the outside corner with a perfect pitch.

"Ball one," the umpire muttered, turning his head aside.

Our fans booed, but it didn't matter. I knew it; the batter knew it; the umpire knew it. I went into the wind-up, zeroed in on Hadley's target, and threw another strike three. This time the ump's fist punched the air. Seconds later, guys mobbed me on the mound, spinning me around and around. I felt like I was a rocket, the mound was a launch pad, and I was set to explode into outer space.

TWO

WHEN WE LINED UP and high-fived the Jesuit High players, I was so excited that I didn't see a single face, not even Fergus Hart's. It was just "Good game . . ." "Good game . . ." "Good game . . ." When that ended, I turned to see my mom up against the fence. Antonio and Curtis flanked her, both waving their hands above their heads. Suja stood a few steps behind, clapping her hands and smiling.

"Laz! Laz! Over here!" Mom called.

I jogged over, fighting the impulse to sprint. "Let's go," Mom shouted. "Time to celebrate."

"Okay, okay. Great. Just let m-me check with Coach."

I looked around and saw Mr. Thurman heading toward us. He gave me a high-five and then turned to my mother. "We're having pizza back at my house. The semifinal game is at seven tonight, so it's nothing big, but we'd love to have you come."

"Thanks," Mom said, "but we've got plans."

Mr. Thurman nodded. "Okay," he said, though it didn't sound as if he thought it was okay. He looked at me. "You need to be back on this field by six."

"Don't worry," Curtis said. "We'll have him here."

Suja stepped forward. Our eyes met. "Got to go," she mouthed. "You were great."

"Thanks," I mouthed back.

She gave me a wave and left.

When we'd all squeezed into the Corolla, Curtis looked back over his shoulder at me, his face contorted. "Something smells a little game-y back there. How about we go to the apartment so you can shower up. Then we'll get lunch."

"You can just drop me off at Jet City," Antonio said. "I've got—"

"You've got nothing," Mom said. "Your brother just won the biggest game of his life, and you're going to be part of the celebration."

Antonio slumped back in his seat, his arm folded across his chest.

I'd been flying, but that brought me down. Thinking about Garrett and Jet City and drugs was not what I wanted to do. As Curtis drove, he went through the game inning by inning. After a few minutes, Antonio added a few comments, and that brought back the good feelings.

When we reached the apartment, I showered fast, changed fast, and was back in the main room within fifteen minutes.

"How's McDonald's sound?" Curtis asked. "I bet you haven't a Big Mac since you moved to Laurelhurst."

The great thing about fast food is that it's fast. Fifteen minutes after we'd gotten back into the Corolla, we were sitting in the sunshine eating juicy burgers at a red plastic table. Little kids, screaming as they ran around the playscape, provided free entertainment. And Curtis was right—I hadn't had a Big Mac since I'd moved to Laurelhurst, and I'd forgotten how great they taste. I took one huge bite after another.

"So explain how this tournament works," Curtis said. "What happens now?"

My mouth was so full I couldn't answer. I took a big glug of the chocolate milk shake, but that only made me cough.

"Don't choke to death," Mom said as I tried to swallow.

Antonio poked me. "No, let him. Think of the headline. *Star pitcher dies as family watches.*" He pulled out his cell and aimed at me. "I'll film the whole thing and put it on YouTube. It'll go viral for sure."

"Use my phone, Antonio," Curtis said as my coughing got worse. "I don't think yours even makes videos."

"Stop it, both of you," Mom said, grinning.

I finally managed to swallow. "Tonight, we p-play the winner of Kentwood–T-Tahoma. If we win, next week we'll play whatever t-team makes it out of Eastern Washington, probably Gonzaga Prep."

"But you won't pitch tonight, right?" Curtis asked.

I shook my head. "No. There are rules about n-number of p-pitches and all that. K-Kevin Griffith pitches tonight."

"They used Laz first," Antonio said, "because Jesuit was the tougher team to beat."

Mom's eyes met Curtis's, and then she turned to me. "Laz,

we have tickets for a show at the Emerald Queen Casino. Queen Latifah. We bought them before we knew about your playoffs. You won't mind us missing the second game? Since you're not pitching?"

When we'd finished eating, it wasn't even four o'clock. I had two hours before I needed to be back at Husky Ballpark. I didn't want to sit around the Woodacres apartment watching TV, but I had nothing else to do—until Antonio saved me.

"I bet Mr. Leskov would want to hear about Laz winning," he said as we drove back to the apartment. "So would the all North Central guys at the community center. If you lend me the Toyota or the pickup, I'll take him there. He can chill out, be the big star, and you and Curtis can head to the concert whenever you want."

Mom twisted in her seat to look at me. "That be okay with you, Laz?"

"S-Sure."

When we pulled up in front of the apartment, Curtis handed the keys of the pickup to Antonio. There were handshakes and hugs, and then Antonio and I were headed east on 130th toward the community center.

"It's going to happen for you," Antonio said as we crossed I-5.

"What?"

"Come on. Don't play dumb. You outpitched that Fergus guy, and he's going to be a first- or second-round pick. They're going to call your name early, Bro. You're going to get some serious bonus money."

I stared out the window at the big trees hanging over the street, their leaves lit up by the bright sunlight. Forty rounds in the draft . . . thirty-two teams . . . more than one thousand names called.

After Antonio pulled into the community center parking lot, we both got out and walked toward the main entrance. We'd finally have a couple of hours together. I had things to say to Antonio. I just hoped I could think clearly and talk without getting stuck on every other word.

Before we reached the stairs leading to the front doors of the community center, Dawit and a couple of his friends spotted us. They'd been shooting hoops on the outside courts, but they stopped playing and came over.

"Hey, Antonio," Dawit said, smiling. "Never see you here."

"My brother just pitched a great game," Antonio said, motioning toward me. "I'm bringing him so he can brag to Mr. Leskov."

For the next couple of minutes Antonio told Dawit and his friend about my game. They nodded, but they didn't really care. Why should they? Then the conversation turned to North Central. During an assembly on Friday, somebody had rolled a shot put down the steps from the top of the auditorium to the floor. "Was that you?" Dawit asked, laughing as he poked at Antonio.

"Nah," Antonio said, but his eyes said something different.

"Yeah, it was," Dawit said. "Thump, thump, thump. Faster and louder. I thought Mrs. Park was going to have a heart attack."

The banter went back and forth. It didn't matter whether Antonio had pulled the stunt or not. He made it his own with his easy way and his easy smile.

Finally Dawit and his friends returned to their basketball game. I started up the steps to the community center, but Antonio stayed behind. "Aren't you g-going in?" I asked. "I thought we c-could shoot some p-pool and j-just hang out."

He screwed up his face. "Truth? I can't. Leskov has banned me."

"B-Banned you? Why?"

His face got more twisted. "He says I'm a bad influence. He doesn't want me hanging around young kids."

"Seriously?"

"Yeah. Seriously."

My chance to talk to him was slipping away. "We c-can go someplace else."

Antonio shook his head. "Things to do. Next week, for sure." He motioned toward the street. "You got money for the bus down to U-Dub?"

I nodded. "Yeah. I'm good. But, we r-really need t-to—"

"Laz," he said, his voice suddenly sharp. "I got no time now. I just don't. And remember, you're the one who moved out, not me. So we'll get together when we get together. Okay?"

My heart was pounding fast. "O-Okay. I'm s-sorry."

The anger left his face. He gave me a half smile. "All right, then. Shine bright, Brother."

Then he returned to the truck and drove out of the parking lot. I stood for a few minutes, feeling lost, before I went inside.

When Mr. Leskov saw me, he took me by the shoulders and shook me, telling me he'd read about me in the newspaper. "You strike three those boys in the playoffs," he shouted.

I tried to explain that I'd already *strike three'd* them, but he didn't understand.

For the next thirty minutes I played foosball and Ping-Pong with some North Central kids I sort of knew. After that, I found a soft chair in the TV room and watched a few innings of a Yankees–Blue Jays game. I tried to recapture at least some of the joy I'd had at the end of the Jesuit game, but it wouldn't come. At five, I changed back into my sweaty uniform and caught the bus down to Husky Ballpark.

THREE

I COULD FEEL THE ENERGY around me during warm-ups. We'd beaten the best team in the state. Now we just had to take care of business against Tahoma. Do that, and we'd be playing at T-Mobile Park on Friday for the state title. I tried to breathe in some of the excitement, but when you know you're not going to play, it's not the same. And the whole thing with Antonio was like a black cloud over my head, pushing my spirits even lower.

Then, just before the game started, Coach Vereen came over. "I had Mr. Thurman go through the scorebook. You threw ninety-three pitches against Jesuit. See what I'm saying?"

I shook my head. "Not r-really."

"The rules say you can throw a hundred and five pitches in a day. That means you've got twelve left. Twelve pitches could be a couple of batters, maybe one full inning." He paused. "If I need someone to close the game, could you do it?"

I felt like I was a character in a video game that had suddenly been booted up. All the gloom disappeared. "My arm is fine, Coach. I can p-pitch."

"You sure? I don't want you hurting yourself."

"No. I'm f-fine. Really. I w-want to p-pitch."

He put his hand on my shoulder and squeezed. "All right, then. Hopefully we won't need you, but if we do . . ."

Tahoma was the home team. I sat on the bench next to Kevin as we batted in the top of the first. His right leg was tap-tap-tapping the ground, and his fingertips were drumming on his thighs. He kept stuffing his mouth with sunflower seeds and machine-gunning the shells out through his teeth.

Tahoma's pitcher was guiding his pitches; our guys were loose and confident. Andrew . . . Jared . . . Ian—all three of them smoked the ball, and all three made outs—two line drives and a hard ground ball. That's how baseball goes sometimes.

"You got 'em," I said to Kevin as he spit out the final batch of sunflower shells and started toward the mound. His eyes were almost glazed over; beads of sweat lined his forehead. Coaches talk about players who rise to the occasion. There had to be guys who fall apart. Kevin had failed twice before. Was he going down a third time?

It sure looked like it. His pitches were everywhere: high, low, wide, tight. He walked the first batter, gave up a hit, and then plunked the number-three hitter in the butt. Hadley went out to calm him; the infielders shouted encouragement. Coach Vereen clapped his hands and called out, "Easy, Kevin. Easy." You can lose a baseball game in the first inning, and we were on the verge.

With the bases loaded, Kevin grooved a fastball over the

heart of the plate. Tahoma's cleanup hitter crushed it, sending a rocket toward Jay at third. If he hadn't stuck his glove up, the ball might have taken off his head. But he did stick his glove up and the ball smacked into the webbing. He stepped on third for the second out and whipped a throw to second base before the base runner could get back.

Triple play!

Everything stopped as spectators and players took in what had happened. Then our fans roared, and our guys hollered and slapped gloves as they ran into the dugout, huge grins on their faces. Tahoma's players dragged themselves out to their positions, their faces like deflated balloons.

We scored twice in the top of the second, both runs coming home on a fly ball to right center that fell between the outfielders. With a two-run lead, Kevin was a little better. He threw strikes, but he still didn't have any zip on his fastball. Tahoma managed runs in the third and the fourth, but we kept scoring. Our lead was 5–2 after three innings, then 6–3 after four.

By the bottom of the fifth, Kevin was taking deep breaths and tugging on his shoulder. The leadoff hitter popped up to short, and the next batter grounded out to first. It looked like he'd get through the inning, but the next two batters reached base, the first on a walk and the second on a line single to left. Coach Vereen had the twins warming up. He walked to the mound to talk to Kevin, his eyes going back and forth between the twins and Kevin, trying to decide who had the best chance of getting the third out. After looking to the bullpen half a dozen times, he left Kevin in.

The Tahoma batter stepped to the plate. The umpire pointed at Kevin. Hadley crouched, gave the signal. Everybody knew it was going to be a fastball, and it was. The Tahoma batter turned on it, sending a high drive to center. Ian raced back, his eyes tracking the ball. On the warning track, he stopped. I thought the ball was gone, a three-run homer. But then Ian retreated one more step and, with his back against the fence, leaped. The ball settled harmlessly into the webbing of his glove. Three more inches, and the game would have been tied, but Ian's fielding gem had turned a home run into a long out.

Kevin hadn't gone more than five innings in any game all season. When he reached the bench, Vereen slapped him on the back. "Way to step up."

Marc Robosky pitched a gut-wrenching sixth. A couple of hits, a couple of walks, a sac fly. When the seventh batter struck out swinging on what would have been ball four, we cheered like crazy, but our lead had been cut to 6–5.

When it came to pitching, Tahoma was in the same spot we were in. They'd used their best starter in the afternoon game, and their second-line pitchers all looked overwhelmed by the moment. Jay smacked a one-out, run-scoring double in the top of the seventh, pushing our lead back to 7–5.

Coach Vereen clapped his hands together and then wandered over to me. "Get loose, Laz."

Mentally, I was ready to go, but physically? The first few throws in the bullpen told me—my arm was tired and my shoulder was stiff. I fought the impulse to rush the warm-up by throwing harder; instead, I threw softer, loosening slowly.

Andrew Robosky took the mound for the bottom of the seventh, and for two batters he looked like a major-league closer, getting the first on a strikeout and the second on a soft roller to second. One more out, and Andrew would have done it. I was in the bullpen area, with a lousy view of the field, but I could see the guys on the bench hanging on to one another, ready to rush the mound.

The last out is never easy. Nerves hit Andrew. He walked the batter on four pitches. He threw two more balls to the hitter after that, and then threw a changeup that the guy ripped into right center for an RBI double.

Laurelhurst 7–Tahoma 6.

Coach Vereen had seen enough. He strode to the mound, took the ball from Andrew, and motioned to me.

I trotted out, acting as if everything was normal, but feeling the strangeness of it all. Pitching in two games in one day. Starting the first and now closing the second.

I don't know if my arm still felt stiff, because I really didn't feel anything. In the far distance I heard the crowd screaming, but that noise was muffled by an even louder roar from inside my head. We were one out from the title game, and it was up to me to get that out.

Hadley gave the target.

I went into my wind-up, delivered.

"Strike one!"

The ball came back. I got set. The target.

"Strike two!"

I took a deep breath, exhaled, and then everything slowed down even more. My movements, the batter's, Hadley's. As I went into my motion, I stayed slow, so slow, and let the ball just ease out of my hand like it was water. The bat moved into the hitting zone just as the pitch dived down and to the left.

"Strike three!"

And then the guys were on me for the second time, and the world was spinning and spinning and I felt as if I were on the greatest ride and the greatest amusement park in the whole world.

FOUR

MY MOM AND ANTONIO and Suja and Curtis either called or texted over the weekend, congratulating me, telling me how happy they were that we'd won the second game and how sad they were that they hadn't been there. At Laurelhurst on Monday everybody was my new best friend, even kids who didn't know a double from a double play. I got high-fives and low-fives and knuckle bumps in the hallways, in the classrooms, at lunch.

Coach Vereen called us into the wrestling room and gave us a talk on focus. "Eat right, sleep right, do your schoolwork. Keep things normal." Then his eyes went to me, or at least it seemed they did. "Some of you will get phone calls from news reporters or TV guys or Internet sites. Just remember. There is no *I* in *team*." Hadley, sitting next to me, dug his elbow into my ribs.

Vereen sat us down on the mats and had us watch World Series highlights, which turned out to be boring. When you know that every play is going to be great, none of them are.

As we left the gym, he handed each of us an envelope. "You

get four passes for the games at T-Mobile. Don't even think of selling them, not even for a Snickers bar."

I did a quick count in my head: Mom, Antonio, Curtis, and Suja. It was sunny and warm, and I didn't feel like sitting in my basement room. I had to get the tickets up to North Central sometime. Why not now?

I texted my mom. She said she'd be at the apartment, but she called while I was on the bus: she was stuck at work. "Antonio should be around, though. You could hang out with him until I get there."

Antonio wasn't at the apartment. I stuck three passes into the mailbox and texted Suja. I was expecting another **Sorry, won't be there,** but her response was immediate. **At home. C U in 10.**

Jet City had more empty spots, more deserted trailers, more trash along the fence. Suja opened the door before I'd taken two steps up her walkway. She hugged me and told me how everybody at North Central High was rooting for me.

A table with green plastic chairs was set up in front of her house. We sat in the unexpected sunshine and talked. The Senior Ball. Graduation. Whitman College. Baseball. Then came a pause. "Laz, I'm sorry, but I've got a physics final coming up."

I jumped to my feet. "I need to g-go anyway." I took her ticket out of my back pocket. "This pass will get you into the championship game. If you want t-to see it."

She stood and took a step toward me. "I'll be there." Then she wrapped her arms around me and gave me another hug.

"Later," I said, and started down the walkway. Her voice called me back.

"I think your brother is at Garrett's. They drove in right before you got here." She paused. "I mean, if you want to talk to him."

She smiled, waved again, and then went into her trailer. Her door closed, leaving me standing on the gravel path.

Did I want to talk to Antonio? He confused everything, making it hard for me to focus. And I needed to focus now more than ever. Waiting until the season ended was the smart thing to do. I took a couple of steps toward Aurora Avenue but then stopped.

He was my brother.

I turned and headed toward Garrett's trailer. As I neared it, I thought Suja must have been wrong. The Subaru wasn't in front; the shades were drawn, the windows closed. As I headed up the walkway, though, I heard voices, one of which was Antonio's.

I knocked.

The voices went quiet.

I knocked again. "It's me. Laz Weathers. Is Antonio there?"

Then I heard what sounded like chains rattling. Next a deadbolt slid back, another lock was released, the door opened, and Antonio slipped outside. As soon as he did, the door closed behind him and the deadbolt clicked into place.

"Has Garrett g-got chains over his d-door?" I asked.

"It's weird here now, Laz," Antonio answered, his eyes

darting from side to side, his voice tense. "Crazies from Aurora come in at night."

"How does his g-grandfather get out with all those locks? Or S-Selena?"

"They're gone. They moved to an apartment in Burien. It's just Garrett here now."

I understood why I hadn't seen either of them at the back fence for a while. Garrett was dealing right from the trailer.

Something must have passed over my face, because Antonio spoke before I had a chance to say anything. "It's ending. Garrett moves out on Saturday. And I'm glad he's going, glad to be done with all this."

It took a moment for me to understand what he was saying. When the meaning did come through, I felt tension pour out of me like water over a dam. "That's g-good," I said, keeping my voice calm. "Really g-good. In fact, it's great." I paused. "The championship g-game is Friday n-night at T-Mobile. I left a ticket for you with Mom. Think you can m-make it?"

Garrett called out something I couldn't make out. "I hope so, Bro. I just can't promise. There are still things that need finishing."

FIVE

TUESDAY MORNING, COACH VEREEN called me out of class to his office. I was working up the courage to ask him to make a DVD for me, but he started talking before I could say anything.

"Got some news I think you're going to like," he said as he handed me printed copies of two emails he'd gotten. "The first is from the San Francisco Giants, the second from the Colorado Rockies. You can read them later. Basically, they both ask the same question. Are you interested in professional baseball?" Coach Vereen paused. "Are you?"

"Yes, sir," I said, keeping my voice calm. "Yes, I am."

He tugged on one of his ears. "The June draft is coming up, so you've got to move fast. I've got a DVD of the Jesuit High game. I'll have one of my TAs make copies. You come back here during your lunch period—the door will be open. Check out a laptop from the library, write a cover letter, include your email address and your phone number, and then send the DVD and the letter to the Giants and the Rockies. Their addresses are on the emails. And send one to Tommy Zeller, too. The scouts also want a letter from me describing your work habits and all that stuff. I'll write it on Saturday"—he stopped and smiled—*"after we win the championship. Got all that?"*

No teacher called on me that morning, which was good, because I barely knew what class I was in. For three hours, all I did was compose a cover letter in my head. When lunch came, I hustled to the library, checked out a computer, and then went to Coach Vereen's office.

The letter took no time. Rookie league, A-Ball, instructional league, Mexican League, Latin America, Japan, Korea, Taiwan —I wrote that I'd play anywhere. I'd be a starter, a middle reliever, a closer. Whatever they wanted me to do, I was all in.

Coach Vereen had left three stamped manila envelopes on the table. I wrote the address of one team onto the envelope, slid the letter and DVD inside, and sealed it. Then I went to the next team and started the process again. I finished just when the bell rang for class.

I was burning with energy all afternoon, so it was great to get out of the building and onto the baseball diamond for practice. I stretched, ran in the outfield, played some long catch, stretched some more, ran some more.

When it was time for the hitters to take batting practice, I was the first pitcher to reach the mound. I felt strong enough to throw my fastball right through Hadley's mitt. As soon as I stepped on the mound, Coach Vereen waved me off. "Go run some laps."

"But I want to p-pitch," I said.

"You're too pumped. You won't be able to dial it down, and you might hurt your arm or hit somebody in the head and kill them. Run some laps."

SIX

IT WAS THE END OF THE YEAR, so teachers were going easy on us. That meant slack time, when I'd rather have had something hard. Even math was no sweat. The last chapter in the text was about biased and unbiased surveys. It was filled with questions like *Marie Schwartz surveys the school soccer teams to find out the favorite sport at Pleasant Valley High. Why is this survey biased?* I could have answered that in sixth grade.

I used some of my extra time to research Gonzaga Prep—the team we'd be facing in the final. The school was in Spokane, a couple of miles from Gonzaga University. They'd won the eastern regional, so they were good, but they'd also lost four games during the year and had four one-run victories. The three- and four-hitters hit for high averages, but didn't have much power. The rest of the lineup looked okay, but just okay.

Sometimes in school I'd be sitting next to a bunch of top students and they'd take turns talking about how they were worried they'd flunked some test or bombed some paper. Then, a day later, they'd pretend to be shocked when they got an A.

I hated it when kids did that, but I played my version of that game a couple of times, scaring myself with the thought that if I had a bad outing against Gonzaga, no team would draft me.

It wasn't true, and I knew it. I'd pitched Laurelhurst to a league title and a regional title and into the state title game. I'd shut down the best teams in the state. My fastball was in the nineties. I had good control. Even if I lost to Gonzaga Prep, I'd shown enough. Teams never have enough pitching, and forty rounds is a lot of rounds.

Some team would draft me.

SEVEN

FRIDAY. CHAMPIONSHIP DAY.

North Central had had pep rallies, but none were anything like the one at Laurelhurst. The walls of the gym were covered with banners. The band blasted out song after song. Players from earlier teams sat on folding chairs set up on the gym floor. Every person chanted *"Pop! Pop! Pop!"* when Vereen entered.

The principal, Mr. Chavez, gave a speech recounting Coach Vereen's career. I knew he had been around for years, but I didn't know that he'd started coaching the year the school opened, making him the only baseball coach in the forty-two-year history of Laurelhurst.

When Mr. Chavez finished, Mr. Thurman took the microphone. "The boosters have a gift for you," he said, and he held up a plaque that showed Coach Vereen's face in profile. "This will be placed above the main entrance to the gymnasium, which has officially been renamed Pop Vereen Gymnasium." More cheering, more stamping of feet. Some of Vereen's old players looked like they were wiping away tears.

Next, former players took turns telling stories about this

team and that team and how Coach Vereen had taught them a lot about baseball but even more about life. The period was about over when Coach Vereen stepped up to the microphone. He had notes in front of him, but all he managed to say was "Thank you." He stepped back, and everyone rose to their feet, clapping and cheering.

That ended the pep rally. The one thing that hadn't been mentioned was the only thing that was missing: the state title. If I pitched my game, it would be a kid from North Central High who made the fairy tale ending come true.

EIGHT

WHEN THE SCHOOL DAY ENDED, all the guys on the team met at the gym. We stretched, ran a little, and then hung out. At four thirty we got the word to change into our game uniforms. Fifteen minutes later we were on the bus, heading to T-Mobile Park.

There's nothing normal about a championship game, so nobody knew how to act. Being quiet seemed wrong, so guys talked, only they talked too loud and they laughed too hard.

We reached the ballpark ninety minutes before the game. A security guy led us through different rooms that were just for the Mariners players. As he walked, he rattled off a list of things we couldn't touch—which was everything. But we could look. The clubhouse, the weight room, the showers, the trainer's room—it was all out of a magazine. At last he led us down a hallway that led into the locker room itself.

In the center area leather sofas and chairs were positioned for watching widescreen TVs suspended from the ceiling. Around the edge were the players' cubicles, each about the size of Antonio's room at the apartment.

When we reached the dugout, I understood why players stand on the top steps during a game. From the bench you can hardly see the field.

My duffle held my street clothes and cell. I shoved it into a corner, and then, for the first time in my life, I stepped onto a major-league field. As I took that step, I thought that someday I might step onto the field as a major-league player. The hairs on my arm and neck stood straight up. Coach Vereen's voice snapped me back into the present. "Let's go. Regular warm-up. Get to it."

I stretched, jogged in the outfield, played pepper. A few people were filtering into the park, but not many. Parents and kids could come right down to the railing and say hello and wish guys luck.

My mom was one of them. I heard her before I saw her. "Laz!" I turned and she was holding her hands above her head, clapping as if she were at a rock concert. "Antonio and Curtis are coming later," she hollered. "We'll be there," she said, pointing to the section directly behind home plate. She made two fists and shook them. "Good luck!"

I waved and then trotted to the outfield to play long catch with Ian. Back and forth the baseball went, the only bond between us, but a strong one. Finally I heard Hadley's voice: "Time to get ready, Laz."

The bullpen was out in left field, cut off from everyone else. I stepped up on the mound as Hadley crouched down behind the plate. The distractions were gone. His glove was the whole world. With every pitch, I felt stronger, more confident.

This was my moment.

Ten minutes before game time Hadley and I jogged to the infield and lined up along first base, waiting for the Laurelhurst band to play the national anthem. I was minutes from the high point of my life.

Then everything crashed.

NINE

SUJA.

She was running down the aisle from the main concourse, holding out her cell phone. "Laz! Laz! You need to hear this!" Her eyes were so wild that everybody on the team, and almost everybody in the stands, was staring at her.

What was she thinking? I couldn't talk to her, not with the game minutes away. I looked down, staring at the dirt, ignoring her. She kept running, kept calling my name. When she reached the railing, she leaned over, stretching her phone out as if I could reach from the first base line to the railing and take it from her.

"Laz, Antonio is in trouble."

My head jerked up. Our eyes met. Her fear grabbed hold of me. I took one small step toward her, then a bigger one, and then I was running. When I reached the railing, she shoved the phone into my hand.

"Who is this?" I asked. "What's h-happening?"

"Laz, it's me. Garrett. I did a stupid thing. A really stupid thing, and I'm sorry."

"Wh-What are you t-talking about?"

"Your brother. I sent him to do a deal, the last deal. I was selling everything. Done. Out. No more. He was supposed to meet the buyer under the Ballard Bridge. But it was all a setup. I've been calling him, but he doesn't answer. You got to get there first. These are bad guys, Laz. Really bad guys. They could do anything."

"Wh—"

"Twenty minutes. It goes down in twenty minutes. He has my Subaru, so I can't get there. Besides, I can't show my face. They want me more than they want him. But they're not after you at all. You see that, right?" He paused. "That's why it's on you."

The phone went dead.

Mom must have heard Suja, must have sensed that something was wrong, because she was working her way toward me, pushing past people, moving as fast as she could. The band had started playing the national anthem.

And then it was Mr. Thurman at the railing, shouldering Suja aside. "What are you doing, Laz? Get back there with your team."

I dropped my glove and started to climb over the railing. "I can't," I said, shouting to be heard over the band. "I have to go."

He grabbed my arm, stopping me. "Are you crazy? The game starts in two minutes."

Mom was racing down the aisle, coming closer. I couldn't hear her, but I could read her lips: *What's wrong?*

"Antonio," I shouted as the last notes of the anthem faded and cheers came up from the thousand or so fans.

Mr. Thurman, his hand still gripping my arm, twisted me so that I was facing the press box. "Major-league scouts are watching you right this minute. Think what you're doing. They're not going to waste a draft pick on a player who walks out on his team."

Mom had reached us. "Take your hands off my son!" she barked.

His grip relaxed. I shook free, got completely over the railing, and started up the aisle. "We've g-got to g-get to the Ballard Bridge," I said to my mom, who was right by my side. "Antonio is in danger."

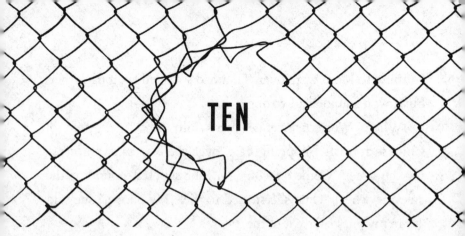

TEN

WE HAD TO DODGE CARS AND TRUCKS to cross First Avenue South. After that we ran to Utah Street, where Mom had parked the Corolla.

Horns blared as she shot out into traffic. She blew through a red light and raced toward Western Avenue and Ballard.

"Explain," she said as she wove in and out of lanes.

"Some g-guys he's meeting. They're g-going to hurt him. Or they m-might."

"What guys, Laz? What are you talking about? Why would anyone want to hurt Antonio?"

"That Garrett kid g-got him m-mixed up with drugs. "

She looked over at me, her eyes blazing. I felt the car accelerate. Then she peppered me with questions.

How long?

Where?

When?

Why hadn't I said anything to her?

That was the hardest question. I remembered Antonio telling me last year that he was sixteen, not six, and the days of running to Mom were over. That had sounded right back then, but now it sounded all wrong.

Where Western Avenue turns into Elliott, a group of Chinese tourists, shopping bags over their arms, were crossing the street. "Come on, come on," she shouted, pounding the steering wheel. Then she turned to me. "My phone," she said. "It's in my purse. Give it to me."

She punched a number on speed dial. The last tourist cleared the street, and she took off. "Curtis, did Antonio show up?" Pause. "Listen, Laz says he's in trouble. Gangs. drugs—I don't understand it all, but that doesn't matter. What matters is that some guys are waiting for him by the Ballard Bridge, and he has no clue." Pause. "It goes to voice mail." Pause. "We're headed there right now." Pause. "No. You call them."

She disconnected.

For a while we were lucky—green light after green light. But the light by Whole Foods turned yellow when we were still a couple hundred yards away. Instead of stopping, Mom floored it and roared through. The animal shelter flew by, and after that, Interbay Golf Center.

The Ballard Bridge was finally in sight.

"What side?" Mom asked.

My body seized up. "I d-don't know."

She bit her lip. "It'll be the other side. More places to hide over there."

She handed me her cell. "Try him again."

I punched in the number.

Voice mail again.

The Ballard Bridge is a drawbridge that opens about a dozen times a day. Cars have to sit and wait while sailboats and fishing boats pass under. As Mom reached the south end of the bridge, I was sure the red lights would flash, the bridge would open, and we'd be stuck for five minutes. I didn't want to think about what would happen to Antonio in those minutes. But then I felt the pavement change to metal grating, and seconds later we were on the Ballard side. A thought flashed into my head.

"Nine-one-one," I said. "We sh—"

"Curtis called," Mom said as she took the off-ramp. She pulled to a stop in front of Mike's Chili.

"Shouldn't we c-circle around?" I asked. "A bunch of streets g-go under the b-bridge. The m-meeting could be at any of them."

She shook her head as she threw open her door. "It's faster on foot."

ELEVEN

WE STARTED BY SEARCHING where Leary Avenue passes under the bridge. The sun was going down, and it is dark below a bridge deck even at noon. I looked into the darkness and saw something moving behind the bridge supports.

Mom saw it, too. "Antonio!" she called out as she rushed toward it. "Antonio!"

I was next to her, but I could barely hear her—the roar from the cars above was as loud as a fighter jet. We pushed aside a deserted shopping cart. "Antonio!" Mom called a third time as again something moved in the darkness.

A voice came back. "Leave me alone."

My eyes had adjusted. A homeless guy, hollow-eyed and holding a moldy sleeping bag, was staring at us.

We headed down a narrow one-way street that led to where Northwest Forty-Sixth crossed under the bridge. The area was smaller and dirtier and smelled like sewage.

"Antonio!" my mother shouted, walking toward Pono Ranch.

I searched in the opposite direction, toward LA Fitness.

"Antonio!" I shouted.

Nothing.

"Antonio!"

"Antonio!"

More nothing. No gang guys, no brother.

I stopped. Was it a false alarm? Had I walked out on my team for nothing?

Mom had turned back and was approaching me. Before she reached me, her phone rang. She turned her back to me and covered one ear so she could take the call.

That's when I heard the laughing. Not funny laughing, but mean laughing. Where was it coming from? I looked across the street and saw an alley I hadn't noticed before. I looked back to Mom. She was still on the phone, her back to me.

I couldn't wait.

A cement truck was rumbling down the street, but I raced across anyway. The driver laid on his horn, but I kept going until I reached the entrance to the alley. At first I had trouble seeing, but then my eyes adjusted to the gloom. At the bottom of the alley, three guys, hoodies up, were kicking at something. When I spotted Garrett's black Subaru parked on the road at the far end of the alley, I knew what they were kicking.

"Stop it!" I screamed as I started toward them. One of the guys took a couple of steps toward me.

"You don't want to come down here," he shouted, waving something in his hand.

I kept moving forward. There were probably forty yards between us, about the distance from second base to home plate.

In all the roar from the cars on the bridge, I could just make out the wailing of police sirens. The guy staring me down heard the sirens, too. "Yo!" he called over his shoulder, his arm pointing in the direction of the sirens. "Let's roll!"

The guy turned back to face me. "I told you to stop!" he screamed. The sirens were louder, the police cars closing in.

Suddenly the guy turned and started running. Then all three them were running, heading down and out of the alley. When they reached the street, the first guy turned back. I heard *pop . . . pop . . . pop,* saw sparks on the ground, and felt a burning pain. I grabbed at my left leg. It was warm and wet—blood. I looked up to see a car speed away, heading east toward the Fremont district. Then I looked down again at my left thigh, at the blood staining my white baseball pants.

"Antonio!" Mom was racing down the alley toward my brother, who was curled in a ball, moaning. She stopped when she saw the blood on my hands and on my jersey. "Laz! What happened!"

"I think m-maybe I g-got shot," I managed.

Mom took off her scarf and shoved it into my hand. "Sit down right there, right where you are. Press down. Hard. I'm going to check Antonio. Then I'll be back."

I nodded.

That's when the bicyclists showed up: two women, at the top of the alley—neon green shirts, flashing white lights. "You need help down there?" one of them called.

• • •

What happened after that is hazy. I heard more sirens, saw a cop car, a second cop car, a medic aide car. I remember one of the bicyclists sitting next to me and the other one putting her coat around my shoulders. I heard Curtis telling me I was going to be okay, and then a paramedic was checking me. Down the alley, I could see another team of paramedics working on Antonio. He was lying flat on his back with a brace around his neck. I remember wondering whether that was a good or bad sign.

A gurney appeared. The paramedics helped me onto it and had me lie down. As they wheeled me to an ambulance, Mom ran her hand over my forehead and said something I couldn't make out. The paramedics slid me into the back of the ambulance and closed the door. I couldn't see Antonio. "Is my brother okay?" I asked, but no one answered.

TWELVE

BALLARD HOSPITAL IS THREE BLOCKS from the Ballard Bridge, so I wasn't in the ambulance more than a couple of minutes. The paramedics talked about starting an IV, but decided against it. "He'll be in the ER before I find a vein," the female paramedic said to her partner. Vomit came to the top of my throat, but I didn't puke.

Once we reached the hospital, the paramedics wheeled me into an examining room and transferred me to something that was part bed and part table. A nurse with red glasses and red hair hooked up an IV; a thin man with a gray beard examined my leg.

"You've got a bullet stuck in your thigh," he said, his voice angry. "But looking at how shallow that wound is, I'd say you got hit on a ricochet. A direct hit to your femoral artery and you could have bled to death before anyone reached you."

"I saw s-sparks on the g-ground j-just before it hit me."

He frowned. "Yeah? Well, those sparks may have saved your life. Now keep still and let me get this out of you."

I lay back. They numbed my leg and then put up a screen so I couldn't see anything, but I could sort of feel the doctor digging around. Finally he stopped. "You'll go to x-ray next. A chunk of your leg is torn up, but your body will take care of that."

"Th-thanks," I said.

He snorted. "You know how you can thank me? Don't get shot. Don't get stabbed. Don't OD. That's how you can thank me."

Mom came while I was waiting for them to take me to the x-ray room. "The doctor says you're going to be fine," she whispered as she leaned in and kissed me. "Just a flesh wound. How are you feeling?"

"I'm okay. H-How's Antonio?"

She started to speak, then choked up, then started again. "He's bleeding inside. They need to operate. I'll be with him for a while, but I'll be back here to check on you, or Curtis will."

A nurse came in. "They're ready to take some pictures."

Mom ruffled my hair and left.

The x-ray technician was a young guy. "You're one lucky dude," he said as he adjusted my leg under the machine. "If that bullet was a few inches over, you'd be singing in the girls' choir —if you get what I mean." He was grinning, but I'd already thought of that, and I didn't think it was funny.

He wheeled me back into my room, told me a nurse would be coming by, and left. Around me, medical equipment hummed. I looked at the clock: it was 8:55. The voices in the hallway sounded farther and farther away.

I closed my eyes.

THIRTEEN

CURTIS WOKE ME. First thing, I asked about Antonio.

"They're going to remove his spleen," he said. "It's not good, but these doctors know what they're doing. You'll stay here until he comes out of surgery, and then your mom or I will take you back to the apartment. A couple of hours. Maybe three. You can do that, right?"

I nodded.

Curtis stepped aside. Behind him was a man I hadn't seen. "This is Detective Wasserman. He's got questions for you. You're grown up, so you do what you want, but here's my advice. If Antonio screwed up, then he screwed up. If you screwed up, then you screwed up. Tell the truth, pay the bills, move on."

After Curtis left, Detective Wasserman asked questions and I answered them. Garrett, his sister, Antonio, Dustin, the back fence, the Subaru—I told him everything. The only time he pushed me was when I said I didn't know what the guys in the alley looked like. "Come on, Laz. White, black, Hispanic? Tall, short, fat, skinny? You must know something."

"They were wearing h-hoodies. It was dark, and besides I wasn't l-looking at them. I was looking at my brother. And then the one g-guy started r-running, and then they were all r-running, and then I g-got shot."

He grunted. "So, you got nothing for me? Is that what you're saying?"

"I'm n-not lying. I'd tell you if I knew." I paused. "M-Maybe Antonio c-can tell you."

He stared me down. "Maybe he can," he said, and then put his notepad away. "Anything you want to ask me?"

I swallowed. "Will Antonio go to j-jail?"

Detective Wasserman shook his head. "By the time those guys got done with him, your brother had nothing. No drugs. No money. No phone. No wallet. Nothing. The guys who beat him took it all. So we've got nothing on him." He pointed his finger at me and almost smiled. "But your brother didn't get off, did he? And neither did you. Both of you could have died tonight. Don't ever forget that."

After he left, I lay back and stared at the ceiling. In biology I'd learned something about the spleen, but I couldn't remember what.

I watched the second hand go round and round the face of the wall clock. It reminded me of runners going from base to base. The championship game was over. I thought about texting Hadley to get the final score, but my cell phone was in my duffle bag, and that was tucked away in a corner of the Mariners dugout. My clothes and wallet were in the duffle, too. And I'd just dropped my new glove at the railing. Would anybody bother to bring my stuff back to Laurelhurst?

FOURTEEN

IT WAS MIDNIGHT when Mom finally came back. Antonio was out of surgery, and he was doing okay, but he'd have to remain at the hospital for a while. "Curtis will stay with him tonight. You and I will go to the apartment and come back in the morning, or at least I will."

"I want to c-come b-back."

"We'll see how you feel."

The nurses made me sit in a wheelchair in the lobby until Mom brought the Corolla to the front of the hospital. They also gave me crutches, though I could tell I wouldn't need them for long. My leg was sore, nothing more.

As Mom drove over Phinney Ridge toward Aurora Avenue, I asked her what the spleen did. She gave a small shake of her head. "It filters the blood. Infections will be a big deal for Antonio for the rest of his life, but the doctor said that if you've got to lose something, the spleen is better than almost anything else."

After that, she went quiet. I leaned my head against the cool glass as the miles clicked away.

Once we were in the apartment, she pointed to Antonio's

room. "Sleep in there. He must have clothes that'll fit you. Sweatpants, at least. Tomorrow we'll get your stuff from those people and get you moved back in here."

"What about the r-rules—"

"Don't worry about that. Right now, the thing you need to do is sleep."

Minutes later, I was lying on Antonio's bed, totally exhausted but somehow wide-awake. Lights from passing cars danced across the ceiling. If I moved my leg a little, it hurt a lot, so I lay flat on my back, thinking first about Antonio and then about the baseball game. I wanted Laurelhurst to win. I wanted Coach Vereen to get his title and Mr. Thurman to see Ian holding the trophy. I wanted Hadley to be part of a championship team. I wanted the kids at Laurelhurst to remember all the games I did pitch, not the one game I walked away from.

Then I remembered: Mom kept her laptop on a table by the sofa.

I could get the score.

As I wriggled out of bed, my leg started throbbing. I hopped out to the front room, opened up the *Seattle Times* webpage, clicked Prep Sports, and then Baseball. The page went blank for a split second before the headline appeared.

Gonzaga Prep Takes State Title
Defeats Laurelhurst 13–10
By Clay Pearson

It took a while for the words to sink in. Ian had a home run and a double. Jay had two doubles and three RBI. Hadley threw out a base stealer and scored a run.

But the pitching?

Eight walks. Eleven hits. Two home runs. Four doubles.

There was no way Gonzaga's hitters would have pounded me like that. No way in the world. I'd have beaten them. I'd have led Laurelhurst to the title. I'd have made the fairy tale come true, and everyone at Laurelhurst knew it. Andrew Robosky was the losing pitcher, but I was the reason we lost.

I was about to log off when I saw, in tiny print just below the box score, one final paragraph.

The Seattle Times has learned that Laurelhurst's star pitcher, 19-year-old Laz Weathers, suffered a gunshot wound Friday night in an incident in Ballard. A seventeen-year-old companion of Weathers (the Seattle Times does not publish the names of juveniles) was hospitalized with serious injuries incurred in the same incident. Seattle Police Department's Drug/Gang Unit is investigating.

I dragged myself back to Antonio's room and lay down on his bed, my head swimming. Sometime in the night, the shakiness gave way to exhaustion, and I fell asleep.

FIFTEEN

WHEN I AWOKE, my mother was moving about in the kitchen. I dressed quickly and hobbled out to join her. "How's the leg?" she asked.

"It hurts, b-but it already hurts less. Any word on Antonio?"

She was adding milk to a cup of steaming coffee. "He's still in the intensive care unit," she said, not looking up. "Curtis is at the hospital. I'm going after I finish this. You feel up to coming?"

"Yeah."

She motioned with her head toward the refrigerator. "There's milk and cereal. Eat something."

I filled a bowl with Wheaties and poured milk over the top. When I sat down at the table, she put her coffee down. "Sorry about your game." She sipped her coffee and waited. I didn't answer. There was nothing to say.

"Laz, call those people you've been living with. Tell them you'll be moving out." She paused. "Do you have your phone with you?"

I shook my head. "It's in my d-duffle bag, and that's at the ballpark."

She got her cell from her purse and slid it to me. "Use mine."

I opened up her phone and then stopped. "I don't know the n-number."

We looked at each other, and then her eyes flashed. "I've got their phone number," she said. "The woman — Catherine — she gave me her business card that day we dropped you off."

Mom took out her wallet, rooted through some cards, and handed one to me. Then she took her coffee to the sofa as I punched in the numbers. Mrs. Thurman answered on the second ring, her voice filled with concern. "Are you all right? We read in the newspaper —"

"I'm f-fine," I said, and then, without stuttering too much, I managed to explain that the doctor said I'd be back to normal within a month. After a pause, I told her that I'd be moving back with my mom.

"I understand," she said. "We're going to Suncadia Resort today. All of us. We need to get away. I'll have Ian box up your belongings and put everything on the front porch, toward the maple tree. If you could drop the house key into the mail slot, that'd be great. And, Laz, Ian brought your duffle back from the ballpark, so you don't have to worry about retrieving that. It'll be on the porch with everything else."

Thirty minutes later I was standing by Antonio's hospital bed. His face was puffy, his eyes black slits. Even his ears were swollen. I listened as the doctor, a tall woman with short black hair and a thin face, told Mom that Antonio had come through the surgery okay, but he was still in bad shape. "Bruised kidney . . . Bruised liver . . . Concussion."

The list went on and on. "We're going to keep him here so we can monitor him closely."

After the doctor left, we pulled up chairs and sat close to Antonio's bed. Occasionally he mumbled something. His eyes would shut for a while, and then he'd open them and mumble something else.

Around noon, Mom told Curtis to go back to the apartment. "You need sleep." Then she looked at me. "Do you think those people have your stuff ready?"

"Yeah."

"What people? What stuff?" Curtis asked.

Antonio moaned.

"Laz will explain," Mom whispered.

I was nervous about being alone in the car with Curtis, afraid he'd blame me for what had happened. But it was the opposite. "You saved my son's life," he said as we drove toward Laurelhurst. "If you hadn't left that game, those punks would have beaten him to death. I owe you. I'll always owe you."

The boxes and my duffle bag were right where Mrs. Thurman said they'd be. Ian had retrieved my new baseball glove, too. He'd put it on top of the duffle, so it was the first thing I saw.

Curtis loaded all my stuff into the truck; he wouldn't let me help. "I hope we get out of here without getting stopped by the police," he said, only half joking, as he backed out of the Thurmans' driveway. "Package theft and all that. My pickup doesn't exactly fit the neighborhood profile."

He relaxed when we were out of Laurelhurst and headed to Aurora Avenue, which is when I got nervous. Would the Woodacres manager kick them out when he found I was living there?

"I'll start looking for a p-place to live," I said when we reached the apartment and Curtis was carrying my stuff inside. "I know I c-can't stay here."

He yawned. "Don't sweat it. The manager likes us; he'll cut us some slack. I'd say you've got until August first. Maybe September first." He raised his arms above his head and yawned again. "I'm going to crash and then head back to the hospital this afternoon. You need anything?"

I shook my head.

He went into the bedroom and closed the door.

Once I was alone, I went through my boxes. I didn't unpack —there was no place to put anything—but I did some organizing. At the bottom of the last box, I felt something metallic: the laptop. I opened it and found a note from Mrs. Thurman. "Keep this, Laz. It's no good to us sitting in a closet."

My cell had a bunch of messages, but only five percent of battery life remained. I connected my phone to Antonio's charger, which was plugged into the one outlet in his room, and then sat with my back against the wall. I was scheduled to work that day, so I called Mr. Matsui.

"The newspaper says you got shot," he said as soon as he heard my voice. "Are you okay?"

"Yeah, I'm okay. I got hit on a r-ricochet, so it's not l-like I was *shot* shot. I can't w-work today, b-but I should be able to w-work n-next weekend."

There was a pause. "Laz, I don't want trouble here. Just a few more weeks and we're closed for good. If some gang is after you . . ."

"Nobody's after m-me. There won't b-be any tr-trouble."

Another pause. "I don't know, Laz. For right now, I think you should just stay away. I'll call you if things change."

After I disconnected, I stared at my cell phone. It was one o'clock on Saturday afternoon. Eighteen hours earlier I'd been standing on the mound at a major-league ballpark, on the verge of a professional baseball career. And what had happened since then? I'd walked out on my team, been shot in an alley, lost my room at the Thurmans, and now I'd lost my job, too.

I didn't regret what I'd done. Those guys would have beaten Antonio to death. Still, I wanted to go to his hospital room, grab him by the shoulders, shake him, and yell at him for totally messing up my life.

While Curtis slept, I read my text messages. The first was from Clay Pearson. **Sorry, Laz. Had to report it. News is news.** After that came a bunch from kids who'd read about the shooting. I skimmed over them, not answering any, but stopped when I got to Suja's:

Anything I can do, just ask.
♥♥♥♥♥♥♥

I typed: **Thx. Will do.**

Later that afternoon, Curtis and I returned to Ballard Hospital. They'd moved Antonio from intensive care to a regular room. His face was still puffy and bruised, but he was able to talk in a whisper.

In the movies, the good guy gets beat up and then a few minutes later he's chasing down the bad guys. Real life doesn't work that way.

He'd sleep and then he'd whisper-talk and then he'd sleep. It seemed as if he was hooked up to about ten machines. Before we left, the same doctor called Mom and Curtis into another room. When they came out, Curtis had his arm around my mom, and their eyes were brighter. "He's out of danger," Mom said to me. "He just needs time."

SIXTEEN

I HAD TO FINISH OUT THE YEAR at Laurelhurst High, but I didn't go back that Monday. Instead I went with my mom to get my leg checked at the Ballard Clinic. When the doctor took the bandage off, the hole in my thigh looked like something a snapping turtle would cause. "No sign of infection," he said. "You'll be back to normal in no time."

Next we went to Ballard Hospital. Antonio was in a new room, hooked up to only one monitor, and his voice was stronger. All that was good, but I could sense Mom growing angrier as he got stronger. She held it in with him, but on the drive home, she let me have it again.

"*See something, say something*. You ever heard that?"

"I've h-heard it."

"And?"

"I g-get it. It's j-just that—" I stopped. "I screwed up. I'm s-sorry."

Silence. Then, in a clipped voice, she said, "It's over, Laz. Finished. I won't beat you up over this again."

No more putting it off—I had to return to Laurelhurst High on Tuesday. Monday night, my stomach churned at the thought of facing everybody. Then I caught a break. Curtis had a job trimming trees in Montlake, a neighborhood close to Laurelhurst. He could give me a ride, which saved me from a miserable bus ride.

His work started early, so he dropped me off at the high school thirty minutes before first period. I was tempted to hide behind the greenhouses and wait for the bell, but that would have been cowardly. So I tried not to limp as I made my way up the front stairs and headed to the library, hoping to find a corner where I could sit down and pretend to be studying.

I didn't make it.

Coach Vereen was heading down the hallway in my direction. As soon as he saw me, he pointed to a classroom. "In there," he said.

I opened the door and stepped inside. A female teacher I didn't know looked up in surprise. "Can I help you?"

Coach Vereen was one step behind me. "Mrs. Garrigan, could I use your classroom for a few minutes? It won't take long."

"Mr. Vereen, I've got a class—"

"Just a few minutes, Mrs. Garrigan." His voice was sharp.

She frowned, sighed, then grabbed her purse and left. "I'll wait right outside the door," she said.

Once we were alone, Coach Vereen pointed to a chair. "Sit down, Weathers."

I sat. He folded his arms across his chest and stared at me.

"I've never misrepresented a player to a major-league team in my life, and I'm not starting now, not in my last week on this job and definitely not for you. So here's what I did, and I want you to hear it from me, up-front. I sent an email to every major-league scout on my contact list. I told them exactly what happened Friday night. That you were supposed to start the title game. That minutes before the opening pitch, you walked out on your teammates. That later you were shot in a drug deal gone wrong." He paused. "Mr. Thurman took you out of North Central High and brought you into his home and into the Laurelhurst community. You had the chance of a lifetime, young man. We got you onto the big stage, but you blew it."

He stared at me, waiting for me to respond, but I wasn't going to stammer out any sort of excuse. What good would it have done? Finally he turned, opened the door, and stepped into the hallway. "We're finished, Mrs. Garrigan. Thank you."

All morning, it was as if I had cotton in my ears. I could hear words, but they were muffled and made no sense. At lunch, I grabbed two slices of pizza and found some empty steps behind the gym where I could eat alone.

If I hadn't been there, I wouldn't have seen Tommy Zeller pull into the parking lot and climb out of his white Ford Explorer. The back door of the gym opened and Coach Vereen and Ian walked out to greet him. They were smiling—all of them.

Tonight was the night—the beginning of the major-league draft. The baseball draft isn't as big a deal as the NFL or NBA drafts; still, ESPN was televising the first two rounds. Zeller being at Laurelhurst had to mean the Mariners were planning to draft Ian.

I dreaded facing Coach Vereen again at gym class, but he had a substitute teacher, a young guy, who opened up the equipment box and then stepped aside. "You can do whatever you want," he said, "so long as you don't get in a fight and you don't get hurt."

I couldn't run, so I wandered over to where some kids were playing Frisbee, stood by a tree and caught Frisbees that came right to me, which weren't many, and then flicked them back.

It was a long bus ride home to an empty apartment—Mom and Curtis were at the hospital. I was bored, and I'd heard Mom complain that the front windows were dirty, so I washed them, but when I finished, they didn't look much better.

I microwaved a Salisbury steak dinner, sat down at the kitchen table, and ate. After I cleaned the dishes, it was six o'clock. The major-league draft was starting. I didn't want to watch, but somehow I *had* to. I flicked Curtis's TV to ESPN and flopped down on the sofa.

Each team had four minutes to make a pick. As the clock ticked, the announcers would evaluate the highest-rated players. Then somebody from the team would phone in the selection, and a guy in a suit would step to the microphone and announce the choice. After that, ESPN would show a camera feed from the kid's home. The player and his family would be jumping around, hugging one another. I could picture the Thurmans in the game room, tense, waiting to hear Ian's name.

The Mariners had the sixteenth pick. At 6:45, the Twins—picking thirteenth—chose a catcher from Biloxi. When a commercial came on, I went to the kitchen and scooped chocolate ice cream into a bowl. I was limping back into the front room as a man stepped to the microphone. "With the fourteenth pick, the San Francisco Giants select Ian Thurman, outfielder, Laurelhurst High School, Seattle."

The TV filled with a feed from Ian's house. His mother, wide-eyed, was hugging him while his father was shoving a Giants cap onto his head. That lasted about twenty seconds and was followed by highlights of Ian hitting and fielding. Then it was the ESPN anchor again. "Next up, the Milwaukee Brewers."

I flicked off the TV and headed outside. It was a warm night. No breeze. Big blue sky with cotton clouds. It was the kind of night that—when you're feeling good about yourself—makes you feel even better. But when you're down, it's as if the world is laughing at you.

I picked up the Interurban Trail, crossed over Aurora Avenue, and walked to the Jewish cemetery. As I turned back, my phone vibrated: a text from Suja. **U doing ok? Call me when u can. Miss u.**

I didn't have the energy to talk to her. I typed: **Things r better. Call Later. Miss u too.**

I hit send and then returned to Woodacres. When I stepped inside the apartment, Mom was unloading groceries. I helped her put things away and then went into Antonio's tiny room.

A couple of minutes later Curtis knocked on the door and

stepped inside. "Hey, I saw that Thurman kid got drafted by the Giants."

I nodded. "First r-round."

He sort of smiled. "Two more days, Laz. Every team needs pitching, and you know that's true. Don't give up."

What good would it have done to tell him about Vereen's email?

"I won't," I said.

"And listen. If nothing comes through, I can get you a job with the tree service while you figure out what you really want to do. Or you could just stay with tree work. It's honest work and pays a decent salary."

SEVENTEEN

THE NEXT DAY, Hadley tracked me down before school. "You heard, right? The Giants snagged him before the Mariners could. He'll get something like four million as a signing bonus. Four million! He won't go to Arizona State now."

In the hallways, kids razzed Ian, calling out requests for cars and phones and trips and clothes and Xboxes. Ian would holler something back, and everybody would laugh like he was some great comedian.

The baseball draft continued on Wednesday. During lunch, word went around that Jay Massine had gone in the ninth round to the Dodgers. "PE today is going to be wild," I heard one kid in my class say. "Party time!"

He was right. Two guys drafted in the first ten rounds—Coach Vereen was sure to do something for them. There might even be reporters and TV and radio guys. Clay Pearson probably.

I couldn't face any of that, so I did what I'd never done in four years—I cut my afternoon classes and took the bus back to Woodacres. But when I got off, instead of going to the apartment,

I walked over to the driving range. If Mr. Matsui told me to go away, I'd go away.

From the parking lot, I could see that new signs had been plastered on the windows: **CLOSING JUNE 15! EVERYTHING MUST GO!**

"Hey," Mr. Matsui said when I stepped in the door. "There he is." Then he looked at the clock on the wall. "Shouldn't you be at school?"

"Half d-day t-today," I said, my voice shaky with the lie. "I thought I'd s-stop in and say hello and g-goodbye."

"I'm glad you did, Laz. I haven't felt good about that phone call." He paused. "If your leg is okay, you could clean up the range one final time. I'd pay you in cash—same hourly rate as usual."

Driving the John Deere made my leg hurt, but I worked three hours anyway. At the back of the driving range, on the Jet City side of the netting, sat one of those demolition machines that has a giant metal mouth at the end of a long yellow arm—a mechanical Godzilla just waiting to chew up the abandoned mobile homes.

After I finished, I went into the pro shop. "Be smart, Laz," Mr. Matsui said as he paid me. "Stay away from that gang stuff."

"I n-never was in any gang stuff," I said, but I could see in his eyes that he didn't believe me.

We shook hands, and I left. I was still in the parking lot when my cell rang. I looked at the screen: *Suja*.

I'd promised to call her and hadn't. I couldn't let it go to voice mail.

For the first few minutes, she asked about Antonio and me. I told her I was doing better and he was doing better, and she told me how glad she was.

"I know you probably don't want to do this, but I need to go over the details for the Senior Ball."

I blanked for a second. I'd forgotten all about the ball.

"S-Suja, I d-don't think I-I c-can—"

"Laz, you just told me you were fine."

"Not for d-dancing."

"We don't have to dance. You're my date. You promised."

"Come on, Suja. K-Kids go without d-dates."

"But I want to go with you. It'll be our goodbye to North Central, to Jet City. We *need* to do this. For closure."

I'd already said my goodbyes to North Central, but I could hear in her voice how much this mattered to her. She'd been a friend for a long time, a better friend than anyone. So instead of saying no, I heard myself say "Okay."

I half listened as she spent five minutes laying out the details of the evening. The only thing that stuck was that they'd pick me up at six thirty at the entrance to Jet City. That was all that mattered. Once they picked me up, I'd just go where everyone else went. "Thanks, Laz," Suja said when she'd finished. "You're going to be glad you said yes. I know you will."

EIGHTEEN

THURSDAY. THE LAST DAY of the baseball draft.

Curtis was still able to give me a ride to school, so I wasn't stuck on the bus in the morning. The teachers weren't teaching anything, at least not to seniors. It was all free time, which meant it was all talk time. The athletes argued about how much money Ian would get and whether Jay would turn pro. Other kids were pumped about going to college in the fall. And it seemed like everybody was headed to France or Costa Rica or Hong Kong over the summer.

At lunch, I took my food back behind the gym. Six more days and the school year would be over. While I worked tree service with Curtis, I'd look for a place to live. I'd seen some **ROOM FOR RENT** signs in the University District. The other people would be UW students. I wouldn't like that, but I'd survive. Later on, maybe I'd do what Mom wanted: go to a community college and learn how to operate a hospital machine or maybe become a paramedic. I wasn't smart enough to be a doctor, but I was smart enough to get injured people to the doctor.

I was lost in my own thoughts, so I didn't see Ian until

he was right in front of me. I jumped to my feet. "Hey, c-congratulations. The G-Giants. That's great. Even if it's not the M-Mariners."

He grinned. "Thanks. Actually, I'm glad it's the Giants. The M's have minor-league teams in Everett and Tacoma. My dad would be at every game. The Giants are going to send me to a team in Virginia."

I swallowed. "S-Sorry about walking out on the championship game."

"That's okay. We got to play at T-Mobile, which was cool." He paused. "It was your brother, right? The other guy they wrote about in the newspaper?"

I nodded.

"What else could you do? You got to go for your brother." He paused. "Listen, I heard about Coach Vereen's email to all the teams. He told my dad, and my dad told me. It sucks. I know how bad he wanted to win, but he didn't have to do that to you."

I shrugged. "Yeah. Well, he d-did."

Ian frowned. "I don't know if it will help you, but when the Giants called me, before I hung up I told their head scout about you."

"T-Told him what?"

"That you're the best pitcher I faced except for maybe Fergus Hart. And that's just *maybe*. I also told him that you aren't a gang guy or a druggie and that they'd be stupid not to draft you."

"You t-t-told him that?"

"Sure. Why not? It's all true."

330

"What d-did he say?"

"He didn't say anything."

The bell rang. Ian gave me a thumbs-up, turned, and headed to his class. I should have thanked him, but I didn't, maybe because I was having so much trouble getting my head around what he'd told me.

I had no chance.

And now I had one again.

On the way to art class, I ducked into the library, logged on to a computer and searched: *Major-League Baseball Draft Day Three*. They were in the middle of round 27. I watched for a couple of minutes as empty slots filled with names. It was going fast.

Art that day was outside—the assignment was to sketch a dogwood tree that was in bloom. As I filled my white page with dark lines, I kept picturing the draft board filling with more names and having fewer empty slots. Kids from Arkansas and Maine, Arizona and Montana. Round 28. Round 29. Round 30. How much could teams really know about any of those guys?

Coach Vereen didn't have a sub that day, but gym class was still free choice. I moved to my out-of-the-way spot by the tree, caught some more Frisbees, and flicked them back to anyone who looked interested. Throughout the period, Coach Vereen moved from group to group, smiling and wishing kids good luck. When he saw me, he walked past as if I weren't even there.

When PE ended, I did a last check at the library before heading to the bus. They were in the middle of round 34. Six more rounds and it would all be over.

NINETEEN

I HEARD MY CELL RING as I was climbing on the bus. Flipping it open, I covered my ear to block out the noise around me. My blood was pounding. Had some team called my name?

"Hello," I screamed, trying to be heard over the bus noise. "Hello!"

A man's voice—but I couldn't hear what he was saying. I ducked down and pressed the phone even harder against my ear. "Hello!"

"Laz, this is Curtis."

It was good news, though, and that helped some. Antonio was being discharged from the hospital. He'd need his room back, which meant I needed to move my boxes behind the sofa in the front room, which is where I'd be sleeping.

"Okay," I said, and disconnected. I sat up and looked out the window. I was glad that Antonio was leaving the hospital. But I felt disappointed, too, as if a vacuum cleaner had reached inside me and sucked out my heart.

A couple of blocks later my cell rang again. "Yeah?" I said, certain it was Curtis with another request.

But it wasn't.

"Am I speaking with Lazarus Weathers?"

"Yes."

"This is Richard Bellamy with the San Francisco Giants."

The bus lurched to a stop. The door hissed open, and a bunch of guys got on, punching one another and laughing loudly. I leaned way forward, so that my head was nearly touching the ground. "Yes, s-sir," I said.

"We've got your name on our draft board here, Lazarus. If we were to select you, we'd require you to take a drug test right away. Would you be willing to do that?"

"Yes, sir," I said.

"And you'd pass it?"

"Yes, sir. I know I would."

"You'd have to take drug tests regularly after that. All baseball players do."

"Yes, sir. I've n-never t-taken drugs. That's no p-problem."

"You're the Seattle kid who got shot, right? In a drug deal."

"Yes, sir."

There was a pause. "All right, Lazarus. Not promising anything, but keep your phone with you."

My mind raced so fast that I almost missed my stop. When I got inside the apartment, I opened my laptop. Round 36 was over. I told myself that more than a hundred names were still to be called, but that wasn't true. The Giants were my only chance, and they had just four more picks.

I plugged my phone into the charger and turned the volume

to high. I moved the sofa out a little from the wall and shoved my boxes behind it.

Then I checked my laptop.

Round 37 was over. The Giants had picked an outfielder from Hawaii.

The door opened. Mom and Curtis came in with Antonio. His stomach was bandaged, so he walked slowly, but he was able to walk. The swelling on his face had come down.

They'd stopped at Red Mill and bought bacon cheeseburgers and fries. Mom got out paper plates and napkins, and we ate at the kitchen table.

I could barely eat; my stomach was as sour as vinegar. Round 38 had to be over. Maybe even round 39.

"Not hungry?" Mom said, motioning toward my plate.

"I ate a l-lot of food at school," I answered. "Class p-parties."

We moved to the front room. Curtis brought up *The Terminator*, Mom's favorite movie. He had the volume high so that everyone could laugh at Arnold Schwarzenegger's accent. I took my cell out of the charger, put it on vibrate, and held it.

"You expecting a call?" Curtis asked.

"No. N-Not really."

He tilted his head. "So why are—"

The hair on my neck stood straight up—the phone had moved in my hand. I jumped to my feet, ran to the bathroom, slammed the door shut, and flipped it open. The screen read *Unknown Number*.

I hit accept.

"This is L-Laz Weathers."

"Hello, Lazarus. This is Rich Bellamy." He paused. "Welcome to the Giants family."

He said other things, too. He'd had three long days; he was tired; he'd call again soon, or somebody from the Giants organization would.

I thanked him, and the phone went dead. I went to the front room, grabbed my laptop from behind the sofa, and took it to the kitchen table. I needed to be sure.

"You're missing the best part," Mom shouted, and then she did her Arnold imitation. *"I'll be back!"*

"G-Give me a m-minute," I said.

I hit refresh, scrolled down.

Round 40 — San Francisco Giants: Lazurus Wethers

They'd spelled my first name wrong, and they'd spelled my last name wrong, but everything was right.

I went into the front room, grabbed the remote from Curtis, and hit pause. Mom groaned. "What are you doing?"

"I've got n-news."

When I told them, Antonio made a fist and shook it in front of his head, saying: "YES! YES! YES! YES! YES! YES!" Mom grabbed me and we danced around the front room. Curtis tapped a plastic fork against his beer and held it high in the air: "To the future Cy Young Award winner, Laz Weathers!"

• • •

That night I hardly slept. The next time I pitched, it would be against professional players, not high school kids. Some of them would be grown men. A wave of panic washed over me. Then I took stock. I was a nineteen-year-old high school graduate, not a kid. I'd pitched my team into the state finals. The San Francisco Giants had drafted me.

I was ready.

TWENTY

THE NEXT MORNING, as Curtis drove me to Laurelhurst, he told me he'd be my agent. "You don't want to represent yourself, and you don't want to pay somebody when I'll do it for free. That is, if you trust me."

"I t-trust you," I said.

His face lit up. "All right. I'll research this, find out how much you should get. I promise you, I will not let them walk over you."

When we reached Laurelhurst, I got out and gave him a wave of thanks.

He leaned toward me. "Hey, Laz," he said through the open window, "I got a question for you."

I put my arms on the door and bent down. "What?"

"How would you feel if your mom and I got married?"

I froze for a moment. "I'd be g-good with it."

"What about Antonio? Do you think he'd be good with it?"

"Yeah, he'd be good with it, too."

"You sure?"

"You should ch-check with him but—yeah—I'm sure."

Curtis smiled. "All right. Then I've just got to convince your mom."

After he drove off, I went up the main stairs into school. My news was right there on my tongue. I wanted to tell Hadley. I wanted to tell Ian. I wanted everybody to know.

And I wanted Coach Vereen to hear.

Every morning I'd seen varsity guys hanging out by the main office or in the halls or in the library. But that morning I didn't see a single baseball player.

I didn't get it, and then Trevor Mann, a kid in my art class, gave me a quizzical look. "What are you doing here?" he asked when he saw me looking around.

"Why w-wouldn't I b-be here?" I said.

"Because the baseball and softball teams are having their end-of-season party at Wild Waves. Didn't anybody tell you?" He paused, and then laughed. "I guess they kicked you off the team for getting shot."

I was surprised to feel a smile come to my face. "I g-guess they did."

As I walked to first period, it felt right not to tell any of the guys about the Giants. To them it wouldn't be a big deal. Because, really, what had I accomplished? Fortieth round. Headed to some low minor-league team in some low minor-league city. At North Central, that would have been a major accomplishment. But at Laurelhurst—with Ian being a first-round pick and other kids going to Harvard and Stanford—it was nothing. If

I'd bubbled over in front of everybody like a can of warm Coke, I'd have made a fool of myself.

Monday would be soon enough.

Or Tuesday.

Or whenever.

My bus that afternoon had to reroute because of an accident on Aurora. I ended up walking the last mile to the apartment. When I opened the front door, Mom and Curtis were sitting side by side on the sofa. "Finally!" Mom said, getting to her feet. "Antonio, come out here. Curtis and I have some news. Then we're all going out to celebrate."

TWENTY-ONE

I TOLD MOM THAT SUJA SAID we weren't supposed to dress up for the Senior Ball, but Mom shook her head. "Who ever heard of going to a ball and not dressing up?"

The Saturday afternoon of the dance, she took me to the Children's Hospital Thrift Shop in Shoreline. For fifteen dollars I got a brand-new gray sports coat. And I mean brand-new—the tags were still attached. She went up and down the racks until she found an almost-new blue dress shirt to go with it. I owned gray pants and black shoes, and Curtis was lending me a tie.

That evening, when I came out to the front room all dressed up, Antonio grinned but kept quiet. Mom wanted pictures of Suja and me. She threatened to come with me to the entrance of Jet City where the shuttle van was picking us up so she could take them herself. To get her to stay home, I had to promise to have somebody take our picture.

I was supposed to be at the entrance to Jet City no later than six thirty. It was just a ten-minute walk, but I left the apartment early. I didn't want to hold things up.

Suja and the other girls were standing under the burned-out

JET CITY sign when I arrived. She was wearing a low-cut purple dress that looked new. Her hair was done up, and she had on lipstick and eye shadow and earrings and a necklace. She was beautiful, but she didn't look like the regular Suja, which made me even more nervous. It was the same with the other girls, Tessa and Jackie. I didn't know either of them well, but they were so dressed up I barely recognized them.

"Who are th-the other g-guys?" I asked Suja, feeling sweat on my forehead and under my arms.

Before she could answer, I spotted Dawit Senai and Tory Nelson, wearing coats and ties, walking toward us.

"Hey! Hey!" Tory called out. "There he is!"

We did a handshake and a quick hug, and I relaxed. Then they talked to the girls a little. More hugs. "Like that dress a lot," Dawit said, gaping at Tessa.

She shoved him, and he turned to me and grabbed my arm. "Take your pants down and show us where you got shot."

"I'm not t-taking my p-pants down."

"Come on," Dawit said. "We're all friends. Did the bullet go through, or did it get stuck in your fat thigh?"

Right then the van pulled up.

Suja took a deep breath. "Here we go."

The driver headed south on Aurora, toward downtown. "I thought we were going to Riley's for dinner," I said.

Suja gave me an irritated look. "Laz, I told you I'd changed that. Barbecue just didn't seem right."

We ended up at a place called Pasta Bella in Ballard. It looked like nothing from the street, but inside you felt like you were in Italy. Real tablecloths, real napkins, real candles. Opera playing quietly in the background, art prints on the wall. The eating area was narrow, with dark rugs and dark walls, but it didn't seem gloomy. It took me a minute, but then it came to me.

Romantic.

That's what it was. It was the first time I'd ever eaten in a romantic restaurant.

The restaurant was so nice that I worried I might not have enough money, but when the menu came, I saw that it wasn't much more expensive than Riley's. The waiter said their specialty was *vongole*. He saw the puzzled look on my face. "Pasta with steamed clams," he explained, not making me feel stupid.

I'd never thought about eating steamed clams, but the evening was supposed to be different, so I ordered them. They were chewy, and sometimes I got some sand, but they were good.

I don't remember much of what we talked about, but I liked being close to Suja. I was getting used to her dress and her makeup and her jewelry. She was Suja again, but a special version of Suja.

As we ate, we talked about the coming year and what we were going to do. Everybody knew about Suja's scholarship to Whitman. She mentioned it, but she wasn't the kind of person to brag. Tessa wanted to be a dental hygienist. Dawit was going to work with his father for a taxi company and attend a tech school in Kirkland at night. Tory and Jackie were both headed to North Seattle Community College.

"What about you?" Jackie asked.

I swallowed, and then I told them I'd been drafted by the San Francisco Giants.

Tory's eyes went wide.

"No way!" Dawit said.

Suja grabbed my hand. "You're going to pitch in the major leagues?"

I shook my head. "N-Not in the m-major l-leagues. In the m-minor leagues. At least t-to b-begin with."

She grabbed my arm and squeezed it tight. "We all knew you were great! Everybody knows it. I'm so happy for you. You should have told us right away."

The bill came. We paid up, the waiter wished us a great evening, and we were back in the shuttle van. I'd just assumed that the ball was in the gym at North Central High. "Where's he g-going?" I whispered to Suja when the driver headed west toward Puget Sound. "N-North Central is the other w-way."

I got her irritated look again. "You didn't listen to anything I said, did you?" Then she smiled. "Just wait. You'll see."

We ended up at a place called The Canal. When the van pulled to a stop at the entrance, I looked around at the other North Central kids who were arriving. They were all dressed up, guys and girls. Everybody looked great, and I was glad my mom had made me buy a sports coat and put on a tie, glad that I looked great, too.

Once inside, Suja and I walked around the ballroom hand in hand, soaking it all in. The theme of the ball was outer space, and the walls were covered with murals of the solar system and supernovas and rockets taking off. The dance floor, which was really two floors because there were two levels, was so polished that it shone like a brand-new Mercedes. Glitter balls suspended from the ceiling sent rays of light in all directions. In the back were tables with fruit and vegetables and punch.

We stepped onto a deck. The sun was sitting on top of the Olympic Mountains, turning Puget Sound a golden blue. Suja squeezed my hand. "Aren't you glad you came?"

I smiled, then we went back inside. A deejay took his position on a small stage. Seconds later the music started, and the sound quality was so good it seemed as if a live band was playing.

We danced some; we talked some; we ate some. We got our picture taken by a professional in front of a fake moon, which would make my mom happy. Kids asked me about Laurelhurst and told me they were glad to see me.

I wanted the night to keep going, but at eleven the music stopped, and Mrs. Park, the principal who had canceled the baseball program, took the microphone from the deejay. "This has been a wonderful evening," she said, and then she went into the standard lecture about not ruining it with drinking or drugs or any other type of irresponsible behavior. "It's been a great year and a great ball. Let's keep it great."

That should have been it, but from out of nowhere Suja appeared on the stage and grabbed the microphone.

"Hey, everybody," she said, "I've got some really amazing news. You guys all remember Laz Weathers, right? He went to

Laurelhurst for the last semester, but he's really a North Central kid."

"He's here!" Dawit cried out, pointing at me. Kids cleared out, and seconds later a spotlight blinded me. I wanted to crawl under the floorboards.

"I just found out tonight," Suja went on, "that the San Francisco whatever-they're-called baseball team picked Laz to be one of their pitchers next year. He's the first North Central High kid who has ever been a major-league ballplayer—or at least he probably is."

I felt my face go red. "N-N-No," I said to the kids around me, but nobody was paying attention because they were too busy slapping me on the back and wishing me luck, and I was smiling and shaking hands and thanking everybody, and the whole time I knew that yeah, they were clapping for me—but they were clapping for themselves, too, and for North Central High, and for making it through and graduating despite everything that had been thrown at them for eighteen years, and my throat was so tight I couldn't have said anything to anybody, but I knew Suja was right, that no matter where I end up in this world, I'll always be a North Central kid.

EPILOGUE

ONE

WHEN I WENT BACK to Laurelhurst on Monday, word had gotten out that the Giants had drafted me. Hadley razzed me about being chosen in the fortieth round. "You'll get the same bonus money as Ian," he joked, "only you'll have three fewer zeroes at the end of your check." Later, though, he told me that there'd been an argument about who'd make it to the majors first—Ian or Jay or me. "My money was on you," Hadley told me, "and nobody took the bet."

Tuesday after school I had a physical for the Giants that included a drug test. That morning during math I broke into a sweat. I remembered that the doctor had given me painkillers when he'd dug the bullet out. Would those drugs still be in my system? I called Mom during lunch. "Nothing to worry about," she told me. "You peed all that out days ago."

Laurelhurst's graduation was Thursday night. I didn't go. I did stop by the library Wednesday to say goodbye to Jesus Ramirez. I hadn't seen him much recently, but I owed him. He was out of his mind with excitement because he'd just gotten accepted at MIT. "I was on their waitlist, but I never thought I'd get in. You don't know how good this feels."

I thought, *Yeah, I do,* but I just congratulated him and let it go.

On Friday night, Mr. Leach, a lawyer for the Giants who was in town to begin negotiations for Ian's deal, came by the apartment with a contract for me. I told him that Curtis was my agent. "Smart," he said, and then he and Curtis sat at the kitchen table. Mom, Antonio, and I went into Antonio's tiny room and sat on his bed. We left the door open so we could hear, but Curtis was so loud we could have heard everything he said with the door shut. "Laz had nothing to do with drugs or gangs. Nothing. He was saving his dumb brother." Then Curtis rattled off my stats for the year, which I didn't even know he had. "Those numbers put him right there with Fergus Hart, and the Twins drafted Hart in the second round. He'll get—what? A couple million? And all you can offer Laz is a measly four thousand?"

I didn't hear Mr. Leach's answer, but I knew what he'd say: that Fergus Hart had been a star pitcher for four years, while I'd been around for three months, and in those three months I'd been investigated by the WIAA, walked out on my team, and been shot in an alley during a drug deal.

They argued back and forth. After twenty minutes Curtis called me out to the kitchen. Mom and Antonio came with me. They were both smiling, as excited as I was, but Curtis had a scowl on his face.

Mr. Leach winked at me. "Laz, the San Francisco Giants are

prepared to offer you a standard minor-league contract as well as a signing bonus of nine thousand dollars, assuming that drug test comes back negative." He paused. "What do you say?"

My heart was trying to explode right through my chest.

"I s-say yes."

Mr. Leach handed me a pen with the orange and black Giants logo on it. "Sign right there," he said, pointing, "and then again there."

I signed.

Next, it was details. I was to report to the Augusta GreenJackets, an A-Ball team in Georgia. "We'll fly you out of Seattle on July first, give you a couple of days to get settled. You won't officially join the team until July fourth." He smiled. "That means there will be a fireworks show for your professional debut. Not bad."

"Where's he going to live?" Mom asked.

Mr. Leach waved his hands around. "Not to worry. We'll handle that. The GreenJackets have an arrangement with a place that is close to the ballpark. Your roommates will be other ballplayers, so you'll get to know them right off. It's in a mobile home park, but the players all say it's nicer than what they expected." He paused. "So what do you say? A trailer okay to start with?"

I caught Mom's eye and then nodded. "A t-trailer is fine."

He gathered up his papers, stood, and shook my hand. "We'll be in touch in the next week to go over the final details. In the meantime, take care of that leg."

Mom and Curtis walked Mr. Leach to his car. Everybody had been grinning from ear to ear, but once they were all outside, Antonio's smile turned into a frown.

"Laz, I should have said this—"

"You don't have t-to say anything, Antonio."

"But I was such a—"

"D-Don't," I said. "It's all over."

He stared at me for a long moment.

"Still brothers?"

"Always."

The door flew open, and Mom and Curtis were back in the apartment.

Mom hugged me again. Curtis took a deep breath, exhaled. "Well, Laz," he said, "you've got a team, a place to stay, and cash in the bank. Not bad. Not bad at all."

TWO

MOM AND CURTIS HAD WORK every day. Antonio had taken incompletes in all his subjects, so when he wasn't sleeping—he was still really weak—he was hitting the books. With a good senior year, the scholarship to Central Washington was still possible, and he was going after it hard.

Everybody else was busy, but for me it was sit around and wait. The driving range had closed. Suja's family had moved. Time crawled.

I checked on the GreenJackets every day. Their hitting was decent, but their pitchers were getting battered, which made me want to get to Georgia immediately.

I was flying out early in the morning on July first—my first time on an airplane. The night before, we went to dinner at Olive Garden. Mom had two glasses of wine, and after the second, she got sad. Why had they stuck me on a team so far away? There had to be someplace closer.

"Timmi, San Francisco is close," Curtis said, and he reached over and gently rubbed her cheek with the side of his hand. "Laz will be pitching for the Giants really soon. He'll be so rich he'll fly us down to see him all the time. First-class. Right. Laz?"

"Sure," I said. "And I'll g-get you b-box s-seats, too."

Mom and Curtis both took the morning off from work so they could drive me to SeaTac airport. Antonio came along, too, even though sitting in the car was probably tough on his insides. As we were heading down 130th toward I-5, we heard a loud, crashing sound.

"What was that?" Mom asked.

We exchanged glances, and then Antonio figured it out.

"It's July. I bet they're knocking down Jet City," he said. "Let's go see."

So we did. Curtis pulled up just outside the entrance and switched off the engine. Two monster machines were rampaging through the trailer court, chewing up the abandoned mobile homes. Neither had reached our trailer yet, but one was closing in. We waited, and then we watched as our home was flattened and a dust cloud rose where it had been. Nobody said anything. We just sat for a while longer and watched as other dust clouds rose where other trailers had been.

Finally Curtis restarted the Corolla. As he pulled the car out into traffic, he accelerated, but then had to brake when a slower car pulled in front of him. "Move it, pal," he said as he slapped the steering wheel. "We've got places to go and things to do."

ACCLAIMED SPORTS CLASSICS FROM CARL DEUKER

An IRA Young Adults' Choice

Texas Lone Star List

"A superb sports novel." —*Kirkus Reviews*

"Deuker continues his run as premier author of provocative YA sports novels. . . . Riveting."

—*The Bulletin*

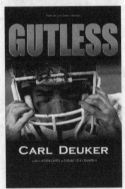

A Junior Library Guild Selection

2017 ILA YA Choices List

"A touchdown for sports collections."

—*School Library Journal*

ALA Best Fiction for YA

A Junior Library Guild Selection

★ "Definitely one for the top shelf."

—*Booklist,* starred review

ALA Best Fiction for YA

A Bulletin of the Center for Children's Books Blue Ribbon Book

"An excellent sports story with a lot more to it than just the game of baseball." —*VOYA*

"Rather than producing a stereotyped high school jock, Deuker portrays Josh as a complex and multidimensional character. . . . A well-crafted sports novel that delivers." —*School Library Journal*

A Booklist Top 10 Sports Book for Youth

"Good baseball books are in short supply for teens; do not let this one slip past." —*VOYA*